# The Opportunity

*Robert Cort*

Clink
Street

*Published by Clink Street Publishing 2020*

*Copyright © 2020*

*First edition.*

*ISBN 978-1-913962-79-1 - paperback*
*ISBN 978-1-913962-80-7 - ebook*

*To Anita, for your patience and support*

# 'The Opportunity'

Ian Caxton is a senior manager at Sotheby's, the world-renowned auction house in London. After successful career moves to Sotheby's branches in New York and Hong Kong, Ian is now based in London and earmarked for the top position.

However, following a chance meeting with Andrei, a very rich Russian art dealer, based in Monaco, suddenly Ian is seriously reassessing all his plans and ambitions. Even his marriage is potentially being threatened!

**'The Opportunity'**, is the first in a collection of five books, charting the life, adventures and career of Ian Caxton. In this first book, Ian is introduced to a new side of the art world. A world of serious wealth, heart pumping adventures and the dark side of the fine art business.

The big question is, will Ian take '**The Opportunity**'? And if he does, what will the consequences be, not only for him, but also for his wife and colleagues as well?!

# Chapter 1

Andrei Petrov had been looking forward to this meeting as he wanted to change people's lives ... forever!

He looked out, through the large bay window, into Maddox Street. This was the first time Andrei had visited The Grapes public house. As he continued to stare through the window he watched the hurrying and scurrying of the London commuters making their way home. Some of them were trying to shelter under their umbrellas from the cold, biting November rain. He lifted up the pint glass and sipped his cold beer. Thoughts drifted back to his former home, Moscow, and how cold it would be there at this moment. If people thought England felt chilly this time of the year, then they ought to experience Moscow in late November. He knew it would be about 20 degrees colder and shuddered at the thought.

A small grin slowly appeared on his tanned face when his thinking returned to the meeting in a few minutes time. He was excited, very excited. Could this man, the man who he was about to meet for the very first time, be the final link in his unique plan? A plan that when accomplished would nett him many millions of extra euros!

From early in his adult life, Andrei had been a chancer, a gambler, but not in the sense of casinos or betting on horses, no, his passion in the early days was investing at the right time in the Russian oil and gas industry. But over the last 20 years his new gambling passion, which he had slowly developed into his personal business, had centred around art and in particular, buying and selling of mostly post 1700 European paintings, both genuine ... and fakes!

Andrei had not returned to Russia for 15 years, certainly not since Putin had decreed the oligarchs were no longer welcome. Whilst he'd made a significant amount of money in the early days from his successful investing in the Russian gas and oil industry, he was not a billionaire. However, he was still very wealthy and quicker than most to notice that the good times were slowly coming to an end in Russia. He timely managed to get his many millions of roubles, euros and dollars out of Russia and into a newly set up Swiss bank account before it was all too late. But of course, he also knew that he could never really relax, or indeed, ever feel totally safe! It was never too late. Any day the Kremlin or the Russian Mafia, might finally decide on revenge. Then for certain, his days in this life would be numbered. His dealings in the art world too had not been without their own risks and a few of his dealings had resulted in a small number of jealous enemies.

His home was now in the Mediterranean playground of Monaco, the paradise for the very rich and the ultimate tax evader. Despite this favoured situation he still spent more days in aeroplanes and visiting clients around the world, than he did in his own home. He usually only came to Britain to meet with his two Russian London based friends and three other very wealthy and important clients. But tonight, he waited patiently and hoped that another UK resident would shortly become a key member of his very select team. A new addition who would make a significant impact on his future.

Andrei looked into the wood panelled room. Some of the city workers were beginning to line the bar and the noise level was slowly increasing. He listened to two suited men standing near to where he was sitting. They were discussing today's events on the stock-market. Evidently the stock market was still as volatile as ever. He wondered why people invested their money there. Art, for those people who knew what they were doing, was much more rewarding.

He enjoyed the English language and had been keen to learn to speak it at school and then college in Moscow. Now, and for the last 15 years, this has been his main conversational language used around the world. He also spoke French, when in Monaco and France and a little Portuguese and Spanish. But it was only with a few Russian friends and colleagues that he had any need to speak his home language any more.

He had first met his two London based Russian friends, Sergei and Boris, during his early stocks and share dealings with Gazprom and Transneft, the giant oil and gas companies. Sergei had worked for Gazprom and Boris for Transneft. Although all three men left Russia at different times, they still kept in touch and have been good friends ever since. Neither Sergei nor Boris have been back to Russia either since Putin had come to power and whilst these two friends do not have the same level of wealth as Andrei, they are rich enough to be able to live quiet, anonymous and very comfortable lives in London.

Andrei continued to watch the people outside and sip his beer. Now in his early 70s he thought his eyesight was still as good as it was in his younger days. He didn't need to wear spectacles and had made deliberate efforts to keep himself generally fit and lean.

He noticed that the rain had now eased and he could catch glimpses of people's faces when they were exposed to the light emitting through the window. He looked at his watch, 6.55 pm, just another five minutes. Again, a grin slowly appeared on his face.

Three weeks earlier in the fine art and private sales offices of Sotheby's in New Bond Street, Viktor Kuznetsov was sitting in the library surrounded by art books and catalogues. Since leaving school Viktor had decided to anglicise his first name and whilst still known as Viktor to his parents, he had dropped the 'k' and replaced it with a 'c' for everybody else. Now to friends and work colleagues he was simply 'Vic'. Although born in Moscow, to Sergei and Ludmilla, Viktor remembered very little of his life there. He and his mother had moved to England when he was four years of age and his father had joined them two years later. Viktor was now 24 years of age and had joined Sotheby's two years ago from Pembroke College, Oxford where he had obtained a First Class Honours degree in Russian History and History of Art.

He was currently two parts through Sotheby's three-year graduate trainee programme and was working in the 'European Pictures 1750–1914' department. Here he was currently researching paintings that had disappeared during the Second World War. When over dinner one evening, he mentioned his work, his father suddenly became very interested and asked lots of questions about what exactly he was doing and what were his findings so far. Such interest surprised Viktor as he didn't know his father was that interested in art that had been lost during the Second World War. Nevertheless, Viktor explained in some detail his current findings and answered his father's subsequent questions. Eventually, however, Viktor became curious and decided to ask a question of his own.

"Why do you want to know?" he asked, sipping his wine and looking at his father suspiciously.

Sergei sat back in his chair and looked at his son. He was quite a big man and still looked somewhat younger than his 64 years.

"Cannot a father be interested in the career of his only child?" His voice was deep and still contained a slight Russian accent, despite the years living in England.

Whilst all the family could speak fluent Russian, it had always been Sergei's insistence that only English should be spoken in the home, unless of course, any of their guests could only speak Russian. As Viktor could not remember any such guests coming to their home, he similarly could not remember any Russian ever being spoken here either.

"Father," said Viktor, "I have been employed at Sotheby's for two years now and this is the first time you have shown such a deep interest."

"I am interested," responded Sergei without further explanation. Viktor knew that this type of blunt response meant his father was not going to expand any further, so he concentrated on eating his dinner.

It was two days later when Sergei began typing an email to his friend Andrei. As he, Andrei and Boris, had always been careful with their communications when living in Russia, they had devised a special cryptic language for written communications which they continued to use to this day.

Translated Sergei wrote:

*'Hello my friend,*

*Are you still interested in possible additions for your art collection?*

*If yes, when are you next coming to Britain?*

*Best wishes.'*

Three hours later Sergei received a reply which he translated:

*'Good to hear from you, my friend.*

*Yes and I am coming to London on the 25th.*
*Dinner on the 26th, 8 pm. Usual place?*
*Keep smiling.'*
Sergei responded immediately:
*'Good.*
*Will make the usual reservation.*
*Keep smiling yourself!'*

When Viktor arrived home from work that evening, his father called him in to his study and told Viktor to close the door. This he did and stood in front of his father's desk. Both his features and his build were very similar to his father's. Indeed, old photographs of Sergei at Viktor's age, showed a striking resemblance. Sergei sat down behind the desk onto a deep seated, high back leather chair and began to speak. "I have been talking with my friend Andrei and he is coming to London in a week's time. I want you to meet him and tell him about the work you are currently doing."

"Do you mean at Sotheby's?" queried Viktor, wondering where this conversation was leading.

"Of course," responded Sergei. "My friend is an avid art collector and I am sure you could help him."

"Help him! What do you mean?" replied Viktor. He was now very concerned as to what was required of him.

Sergei leaned forward and put his arms on the desk. He looked up to Viktor and said, "Now listen. This meeting could be very advantageous for you and ... possibly financially, very rewarding as well!"

Sergei leaned back in his chair once again and pointed to the empty seat next to his desk. "Sit down and I will explain."

For two days Viktor could think of nothing else other than the conversation he had had with his father. After much thought, he decided he needed to get someone else's opinion and from someone who was far more knowledgeable than he was on this matter. He considered friends and other colleagues in the office, but decided that those who he knew well were largely at his level and therefore had little or no more knowledge on the subject than he did. But then suddenly he had an inspirational idea. But of course, he thought, and it might just work! But the problem now is, how do I approach him?

# Chapter 2

The 'European Pictures 1750–1914' department at Sotheby's was the responsibility of 35-year-old Ian Caxton. Ian had recently been promoted to Assistant Director, UK. He had already been singled out by senior management as a strong contender for the very top job!

He was fluent in German and Russian and had obtained a First Class Honours degree in Modern Languages from St John's College, Oxford and a Masters degree with Distinction, in Art History from the London Courtauld Institute of Art. Following promotion, he had recently returned to London after spending time at Sotheby's New York and Hong Kong locations.

Ian's lifestyle had always been somewhat extravagant and he was now finding the cost of living back in London challenging. Whilst his promotion was an excellent career move, he now realised that losing some of the 'expat' benefits was a serious issue and he was now considering all his future options. He knew he was well thought of by senior management at Sotheby's and that greater earning opportunities would potentially be there for him in the years to come, but Ian was looking more to the present and not to the years to come. He had married Emma two years ago and her financial demands had exacerbated the situation. Emma had been born into a well-respected and wealthy Cotswold family and she was certainly not prepared to compromise her living standards just because she was now married.

Ian sat in the company's board room and was discussing an upcoming auction of Constable and Turner paintings and sketches with his boss, Michael Hopkins.

"So, Ian, all in all we ought to get the top prices. The advertising seems to have gone well and there's a great deal of interest," said Michael, looking over his reading glasses at Ian. He passed the file back to Ian. "Excellent, we need this one to be a great success."

Ian collected the file and put it in his folder. "Yes, I am really confident this is going to be the biggest so far this year. Could gross over a 100 million."

Michael stood up and as he did so spoke in a more relaxed manner. "So how are you settling back into the London scene once again?"

Ian also rose from the table and picked up his folder. "Takes a bit of getting used to," he replied, "I'd forgotten all about the poor commuter train service and even by Hong Kong standards, London seems more crowded than ever. I may have to look for a flat nearby." Ian was careful not to be too negative to his boss. He followed Michael to the door. Although just under six feet in height, Ian still stood above his boss by about four inches.

"Have you discussed the flat situation with Emma?"

"No, it's just a thought at the moment, I also need to investigate the costs involved."

"Changing the subject, I was talking to your young trainee, Vic the other day. Seems to be a bright prospect."

"Yes, he is." replied Ian. "He's working on a project trying to identify paintings that went missing during the Second World War. I have a meeting with him tomorrow morning so I will find out more about what he has found out then."

The two men went their separate ways and whilst walking back to his office Ian thought about what he had just said to his boss and also about the possibility of obtaining a flat closer to New Bond Street. Buying would be out of the question, especially as the mortgage on his existing house in Esher had many years still to run, but renting might just be a possibility. Whilst this move would certainly save money on train fares and travelling time, overall it would be yet another expense that he would struggle to justify, although if it was closer to Harrods, Emma just might be a little more receptive to the idea.

When Ian returned to his desk he found two telephone messages left by Penny Harmer, his PA. One could wait, he thought, but the other was from Oscar Ding, a former colleague in Hong Kong. Ian looked at his watch and decided it would be late evening in Hong Kong so he'd ring him later. He leant back in his chair and folded his hands together behind the back of his head and unconsciously began to caress some of the strands of his light brown hair. He looked across the room to a large photograph on the wall of Hong Kong harbour at night. He had taken many photographs of this view from Kowloon, looking across the water to Hong Kong island, but decided this one had particularly captured the mood he remembered so well. All the high-rise buildings were lit up in a multitude of colourful lights and lasers, reflecting almost a perfect image in the harbour water. Two Star Ferries were silhouetted in the foreground, their green and white colouring almost disappearing into the grey of the darkness. Even now Ian could still smell the atmosphere, the excitement and vibrancy of the place. He seriously wondered if he had made the right decision to come back to the UK.

Ian's meeting with Viktor was arranged for 10 am. It was now 9.50 and he was just finishing reading Viktor's report. It was well researched and quite detailed on the paintings that had gone missing, but lacked depth of background information and some suggestive thought as to what Sotheby's should do with this information. Ian made some notes until there was a knock on his door. The door was usually open and Ian called, "Come in Vic and sit down." He pointed to the chair opposite him. This was the first report Viktor had completed for his boss in the brief time he had been in this department and he was nervous as to how he would react.

"I've just finished reading your report. It's a very interesting read," said Ian, flicking through the pages.

"Thank you," replied Viktor. He slowly began to relax.

"I've made a few notes for us to discuss."

"Okay"

"Firstly, can you tell me a bit more about how these pictures became lost in the first place."

Viktor put down his notes and settled in his chair and began to explain his findings.

"Well, during the Second World War the German Nazis not only occupied many countries on the mainland of Europe causing terror and mass exterminations, but they were also responsible for one of the largest acts of art theft and lootings in the century. During the late 1930s and the first half of the 1940s, they plundered and confiscated well over 500,000 paintings and various other works of art from private collections, churches and museums all across the face of Europe. It was highly organised, largely carried out by the Gestapo and supported by Hitler. He in particular craved many of the Old Masters classical paintings, but also some of the 18th and 19th century artists too. He hated so-called modern, abstract art, which he called 'degenerate art'. These paintings were either swapped for the more classical masters paintings, sold for cash to fund the expanding Nazi regime, or just destroyed." Viktor shifted in his seat and picked up his notes, glancing down to refresh his memory, he continued. "Hitler also planned a special museum in Linz, where after the war these paintings would be displayed. Goering too, was apparently an avid collector and at the outbreak of the war a special team was assembled in France and he took personal command. Their aim was to identify and loot as much of this art as was possible. Lorries, trains and even the Luftwaffe were commandeered to transport the fruits of their plundering to Germany. Gradually more paintings were identified in other European countries and so the thefts continued. In Britain orders were sent out from the government and many collections of paintings in the UK were packed and moved to secret hiding locations, just in case."

Penny arrived with two cups of coffee and placed them on Ian's desk. Penny had joined Sotheby's direct from university at the same time as Ian had arrived from Hong Kong. Ian had liked her straight the way and they now worked well together. She was attractive, ambitious and very bright, all qualities Ian respected. "Thank you," he said, with a smile.

After Penny had left Viktor continued. "It is estimated that there are still well over 100,000 stolen paintings from this period, but in reality, nobody knows for sure what the total is. Some reports say it could be twice this figure. What is more certain is that lots of these paintings are now in Russia. When the Soviets left Germany, it is widely thought that Stalin ordered many of these paintings to be recovered, but once they arrived in the Soviet Union they were never repatriated. Similarly, in America and anywhere else where art is bought and sold, paintings from this era are to this day, hanging on the walls of private collectors or just lost in the basements of museums and art galleries."

Viktor stopped talking to sip his coffee. "In many cases records of the original owners have disappeared and provenances have been falsified and completely rewritten.

Switzerland became a notorious clearing house for stolen art and during the war many Swiss dealers cooperated with the Nazis in selling the plundered modern art. These dealers turned a blind eye to where the paintings would have come from and spent much time creating new provenances. Existing provenances, some easier to fake than others, were obliterated. Labels on the back of paintings could be changed. There grew a network of dealers and so-called experts and they were able to provide new authentication – which as we know, is critical for all paintings' valuations." Viktor sipped another mouthful of his coffee. This gave Ian a chance to speak.

"Okay, so what's happened since?" Ian was keen to hear the depth of Viktor's investigations.

Viktor flicked through his notes and continued. "In 1999 the 'Commission for Looted Art in Europe' was established with the prime aim of recovering and achieving restitution of the lost artwork. It has had some success recovering more than 3000 items. However, for any organisation or individual to be successful in claiming back their stolen painting, it is necessary for the Commission to firstly authenticate the painting, establish it's correct provenance and then be satisfied that the claimant is in fact fully entitled to the work."

"Yes," interrupted Ian, "About ten years ago Sotheby's were asked to help one of our clients. From our records going back to the 1920s were able to assist them achieve restitution of two paintings. One was a Van Gogh and the other, I think, was a Matisse. If I remember correctly, both had been sold by the Nazis to a Swiss dealer, because they were considered 'degenerate'. Any paintings that had anything synonymous with Jewish painters or Jewish subject matter, were also thrown out of the Nazi collection and sold." Ian gave Viktor a chance to continue and sipped his own coffee.

"Interesting," replied Viktor. "So, Sotheby's have been involved with some of the earlier restitutions."

"Oh yes, our auction records go back many years showing who bought what painting and for what price. Invaluable information when trying to re-track ownership and true provenance."

"Of course," continued Viktor, "but there are still many tens of thousands of paintings that are still unaccounted for and even if they did come to light the original owners may well have died by now and their families, if they had any, could be completely unaware of their potential inheritance."

"That's true, but the really valuable paintings are well known within the industry, so there would still be records of some sort." replied Ian. He then finished the last of his coffee before continuing. "So where does that leave us? Any ideas as to what we should be doing with the list of all these paintings that you have identified?"

"Actually, I have. Do you mind if I close the door as there are some questions I would like to ask you in private."

Ian was somewhat surprised. "No go ahead, I'm intrigued."

# Chapter 3

Viktor closed the door and returned to his seat. He explained to his boss about the conversation he'd had with his father and the doubts and concerns he had due to his own inexperience. At this stage of his career it would be way out of his depth.

Ian looked at his watch and said, "Look it's lunchtime, let's go to The Grapes and I will buy you a sandwich. We can carry on our discussion there."

The two men left their notes on Ian's desk and exited the building. On emerging into New Bond Street, they turned right. A hazy sunshine tried to break through the grey clouds. It was still warm for early November, but rain had been forecast for later.

"Have you been to The Grapes before?" asked Ian.

"Yes, but the last time was a few weeks ago now. A couple of us called in for a pint one evening after work."

"They do a good pint and nice sandwiches too."

The two men arrived at the junction with Maddox Street and turned right again. The Grapes was about another 100 metres on the left-hand side. They entered the wooden pan-elled saloon and walked up to the bar. It was still early, but there were a number of customers sitting at the tables and standing at the bar. Ian picked up a sandwich menu and gave it to Viktor. "What do you fancy to drink?"

Viktor was conscious he had a busy afternoon ahead of him so said he better just have a Diet Coke. Ian decided he needed a pint of beer.

The two men selected and ordered their sandwiches and picked up their drinks. They saw a table free in the corner and walked over. After sitting down Ian reopened the conversation they were having in the office. "So, let me see if I've got this right. Your father's friend, Andrei, is Russian, but lives in Monaco and collects and trades paintings mainly from the 18$^{th}$ and 19$^{th}$ century. When he lived in Russia, he and a friend Boris had a number of connections with the art underworld and were able to acquire some of the paintings that were formerly part of the Nazi haul." Ian stopped talking as the sandwiches were delivered.

Both men took bites from their food and after emptying his mouth, Ian leaned back in his chair and continued. "Andrei now trades some of his collection on the black market, buying and selling paintings to other known dubious collectors. Your father has told Andrei of your employment at Sotheby's and the work you have been researching and he is now very keen to learn about the pictures you have found and wants to meet with you." Ian picked up his sandwich and started to eat again.

"Yes," said Viktor. "That's about it. But I am doubtful Sotheby's would want to be involved in what could well be illegal trading. In fact, I'm not sure I want to be involved either."

Ian finished his sandwich and after taking sips of his beer he said in a low voice. "Do you want me to have a word with your father?"

"That would be great," replied Viktor. He quickly saw the benefits for himself. It would also take some of the pressure off his shoulders. "But why would you do that?"

Ian took another sip of his beer and leant back in his seat.

Since Viktor had first mentioned his problem in his office, he had been thinking that maybe, just maybe, it could be an opportunity not to be ignored or dismissed at first hand. Indeed it may be just the sort of opportunity that could generate the level of additional income he was looking for. However, he needed to discuss many more details with the Russians and in particular, what would be required of him, before he could make any final decisions. It was certainly worth progressing at this stage.

After a short pause Ian replied, "Well, it may just solve your problem with your father and I am very intrigued to know what exactly your father and this Andrei are getting up to."

"I do not want to get my father into trouble." replied Viktor. He was now wondering if it had been a wise decision to involve his boss, and indeed Sotheby's.

"Let's just say this would all be very unofficial," whispered Ian. "Nothing to do with Sotheby's."

# Chapter 4

That evening Viktor met with his father in his office and explained that he was not really qualified or experienced enough to be involved in Andrei's project. He also told him about the conversation he'd had with Ian and the interest his boss had shown in the situation. He explained how Ian was far more qualified and experienced than him and Ian's knowledge of 18th and 19th century paintings was probably the best at Sotheby's.

Sergei leaned back in his chair and listened patiently to his son's explanation without interruption. Once Viktor had finished talking Sergei thought about his suggestion. He stood up from his seat, stretched his large frame and walked around his office in silence.

He returned to Viktor's side and looking down, he began to speak. "I doubt Andrei would want to deal directly with Sotheby's. He does not work in the 'official' way, otherwise he would have dealt with the likes of Sotheby's or Christie's himself. I will have to speak to him and see what he says."

Next morning Viktor went to Ian's office and gave him a resume of his conversation with his father. Ian listened and then said he would look forward to hearing more in due course.

On the evening of the 26th Sergei left his house in Eaton Square, Belgravia and hailed a taxi. His destination was the

Cipriani London restaurant. This had been a regular meeting place for Sergei, Andrei, Boris plus one or two other Russian colleagues for many years. Although the restaurant had to change its name to C London because of a High Court decision, to most patrons it was still known unofficially as the Cipriani. The restaurant over the years had become a melting pot for the good, the great, and the nouveau riche. It was not only a very popular venue for a number of international celebrities, but a location where some of the most wealthy, mysterious and influential Russians could also be found dining.

Andrei was sitting at their usual table in a corner away from the glare that the celebrities favoured. When he spotted Sergei walking towards him, he stood up and gave a huge smile. "My friend, it has been too long". The two men shook hands and gave each other a manly hug.

"Yes indeed," replied Sergei. "You are looking very fit and tanned as usual!"

"The climate in Monaco, my friend, is excellent. So good for my skin." replied Andrei with a big smile and rubbing the side of his face. "So how is that lovely wife of yours, Ludmilla, and young Viktor, he is progressing well? He must be, what, 20 now?"

"Ludmilla is fine and sends her regards. Viktor is actually 24!"

"My, my," replied Andrei. "How time flies."

"And you my friend, how are you keeping?"

"Keeping very well thank you. Lots of lovely rich widows in Monaco you know!"

"You do not change Andrei."

"No, I do not and I also still enjoy dabbling in my paintings too."

"Interesting you should say that because Viktor is working at Sotheby's."

"Ah, so that is what you were hinting at in your email?" said Andrei, pouring a glass of red wine for Sergei. The wine was Sergei's favourite claret and the group's usual drink when dining at this restaurant.

"Yes, but the situation I was thinking about has changed slightly." Sergei paused, took a sip of his wine and let the flavour develop on his palate before continuing. "I had thought that Viktor, with his Sotheby's connections, might be useful helping you to enlarge your collection."

"I see, so what happened to change this thought?"

"Let's order our food and I will then tell you of a new possible opportunity"

The two men selected their food from the table d'hote menu and after giving their orders to the waiter, Sergei took another sip of his wine before continuing and explaining the details to Andrei of his conversation with Viktor. When he had finished Andrei pondered on this information and then asked, "But we do not know this Caxton man. Can he be trusted?"

"Viktor thinks he can be. He also thinks his boss is very keen to explore any opportunity to increase his income. However, he did say to Viktor that he was not keen to involve, or be seen to be involving, his employers." Sergei stopped talking to let Andrei consider the proposal. After a short time he then continued, "It might be a good idea if you both had a meeting and you could then make your own decision."

Both men sat in silence and drank their wine. Eventually Andrei said, "You know my friend, it may just work. I will meet up with this Caxton man and see what he says he can offer."

Andrei and Sergei enjoyed their food and changed the discussion to each other's lives and events. Finally, at the end of the meal, the two men walked towards the exit. As they left the building Sergei said, "I will ask Viktor to speak with Caxton and arrange a meeting for you both."

"Excellent my friend and thank you. I'm in London for the next four days."

Over breakfast the next morning Sergei told Viktor the details of his meeting with Andrei and Viktor agreed to speak with his boss.

Next day, as Viktor was leaving the Sotheby's offices for lunch, he saw Ian just ahead of him in New Bond Street. He quickly caught up and told him of his father's meeting with Andrei Petrov and that Andrei would be interested in meeting with him. He also said that Andrei was leaving London and going back to Monaco in three days' time.

Ian told Viktor that he was free both early evenings tomorrow or the next day. He suggested meeting at The Grapes at about 7 pm, but if Mr Petrov wanted to meet somewhere else, then that was fine with him.

Viktor promised to tell his father. His father would then get in touch with Mr Petrov this evening.

# Chapter 5

Sergei telephoned Andrei and the meeting was agreed. Sergei would meet Viktor and Ian Caxton at Sotheby's and the three of them would walk the short distance to The Grapes.

At 6.45 pm the following evening, Viktor and Sergei were in the reception area of Sotheby's talking when Ian joined them. Viktor introduced his father to Ian and after exchanging pleasantries the three men left the building and exited into New Bond Street. It had just stopped raining and the air, whilst cooler, was also a little fresher. They walked side by side. Ian was speaking with Viktor whilst Sergei watched the pedestrians passing by him and also took particular attention to the traffic. For most of his adult life Sergei had been alert, and wary of strangers. He had heard about fellow Russians who had been bungled into passing cars and never to be seen again or poisoned 'accidentally' by a jab from an innocent umbrella. He was keen for his name not to be added to this list of casualties. Whilst in business in Russia he had made a few enemies, but hoped that most of these had now forgotten all about him or better still, were dead. But he never could be totally sure and therefore remained careful.

Just before 7 pm the three men entered The Grapes and

Sergei spotted Andrei sitting at a table next to the large bay window. Andrei rose from his seat and greeted his old friend. Sergei introduced Ian and pointed to Viktor. "As you can see, my son is a little bigger now."

"Yes, indeed." said Andrei. "He must have grown 50 centimetres since I last saw him!"

Viktor felt somewhat embarrassed and when he looked at Ian, his boss was giving him a knowing smile. Viktor volunteered to get some drinks and quickly disappeared to the bar. Until he returned Andrei asked Ian about his career and Ian gave a summary of his time at Sotheby's.

Once Viktor had returned to his seat, Andrei wanted to know more details about Ian's experience and in particular his knowledge of 18th and 19th century paintings. Ian explained his involvement with clients and in particular his experience of assessing whether the pictures were genuine or fakes. He also described how he handles valuations, acquisitions, de-accessions and promotions for auctions and private sales.

Andrei was impressed with Ian's confidence and knowledge, but wanted to know if he would be prepared to work wider than just under the remit of what services Sotheby's had to offer.

"That depends," replied Ian, "on what exactly will be required of me, the time involved and what would be my financial gain."

"And what about legality?" queried Andrei. "Would you be prepared to break the law?"

"Again, it would depend," replied Ian. "It would be determined on whether I thought there would be a good chance of being caught … and the financial gain. Without knowing specifics, I can't give you a more definite answer."

"That's fair." replied Andrei. "Okay, I'll tell you of my plan and the proposition. You can then decide."

Over the next 20 minutes Andrei explained in some detail his plan and where he saw Ian's involvement. The three men listened without interruption.

When Andrei had finished talking Ian drank the remains of his beer and stood up. The three others looked up thinking Ian was about to leave. However, Ian surprised them all. "Let me get some more drinks," he said. "This all sounds very interesting."

The meeting went well and all four men agreed their immediate roles. Andrei would be flying back to Monaco and contact his colleagues in Moscow. Sergei would provide a focal point of reference in the UK and Viktor the link between his father and Ian. Ian's immediate task would be to speak with his wife.

On the commute home later that evening, Ian pondered on his decision and what he was going to say to Emma. If he told her the whole truth then it would almost certainly cause a problem as he knew Emma would be very worried and would certainly try to talk him out of such a venture. But on the other hand, he now felt committed and indeed, wanted to be involved with Andrei's plans. Besides if all went well, he and Emma would be more financially secure for the future. He had no intention of telling Emma deliberate lies, but after more thought, decided maybe just one small 'white' lie may solve his immediate predicament. Also, as it was now much later than he usually arrived home from work, he decided not to raise the subject until over dinner the following evening. It would also, he concluded, buy him some more thinking time.

The next morning Ian did not go into London as he had an appointment with a large financial company in Reading, Baxter & Co. Their CEO, Sir Paul Broadway, was looking to raise extra capital to fund his business expansion plans. One option he was considering was to sell a number of the company's paintings. The number of paintings in the collection had steadily increased during the past 50 years. Several previous chairmen had made purchases out of the strong profits during the good times. Now Sir Paul, with the backing of the current chairman, had decided it was time to realise their financial worth. Also, the insurance premiums and additional security requirement costs were ever increasing and needed to be redressed.

A number of fine art sales companies were considered and contacted, but after outlining their specialist skills, expertise and experience, Sotheby's were one of just two companies invited to provide their opinions and proposals.

As Baxter & Co's collection of 53 pictures were all painted during the 1750–1920 period, the original request landed on Ian's desk. His department had put together their presentation report and Ian signed off the final draft. A week later Ian received a telephone call asking if he would visit Baxter & Co's offices and meet with the company's CEO.

As Ian drove his 7 series BMW along the M4, he once again began to think about what he would say to Emma later over dinner. Last evening, he had suggested they eat out and he'd proposed the Two Swans restaurant overlooking the River Thames, on the outskirts of Marlow. Emma was working that day in Marlow and it was on the way home for Ian, so it was a convenient, albeit expensive option.

Ian arrived at Baxter & Co's modern and somewhat palatial offices, for his 10 am appointment. He was met in reception by the CEO's PA, John Chambers, who welcomed Ian and introduced himself. John was about 25, Ian guessed, tall, confident and well dressed in a three-piece navy suit. Ian was escorted to the boardroom where Sir Paul was already waiting. Ian had not met Sir Paul before but he was aware that he was 55 years old. Penny had put together a comprehensive report of the firm for Ian and he'd noted that Sir Paul had been CEO for just over a year, having previously been Baxter & Co's finance director.

The two men shook hands and Ian noted that the PA still remained. The three men all sat down at the table and Ian retrieved a file from his briefcase.

Sir Paul began by opening a weighty folder and said, "We are looking to sell most of the company's art collection and this folder has all the files relating to each picture. John will discuss these details with you, show you around the office and point out the relevant paintings. I will meet with you back here at three o'clock. You can then tell me your initial thoughts."

Ian nodded to Sir Paul and then looked across to John. Sir Paul left the room and John picked up the thick folder left by Sir Paul and sat next to Ian.

Over the next two hours the two men went through the folder and Ian made notes and asked a number of questions.

When Ian was happy with the information obtained, John suggested they have lunch. He would then give Ian the guided tour.

Just before three o'clock John and Ian returned to the boardroom and three minutes later Sir Paul joined them.

"So, what do you think?" asked Sir Paul as he walked towards his chair.

For the first time Ian noticed that Sir Paul had a slight limp. "It's an interesting collection. Do you have any preference as to how you want the pictures sold? We can put together a special catalogue for an auction or maybe you would like us to find private buyers?"

"The Directors are not very keen on a publicised auction. Our competitors may think we are in financial difficulties – which of course we are not. We still want the best price but … I'm sure you can achieve that anyway via private buyers."

Ian looked at his notes. "There are about 25 of your

pictures which I am sure we can sell privately and quite quickly, but the rest, whilst they do have their attractions, require a more specialist market, which may mean a longer time span and more work on our behalf."

Sir Paul looked at John who had remained silent so far. "What's your view John?"

John Chambers looked from Sir Paul to Ian. "If you want the top prices it's still better to go down the auction route. It would be riskier, but looking at Sotheby's previous auction results, you would most likely get worldwide interest and exposure."

The room went quiet. Sir Paul pondered on his decision. "You say about 25 might be sold quickly by private sales … and at a good price?"

Ian nodded and Sir Paul continued. "Right. This is what we'll do. I want you to report to me with an estimated market value of each of the 25 pictures, both if we sold at auction and separately, via a private buyer."

Ian nodded again and responded. "That's fine Sir Paul, we can present our initial report within the week. What about the other 28?"

"Put those in the report too with your estimated auction price."

Later, as Ian drove his car away from Baxter's, his mind had now switched to his dinner meeting with his wife. He was now sure what he was going to say to her.

Ian arrived at the Two Swans, parked his car and looked at his watch. He was about 30 minutes early so decided to take the opportunity to send emails, via his mobile phone, to both Penny and Viktor. He summarised how the meeting had gone at Baxter's and gave them instructions on what to do tomorrow. He looked at his watch again. Ten minutes. He still couldn't see his wife's car in the car park, however, he decided to go into the restaurant anyway.

The restaurant had a cosy atmosphere and a large open log fire. On some of the walls were old landscape watercolour paintings depicting local scenes along the river. The room was already quite busy but Ian was shown straight to an empty table in an alcove. He sat with his back to the wall in order to see fully across the room and also be able to spot Emma when she arrived. He ordered a gin and tonic.

Ten minutes later Emma arrived, a little flustered. She joined Ian apologising and complaining about the volume of traffic in Marlow.

They both ordered their food and a glass of Chablis. Ian then enquired how her day had been.

Emma was a partner in a small accounting firm and her clients were mainly linked to the art world. She and Ian had met five years ago in New York when Ian was responsible for putting together an auction of modern paintings and Emma had been invited by one of her largest clients, Beckworth & Co., the fine art brokers, to join them for the two days of the auction. After the first day Emma was introduced to Ian. Ian knew Beckworth & Co. quite well as they attended a number of his auctions on the behalf of their clients.

It was Emma's first visit to New York and at the end of the second day Ian had suggested she stay on for the weekend and he would show her the sights. After just two days Ian had decided Emma was very special. She was beautiful, bright and interesting. Their romance duly blossomed and despite Ian's work taking him on to Hong Kong, their relationship remained strong and they were married on Emma's 28th birthday. Despite marriage, Emma told Ian she was not keen on moving to Hong Kong, but wanted to stay in England and continue to develop her own career.

Ian knew he only had a short time before his next transfer move, so he went back to Hong Kong on his own. Ten months later he was transferred back to the UK.

"It's been a good day, I think I have picked up another client, Carberry's, the fine art dealers in Marlow," said Emma.

"Excellent, they are a nice company. Tom Davies at Sotheby's, used to deal with them and he always had a good word for them."

Neither of them had a starter and after they had finished their main courses, Ian began to explain that he would have to go to Moscow in about ten days' time. He said that there was a group of Russians who were looking to sell a large collection of paintings and wanted Sotheby's to give them advice.

"How long will you be away?"

"I'm not sure, it might be a week."

"Oh! What if I came out for a few days with you? I have never been to Russia?"

Ian was expecting this suggestion and replied. "Problem is you need a visa. Mine is still current, but it can take several weeks to get a new one."

Emma's excitement was shattered. "Okay, but we must go there together soon."

"I promise," replied Ian. However, Emma could not see his fingers crossed under the table.

# Chapter 6

Two days later Viktor reported to Ian on his findings about the 25 Baxter paintings. Viktor went through each painting with his suggested valuations, both being sold at auction and by private sale. When he'd finished Ian nodded and said, "You have done a good job here Vic. Leave the file with me would you. Mind I don't think I'll need to change much."

When Viktor had departed, Ian photocopied the report and began to annotate notes and comments on the copied version. He also started to type a letter on his laptop to Sir Paul at Baxter's.

On the same day in Monaco, Andrei had just finished talking on the telephone, with two of his art connections in Moscow. It was always difficult to discuss details with his colleagues in Russia, as nobody knew for certain if anyone in 'authority' was listening in on their telephone conversations. Such discussions were therefore spread over a number of different calls, via different phones and deliberately vague, but nevertheless understood by both Andrei and his colleagues. Andrei opened up his laptop. He would email Sergei with the good news.

Later that evening Sergei asked Viktor to join him in his office. He explained the details of Andrei's email and suggested he speak to Ian the next day.

It was just after 8 am the next morning when Viktor arrived at Sotheby's and he went straight to his boss's office. Unfortunately Ian had not yet arrived. Viktor decided to go back to his own desk and speak to Ian later. However, just as he was leaving Penny arrived and explained that Ian would not be in the office until later that morning. Viktor asked her if she would mention to Ian that he would like to speak to him.

At 12.30 pm Viktor's telephone rang. It was Ian and they agreed to meet at The Grapes at one o'clock.

At The Grapes Viktor conveyed the message from his father. In summary, Ian was required to be in Moscow in four days' time. Sergei had obtained a business class BA flight ticket and had booked him in at the Hotel National. Viktor handed Ian the booking reference details. The flight was due to leave Heathrow at 5.30 pm, but he was required to meet Andrei in Terminal 5 departures at 1 pm as Andrei wanted to inform Ian of the Moscow arrangements.

Ian also wanted to speak to Andrei about Baxter's paintings. Things were beginning to happen.

When Ian arrived back in his office he informed Penny that he would be taking a week's holiday. He mentioned nothing about Moscow but suggested she and Viktor look out for a response to his email from Baxter's with regard to the company's paintings. He explained that he had emailed Viktor's report to Sir Paul and was awaiting their response. He instructed Penny, once she'd received the reply, to email it immediately on to him, holiday or no holiday.

Ian arrived by taxi at Heathrow airport, Terminal 5 at 12.50 pm in preparation for his flight to Moscow. He had spent the previous evening sorting through his wardrobe to find the thickest clothes, but eventually decided to pack based on layers of clothing. That way he could adapt to Moscow's winter weather circumstances more easily.

He pushed through the doors below the large 'Departures' sign pulling his suitcase on wheels and holding a carry-on cabin bag. He entered a vast building and into what looked like a small football crowd of people milling around in all directions. Although he looked around for the familiar figure of Andrei, he realised that this was going to be a difficult task. He therefore wandered over to the main flight indicator board. He placed his cabin bag onto his suitcase and scanned down for his flight to Moscow, making sure his flight was still on time. Eventually he found the BA reference number and was pleased to see it was still timed for departure at 17.30. He once again looked all around for any signs of Andrei, but still struggled to see very far due to the mass of fellow travellers. He checked his phone but there were no recent messages.

He put his phone back in his overcoat pocket and bent down to his cabin bag, unzipped the outer pocket and retrieved his passport ready for passport control. When he resumed his normal height, a tall man, probably in his late 50s Ian guessed, wearing a trilby hat and sporting a strong black and grey beard, was facing him.

"Hello Mr Caxton, my name is Boris Pushkin. I am a colleague of Sergei and Andrei." His voice was husky and although the English was clear, there was, like Sergei, the hint of a Russian accent coming through. Boris held out a large hand towards Ian to shake hands. Ian looked into the man's face and hesitantly, shook his hand.

"I was not expecting to meet you Mr Pushkin," replied Ian somewhat warily.

"No, you were expecting Andrei, but the plans have changed slightly. Andrei is still in Monaco and now wants you to meet him at Nice airport. Your flights have been amended and you will now fly from Paris to Moscow later this evening."

This was not what Ian was expecting at all. It was sounding rather odd and he seriously considered whether to abandon the trip altogether and to go back home. However, he decided to hear what else Boris had to say before finally making that decision.

Boris continued, "Andrei sends his profound apologies but will explain all when you arrive at Nice. Here are your new flight e-tickets to Nice, Paris and Moscow."

Ian looked at each ticket individually to buy him some thinking time.

"Also," said Boris, as he produced an envelope from the inside of his thick overcoat pocket. "Here is some compensation for your inconvenience."

Ian looked inside the envelope at a mixture of £50 and US$100 notes. He guessed they must add up to more than £10,000!

Ian stood facing Boris with the tickets and money still in his hand. Finally, he put them both into his coat pocket and decided that since he had come this far, he might as well at least go to Nice.

Boris continued again, "Your flight to Nice leaves in 55 minutes, so I suggest you make your way to passport control immediately. Goodbye Mr Caxton. I hope you have a good flight." At this Boris turned away and quickly disappeared into the crowd.

Ian stood still for a few minutes and then looked up at the indicator board once again. This time he searched for the Nice flight. Once he had found the flight number he also noticed that at the end of the entry there was a flashing 'boarding now' instruction. He quickly zipped up the pocket of his cabin bag and headed to check in his suitcase and then on to passport control.

Once he had settled himself down in his Business Class seat he looked out of the window and waited for take-off.

He began to wonder if he had made the right decision. He really didn't know these Russians and he was now seriously wondering if Andrei would indeed be at Nice airport. A few minutes later he pulled out the envelope from his jacket pocket and removed the money. He counted £7000 and US$15,000. Oh well he thought, at least I have some compensation. A few minutes later the aeroplane was hurtling down the runway. Too late to change my mind now.

As Ian strode into the arrival area of Nice airport he was relieved to see Andrei's smiling face and he walked towards him.

"Hello my friend, I hope you had a good flight. Sorry for the 'cloak and dagger' changes." The two men shook hands and Andrei pointed to the exit. "Come, my car is just outside."

Ian pulled his case and walked with Andrei towards the large glass exit doors. As the two men stepped outside, Ian immediately noticed the warm sunshine and began squinting at the strong Mediterranean late afternoon sunlight. Andrei pointed to a dark green Rolls Royce parked next to where a uniformed chauffeur was standing guard. As the chauffeur went to take charge of Ian's suitcase and cabin bag, Ian firstly removed a brown file. Andrei and Ian climbed into the rear seats and the chauffeur closed the door and put Ian's bags into the car's boot.

When the two men had settled down, the car moved away from the airport. Andrei pressed a button on his armrest and a dark glass screen slowly raised between the front and rear compartments of the car creating a sound-proof area in the rear.

"So, Andrei, why all the changes?" asked Ian, now sitting back, a bit more relaxed and enjoying the comfort of the soft leather seating and the cool air-conditioning.

"My friend, yesterday my plans were to fly to London. As well as meeting with you I had a meeting lined up with a potential buyer for three of my paintings. Unfortunately, Boris, who you met at Heathrow, advised me that he had found out that this buyer had connections with the Russian Mafia. Needless to say, I try to keep well away from them and certainly do not want to step on their toes."

Ian looked at Andrei with surprise. He really didn't want to get mixed up with the Russian Mafia either! What had he let himself in for?!

"Do not worry my friend," continued Andrei, "we will not be involved with them."

"Andrei, this is all becoming much more alarming than you indicated when we first met."

"My friend I promise you, you will not be involved with the Mafia. Let me explain in more detail now, what I want from you. As I told you in London there is a large collection of paintings stored in Moscow and I want you to use your professional knowledge to evaluate them for me. These paintings were collected from the Nazis at the end of the Second World War. I want to know which are real and which are fakes and I want to know their value. The rest is then up to me and my colleagues to acquire them. I already have some potential buyers. These buyers are not interested in selling on, they are mostly wealthy collectors who only want to own them ... and they do not ask questions."

"Where are these paintings stored?"

"That is the most interesting part. They are stored in the Kremlin!"

"What?!" exclaimed Ian. He looked at Andrei in astonishment! "How on earth am I going to be able to see and evaluate them properly?"

"Let me firstly give you a little history lesson about the Kremlin, my friend."

Ian stared at Andrei and wondered what his bombshell would reveal!

"Did you know, my friend, that the Kremlin has, for hundreds of years, been a city within a city? It was firstly designed and built as a fortress and as such, was able to sustain itself during long sieges. The original Italian designers made sure that as well as building high and strong city walls, there were also more basic necessities installed too, such as an adequate supply of drinking water. They found a spring next to what became the Arsenal Tower and from this source, pipes were laid and water transferred, to many underground collection galleries and chambers within the Kremlin site. Over the years, however, this system gradually failed and new sources of water had to be discovered and new waterways, tunnels and passageways were built. Some were even connected to the Moscow River. Also, over these same centuries a vast network of other passageways, crypts, chambers, secret tunnels and hidden doors were built creating a second Kremlin – a subterranean Kremlin. Many of these passages were designed for emergency entrance and exit to and from the Kremlin. Some went down to the river and others came out at various points in the Kitaigorod section of Moscow. Sometimes these tunnels arrived into an individual's private property, located well outside the Kremlin walls. These tunnels had heavy iron doors and substantial padlocks thus allowing access only by the keyholders. Behind these doors were not only the numerous passageways but also many were constructed and designed as strong rooms. Here, the royal family, rich boyars and other wealthy individuals, could hide all their prized possessions."

Ian was already aware of some of these facts but was still intrigued to know where Andrei's story was going.

Andrei continued, "Although it is known that a number of these Kremlin passageways linked the cathedrals, palaces and most of the major towers within the Kremlin, over recent centuries a number of important Kremlin buildings have had to be reconstructed. The result is that lots of these passageways had to be sealed up. It is now almost impossible to access thoroughly the old underground Kremlin without potentially seriously damaging, or destroying, the foundations of many of these important and ancient buildings. Over the last 300 years sporadic efforts have been made to uncover more of the hidden underground city but these have usually failed due to the constant danger of a building collapsing or being permanently damaged."

Ian sat quietly waiting for the next revelation.

"However," continued Andrei, "a number of the many chambers are still accessible and still in use today. They are used to store all sorts of valuables, including, of course, many former Nazi looted paintings!"

"But there is no way we can get access to these chambers surely?"

"Ah, my friend," replied Andrei with a smile, "but we do have access!"

# Chapter 7

Later that evening Ian's flight from Paris was quiet and uneventful, unlike the journey from Nice to Paris when his flight had been delayed. Although his suitcase was automatically transferred to his Moscow flight, he had to rush to the departure gate and was the last passenger to get on board. Once he had settled into his Business Class seat and caught his breath, he again wondered what he had got himself into.

He had been with Andrei, in his car, for just over an hour before he had to check in for the short trip to Paris. It was only in the last minutes of their meeting that Ian was able to hand over the copied file of Baxter's paintings to him. Ian suggested that he might be interested in buying some of these paintings privately. Andrei thanked him and said he would have a look and do some research, but he was not making any promises.

Ian checked his watch when the plane commenced its descent to Domodedovo Moscow Airport. He fastened his seatbelt and looked out of the window. There were very few clouds and the sky was very dark bar for a soft orange glow on the horizon ahead. He turned his head back and closed his eyes. He tried to relax and then thought of Emma. A small smile appeared on his face as he wondered what she would have made of his eventful day and indeed, what she would have said to him! How was he ever going to explain all this to her?

He opened his eyes as the plane's wheels hit the runway. He remembered Andrei telling him that he would be met by Dimitri Ivanov in 'Arrivals' and Andrei had given him a photograph of the same man. He was told that Dimitri could speak reasonable English, but Ian was not too worried because he was confident his own knowledge of the Russian language would help with communications. The plan was for Dimitri to take him to the Hotel National, located just to the north of the Kremlin and Red Square. He was booked into the hotel for five nights. Andrei had given Ian his return e-ticket flight back direct to Heathrow. Whatever else Andrei was, thought Ian, he was certainly organised.

Once Ian had exited the plane he had to join a queue for passport control. The Russian official examined his passport page by page and noticed that Ian had been to Russia three times before and his visa did not expire for seven months. He asked Ian several questions, which Ian answered in Russian. His passport was then stamped and he was told to carry on. Ian collected his suitcase and headed for customs, where he had nothing to declare. After customs he walked towards the large double doors which had a large 'EXIT' sign located directly above. He followed a family through the doors and emerged into the public area.

A number of people were holding up cards with names on, but Ian could not see his name, or indeed the face on the photograph he kept glancing at. He moved slowly into the milling crowd and wondered if any international airport was ever quiet nowadays, whatever the time of day … or night! Suddenly he felt a light tap on his shoulder and when he turned around he recognised the young face from the photograph. The same blond short cut hairstyle, fair complexion and late 20-something features.

"Welcome to Moscow, Mr Caxton." The English words were clear and deep in tone, but again with the obvious Russian accent.

"Hello Dimitri, where are we going?"

"Ah, so you are testing me already. That's good. Do not trust anyone here. To answer your question, however, I am taking you to the Hotel National."

It was just after 3 am local time, when Ian was dropped off at the hotel. Dimitri said he would meet him again at 10 am the next morning in the reception area and wished him a good night's sleep.

When Ian finally arrived in his room he still felt wide awake and checked his watch for UK time.

He calculated that it was too late in the evening at home, so rather than ring Emma he decided to email her. He kept his story short and a little vague, and didn't mention his diversion and extra flights! At least, he thought, Emma would be aware that he had arrived safely. Whilst still connected to the internet, he checked through other emails but the next thing Ian knew was when his telephone rang and an electronic message announced his early morning call. Ian looked at his watch, 7.30 am. He was laying on the bed and still in his travelling clothes from the previous day. He quickly undressed, showered, shaved, put on fresh clothes and made his way through the hotel for breakfast. As he walked along the corridor he wondered what new surprises were going to be in store for him today.

Dimitri duly arrived in reception just before 10am and spotted Ian sitting in a corner of the reception area flicking through a magazine. As he approached, Ian looked up and got to his feet. The two men shook hands and after discussing the comfort of Ian's room and his breakfast, Dimitri suggested they go for a walk. The day was very cold but there was a lovely clear, blue sky. The two men briefly walked through Manezhnaya Square and came to the front of the famous Resurrection Gate. Ian also noticed the Kilometre Zero sign and Dimitri explained that this is deemed to be the exact centre of Moscow and the starting point for measuring all distances in Russia.

The two men walked under the Resurrection Gate's entranceway which led through to Red Square. Ian knew that this famous gateway is historically considered to be the front gate of the city. Although originally built in 1680, it was rebuilt again in 1995 and the twin red towers topped with green tent-like spires are an exact copy of the original. The gate's arch establishes a visual link between two other remarkable buildings – the State Historical Museum and the Museum of the War of 1812, whilst the small chapel by the gate houses is one of the most venerated icons – the Iveron Icon of the Mother of God.

Once in Red Square, Ian stopped and stared at the view. Although he had seen this view several times before, the impact never failed to amaze him. It is one of the true great panoramic views in the world. To his right are the walls of the Kremlin over which Ian could just see the tops of spires and towers of the palaces, cathedrals and other buildings situated within the grounds of the Kremlin. In the foreground sits the cube-like red and black building of the Lenin Mausoleum. Ahead, and some 500 metres in the far distance across Red Square, is St Basil's Cathedral, with its riot of gables and twisting, multicoloured onion shaped domes. Commissioned in 1552 by Ivan the Terrible, it was originally called the 'Cathedral of the Intercession' but now is more fondly referred to as simply 'St Basil's' – the 'holy fool', whose remains are interred within the building!

Turning his head to the left Ian looked at the huge, internationally renowned 'GUM Building'. It's full and correct name 'Gosudartvennyy universalnyy magazin' was built between 1889–93 on the site of a former covered market. There were once situated here, more than 1000 shops selling all manner of products, but during Stalin's rule the shops were closed and the building requisitioned and used as offices. Today, and despite Russia still officially being a Communist country, many world-famous Western retail shops, restaurants and cafes can be found on the ground floor.

After a few minutes Dimitri spoke, "Fabulous view isn't it?"

"Yes indeed," replied Ian. "Just incredible. It never ceases to amaze me."

"We are standing on many secrets and surrounded by many, many more! Come I will explain."

The two men headed for the nearest entrance to the GUM building. Once inside Ian could see the building was divided into three separate arcades, with archways, wrought-iron railings and stuccoed galleries. The history was obvious and had been well preserved, but the shops were most certainly 21st century. The two men walked along the ground floor. Looking through the windows of each of the shops, Ian thought that this could easily be London … or Tokyo, or even Hong Kong. It was truly international.

When the two men arrived at the front of yet another store, which had the name 'Harvey's' printed in gold above the entrance door, Dimitri stopped briefly. He then pushed the door open and entered, holding the door open until Ian had followed through. They both walked towards the rear of the shop and stopped. Dimitri pretended to look at some clothing and then turned around and whispered,

"Behind me there is a green wooden door." Ian looked over Dimitri's shoulder to a row of clothing racks almost covering the whole length of the rear of the shop. He then spotted a small gap at the far end where there was a partial view of a green wooden door. Dimitri continued, "Through that door it leads to the basement where the shop's stock is stored. The walls of the basement are two to three hundred years old but have been improved to keep out possible damp and the rats. However, located in the basement's far wall, facing Red Square, there is a small iron doorway. It is very old, slightly rusted but nevertheless, very strong. It had been locked for many years."

"You said 'had' been locked."

"A very long story, but what you need to know is, we have a key!"

# Chapter 8

When the two men exited from Harvey's shop, Dimitri suggested they have a coffee and he would explain more.

Dimitri led Ian to a nearby cafe and as they were entering he said this cafe's cappuccinos were excellent. So at the counter Ian agreed to Dimitri's recommendation and two cappuccinos were ordered. Whilst the coffees were made, Ian looked around the room. The cafe had all the outward signs of being 21st century, but he also wondered about its history and what tales it could tell.

When their order was completed they both collected their drinks and found a quiet corner away from the main crowd of customers. Dimitri began to speak, "You are aware that under large parts of the Kremlin and surrounding areas, there is an underground world of secret tunnels, passageways, crypts and chambers?" Ian nodded and waited for Dimitri to continue. "We also know that in two particular chambers there are stored a collection of over 200 paintings, most, if not all, were brought back from Germany at the end of the Second World War. The problem was that although we had a good idea of where these chambers were, we could not find any access, except from within the Kremlin. The main access is within the Senate building, which is heavily guarded and almost impossible to get into without proper authorisation."

Ian nodded whilst Dimitri sipped his coffee. He then continued. "After many months of research and investigations we came across several old maps which gave more details of the tunnels and chambers. One in particular showed a possible route from the Senate, under Red Square and into the GUM building. The breakthrough we were looking for. We calculated that the tunnel must come out into one of three shops. Secretly we managed to access the three basements of these shops and found that this tunnel actually came out into Harvey's basement. The main issue now was getting through the iron door which was very securely locked."

Dimitri took another sip of his coffee before continuing. "One of the maps showed that an old drain situated under Red Square might actually lead to a nearby tunnel, which we were sure would lead to the far side of our iron door. Obviously we could not just lift up the drain cover in the middle of Red Square without causing curiosity from the guards outside Lenin's Mausoleum. So eventually it was decided that if we got a group of men together to gather around the drain cover area about 11.30 am – this time is the most popular time for tourists to visit the area – two of them might be able to hide from view, lift the drain cover and slip inside in a short period of time. The group could then disperse before alarming the guards. This is what happened and two of our colleagues were able to climb into the drain. They eventually found the correct tunnel but as it was very narrow and not very high it took quite some time before they found what they thought was the iron door to Harvey's basement. It was then that we had a massive piece of luck. The tunnel is constructed of stones, bricks. rubble and oak beams. Near the door, we found a loose stone in the wall and when it was gently pulled out, there was a fragile, rusty key hidden in the cavity. Our colleague carefully wrapped the key in his handkerchief and they made their way back to the drain cover. At 2 pm the guards change their watch outside the mausoleum, so that was the agreed time to get the two men out of the drain. The group of men reassembled around the drain covering and one tapped on the metal cover. When he heard the men respond, the lid was lifted and the two men were then able to escape from the drain. The fragile key was then taken to another colleague, who is a key cutter, and he was able to make an exact copy. Several days later we managed to regain access to Harvey's basement and tried the new key. The lock and the door proved extremely stiff to move. But the new key eventually worked and the door was gradually opened."

"Wow," said Ian. "So have you managed to get to the chambers where the paintings are stored?"

"No, unfortunately not yet. We have been able to trace a route through the tunnels which arrives at another door, but it looks as though this door is padlocked from the other side. We need to be able to open this first to enable us to get into the passageway. We think that this passageway then leads to the Senate's chambers."

"So how will I be able to see the paintings?"

"Tonight there is a large meeting of Russian dignitaries in the Senate building and the authorities are increasing the number of security guards for the event. Two of our team will be part of the extra security group. We have been able to acquire a key to the chambers and one of our men is going to access the main chamber and the tunnels and see if we can get to the locked door and remove the padlock."

"You should then get access to the Senate chambers from Harvey's basement?"

"That is our hope."

Ian sat back in his chair, finished his coffee and after a short pause said, "So what happens if this fails?"

"It won't." said Dimitri confidently.

Ian wasn't quite so positive. "So what do we do until then?"

"There's nothing you can do for the moment. I will meet you in your hotel reception tomorrow morning at 10 am, as we did earlier. I am sure there will then be some good news to tell you!"

Ian spent the rest of the day visiting the 19th century European Art museum situated on the Ulitsa Volkhonka and the Pashkov House. He had never visited this house before, but he was aware that the Pashkov House is a magnificent mansion built in the Neoclassical style in the late 1700s. It was once one of the finest private houses in Moscow.

After he completed his house tour Ian stood and stared at the view to the east of the city. From the wonderful hilltop location he could see deep into the Kremlin grounds and could just make out a small portion of the Senate building. He stared at the building for some time and wondered what tomorrow would bring. A cold breeze was getting up and was now blowing through his hair. He pushed it back with both hands, pulled up the collar of his overcoat and decided it was time to head back to his hotel. Back to a hot meal and a long hot soak in the bath!

# Chapter 9

Next morning, after his hotel breakfast, Ian returned to his room and composed a brief email to Emma. Again, he was deliberately vague about what exactly he was up to, but he did advise her the details of his BA return flight to Heathrow. He was becoming more and more uncomfortable about the deception, but finally decided that at least now he could justify his vagueness, because he didn't know if anyone was likely to be looking in on his emails!

At 10 am Ian arrived in reception and spotted Dimitri standing with his back to him, looking out the window. As Ian walked towards him, Dimitri turned around and the two men exchanged greetings. Dimitri suggested they go for a walk. Once outside Ian felt the same chill in the air he had experienced the previous evening. He wondered if it was going to snow.

The two men followed yesterday's route to Red Square. There they stopped almost in the middle. Once happy that it was unlikely that they would be overheard, Dimitri explained what had happened at the Senate building the previous night. "It's good news. Our man was able to access the two chambers and has taken some photographs of the layout. These photographs show that the two chambers are connected by a short passageway and at the rear of the second chamber there is a heavy oak door which was partly hidden by some old picture frames and cloth sheets. The door is secured on the chamber side by an old padlock. This was anticipated and our colleague was able to cut it off and pull at the door. Surprisingly, and especially after all these years, the door swung open quite easily and he followed the tunnel. It was cold and slightly damp, but he eventually came to our problem iron door. Again this was locked, and as we had guessed, by a very old padlock. Our colleague was able to cut this off. The iron door proved more difficult but eventually it swung open halfway before jamming on a rock buried in the tunnel floor. Using his padlock cutter, he was able to prise this obstacle out of the floor. The door could then be fully opened."

Ian listened intently to every word Dimitri was saying and, whilst he had some questions, he decided to wait until Dimitri had finished.

"Our colleague closed the door, but left it unlocked and left the padlock on the floor. He then made his way back to the chambers. Once back inside he closed the tunnel door and re-covered it with the picture frames and the cloth sheets making sure nobody could see that the padlock was missing. He then returned to the Senate access door and retrieved a small electronic device from his pocket which, when a button was pressed, his colleague felt a light and quiet vibration on his similar device. Once the area was signalled clear, the door was unlocked and our colleague re-entered the Senate room. After cleaning dust off his uniform, the two guards resumed their temporary duties."

"Have you got the photographs of the chambers?"

"Not with me but you can see them later."

"Do you have any idea of the list of paintings that are stored there?"

"We do have an old inventory, but we are not sure how

up-to-date it is. We understand, some of these paintings are periodically swapped and some have certainly been sold since the inventory was written. However, we do still think there are well over 200 paintings stored there."

"I would like to see this inventory, it could be very useful."

"I will take you to one of our safe houses and you can then inspect the photographs and the inventory."

"Excellent," said Ian.

Dimitri led Ian towards St Basil's Cathedral before they turned left and along the Ulitsa Varvarka. From there the two men turned down several streets before Dimitri stopped outside the 'History of Moscow' museum. He looked all around him and once he was happy nobody appeared to be following them, he turned away from Ian and made a telephone call, speaking in Russian on his mobile. Ian managed to understand one or two words, but the dialect was too strong. It was obvious he was not meant to be hearing what was being said.

After Dimitri finished the call he asked Ian to follow him. After about 50 metres Ian saw that a black front door to a large building was slightly ajar. Dimitri pushed it open and went in. Ian, somewhat hesitantly, followed through. The front living room was sparsely furnished and it was generally quite dark and gloomy with very little daylight shining through the windows ... and it was cold ... very cold. Dimitri led Ian through to the back room which seemed even gloomier. This was not warm either and Ian assumed it was not heated, or the heating had been switched off for some time. He wondered if anyone lived here and also who had opened the front door as there appeared to be no one else in the building, unless of course, someone was upstairs.

Dimitri pointed to a table and suggested Ian sat down. Dimitri disappeared from the room for two minutes and then returned with two brown cardboard folders. He walked over to the table, sat down opposite Ian and handed over the two folders, one at a time.

"Here are the photographs of the two chambers. This other file contains a copy of the old inventory."

Ian took both folders and opened up the inventory file. He removed what looked like about 20 sheets of typed A4 paper.

"Can I have a light on? It's too dark in here to read these?"

"There is no electricity here. You can take that copy with you and read it in your hotel."

Ian put the papers back in their folder and then removed the contents from the second folder. There were five black and white, or more precisely dark and light grey, photographs. Again he struggled to see the details of the photographs in the room's gloomy light. He could just make out two rectangular low ceiling rooms with white or light walls. Stacked vertically against most of the walls were rows and rows of framed paintings all of different sizes. Each painting appeared to have either a plywood or double thickness cardboard sheet separating each picture. He could also see in the far chamber the door which he assumed led to the underground tunnel. It was almost hidden by old picture frames and a pile of cloths. Ian's immediate reaction was what sort of condition were these paintings being kept in? Basement's, unless they were properly heated and ventilated, would devalue paintings within weeks, never mind years!

After Ian had viewed all five photographs Dimitri announced, "look as long as you want, but they cannot leave this building."

Ian looked through them once more, but decided they offered little use for him. He packed them back in the folder and returned it to Dimitri.

"I'm concerned about the conditions that these paintings are being kept in. They might be damaged and virtually worthless. Oil-based paintings not only need to breathe but all artwork can be adversely affected by excess humidity and dampness. Basements are notorious for causing humidity damage."

"You cannot see from those photographs, but the chambers have had special humidity and air-controlled climate units installed. They are stored in conditions similar to those you would find in a proper museum basement."

Ian was not convinced, and once again, wondered if this whole exercise was going to turn out to be a complete waste of everybody's time.

When Ian decided to leave the house Dimitri said he would be staying on as he had some work to do there. Ian promised Dimitri that he would read the whole of the inventory file and report his findings when they met later that evening.

Ian departed back via the front door that he'd entered through earlier. Despite the low temperature outside, he thought it still felt warmer than inside the house!

He carried the inventory folder under his arm and took a slightly quicker route back to his hotel. He felt exceptionally cold and dreamed of a long, hot soak in the bath.

Ian arrived back at the hotel and went immediately up to his room. He put the folder on his desk and went into the bathroom and turned on the two bath taps. He then ordered food from room service and opened a can of beer from his mini bar. After pouring the beer into a glass, he drank half the contents. He then opened the folder, removed the papers and glanced through each sheet before re-ordering them, as far as possible, by the name of the artist. He checked on his bath and was satisfied with the temperature.

He was just about to read the details on the first sheet when there was a knock on the door. It was room service delivering a tray containing his sandwich, hot soup and a small bowl of salad, which he placed on the desk. He then began to eat the soup and read the first sheet of paper. As he read through the details of each painting he made several notes. The hot soup felt good and it warmed him up. He now got undressed and climbed into the steaming bath. He lay back, closed his eyes and reflected on a most unusual day.

Twenty minutes later, Ian got out of the bath feeling fully refreshed and warm again. After drying and putting on a clean set of clothes, he ate his sandwich, salad and finished the glass of beer. Returning back to the inventory, he discovered the largest number of pictures were painted by the artists Renoir and Van Gogh, although there were also several entries attributed to Cezanne, Monet, Moreau, Nicholson, Whistler and other lesser artists. However, what really surprised him was to find Matisse, Picasso, Gauguin and Juan Gris paintings also listed. Being modern art painters, Ian knew the Nazis would not have bothered with them, so he wondered if they were part of another collection.

He spent most of the afternoon reading and making more notes. Of course, he thought, some of this exercise could still be a waste of time, as he still didn't know which of these paintings were still stored in the chambers.

At 7 pm Ian received a telephone call on his mobile. It was Dimitri and the two men agreed to discuss Ian's findings over dinner. Dimitri told Ian that he had made a reservation in the hotel's Dr. Zhivago restaurant for 7.45 pm. He thought Ian would enjoy the modern Russian cuisine that was served there.

Ian finished the last of his notes and walked into the restaurant just before 7.45 pm. Dimitri was already seated and Ian walked over to join him. The restaurant was not overly busy and Dimitri had found a quiet corner table. The two men ordered drinks and their food. Ian began to explain his findings from the inventory. He told Dimitri that if the pictures were indeed painted by the named artists, and not fakes, and were stored in the correct humidity conditions, then it was potentially a fabulous collection. However, he then went on to explain that he was fairly certain some, if not many, of the pictures on the inventory would also be found on the Commission for Looted Art in Europe database. Therefore selling them may be very difficult, especially through the main galleries and auction houses.

Dimitri listened and then shrugged his shoulders, "It does not matter which, or if any, of these paintings are on this database. We have a different group of potential buyers. These people are not too interested in history, they just want the pictures. Our only concern is, are they real or fakes! That information will determine the final price we can get."

Ian was a little surprised with Dimitri's comment. This was certainly a different art world to the one he had been used to dealing in. "So when can I see these paintings?"

"Tomorrow is Sunday and Harvey's will be closed all day. We are able to access the shop and basement from 9 am."

"What about alarms and guards?"

"No problem, all taken care of. We have a contact who is able to temporarily disarm the shop's alarm system. However, we do need to be out of the premises by midnight as that is the time when the alarm has to be reactivated."

"And if we are not out by midnight?"

"Then we have a serious problem!"

# Chapter 10

Ian agreed to meet with Dimitri the next morning in the hotel's reception at 8.30 am. He had previously explained to Dimitri that he would need a LED head torch with adjustable strap, at least two fully charged hand torches, good quantities of clean drinking water, towels, two magnifying glasses, two pairs of clear safety glasses and a large rucksack.

When Dimitri arrived at the hotel he came empty-handed explaining that all Ian's requirements had already been taken to Harvey's. It would not be sensible to carry them to and from the hotel. It might look like suspicious behaviour! Ian, however, already had a shoulder bag containing the inventory, a woolly hat, five ballpoint pens and extra writing paper from his hotel room.

The two men walked their usual route to the GUM building. It was still early morning and there were very few people about. It was very cold but again, a clear day. Although the sun had just risen, it had very little heat in it and so the overnight heavy frost still covered most of the ground in Red Square. When they arrived at Harvey's shop, Dimitri looked around him and when he was sure all was quiet, he tapped twice and then three times on the door. It was immediately opened and Dimitri and Ian went through. The door was closed and instantly locked.

There were no lights on in the shop but an outside light in the corridor sent a shaft of dim light across the shop's ceiling. There was just sufficient light for Ian to spot two other men standing in the shadows. Dimitri put his finger to his lips and the four men quietly walked to the back of the shop and to the green door. The first man retrieved a key from his pocket, unlocked the door and three of them went through to the basement. The fourth member stayed in the shop. Dimitri grasped a small torch from his back pocket and switched it on. He whispered to Ian and introduced Ivan. Both men nodded. Dimitri then shone the beam to a collection of articles near the basement door. Ian could see straight away that they were the items he had requested earlier. The three men walked over to the door and Ian checked he had everything he had ordered. Once satisfied he put on his woolly hat, LED head torch and a pair of the clear safety glasses. Most of the other items of equipment were then distributed between the two men and Ivan unlocked the basement door. Ian stowed his remaining items in the large rucksack. As the door gently eased open they felt an immediate chill and the distinctly musty air blow into their faces.

Ivan switched on his own larger hand torch and placed a smaller torch into his pocket. He shone the larger beam into the tunnel and stepped through the door and onto the dried mud and cobblestones. Ian followed and then Dimitri brought up the rear, quietly closing the door behind him. Dimitri whispered to Ian that Ivan had done this trip before and knew the route. Ian nodded and the men moved forward. Fortunately, the tunnel was just wide enough for one man but each of them had to make sure they kept their heads down as the tunnel's roof was quite low and had some protruding rocks. Dimitri whispered to Ian, "When these tunnels were first constructed the average human being's height was not as tall as we are today."

Ian smiled and nodded. He needed to keep up with Ivan.

They progressed slowly, trying to make as little noise as possible. Ivan stopped and raised his hand for his colleagues to stop too. Ian guessed they must be about halfway across Red Square. Immediately in front of Ivan there was a junction with two tunnels, one going at right angles to the left and one slightly to the right. Each of the two tunnels were blocked by wrought iron doors. Ivan went to the right-hand door and gave it a gentle push. The iron door slowly creaked open and the three men progressed into the next tunnel. As he ducked under the low door frame, Ian spotted the old padlock on the floor. Slowly and quietly they continued to walk but then had to semi-crawl their way along a short section of the tunnel. Ivan suddenly stopped again and whispered in Russian that they would take a short break. The three men sat on the mud and stone floor. Ian took the opportunity to stretch his neck and shoulders and take a drink from his bottle of water.

As the three men sat quietly, they could hear some muffled voices. Ivan whispered that they were probably tourists they could hear above – in the Kremlin grounds! Ian and Dimitri looked at each other and both seemed to smile and raise their eyebrows at the same time. Ivan then reported that they had only about 30 metres still to go. He got up, switched his torch back on and directed it ahead into the dark tunnel. Ian put his rucksack back on over his shoulders and headed after Ivan with Dimitri close behind.

Within a few minutes they arrived at an old oak door which Ian guessed was the entrance to the Senate chambers. Ivan listened for any sign of voices or activity in the chambers. After about 30 seconds he whispered in Russian explaining that the door opens into the basement so when he opens the door some of the old picture frames may move. He would open the door very slowly and hope he could reach through and stop any falling and causing a noise. The other two men nodded their understanding.

Slowly Ivan turned the door's handle and then gently pushed. There was no noise from the chamber and so he tried to look over the small gap he had created at the top. Satisfied there appeared to be nobody in the chambers, he slowly pushed on the door again but this time he managed to also ease his right arm through the gap and catch hold of two of the frames. Slowly the door opened a little more until Ivan could squeeze through and move the remaining frames and the pile of cloths. The two other men followed through and Dimitri closed the door quietly behind him.

The chamber was about three metres high, so Ian stood up to his full height, stretched, removed his head torch and switched on his hand torch. He looked around the chamber and could see the short passageway leading through to the second chamber. Against all the walls were stacked rows and rows of paintings. He noticed that the damp, musty smell that they had experienced in the tunnels had now disappeared and had been replaced by a much fresher, but still chilly air. Reading his mind, Dimitri pointed to two metal boxes located in the passage between the two chambers. Ian nodded when he heard the faint hum from the special air conditioning and dehumidifying units.

Ian removed his inventory, pens and paper from his rucksack. Ivan went through to the other chamber and sat close to the door which led up into the Senate building. It was his job to listen for voices or any footsteps from above. Ian and Dimitri started to investigate the paintings. Dimitri followed Ian's instructions and slowly they looked at each painting together. Where the painting was on the inventory Ian made additional notes about the condition and whether he thought it was authentic. If the painting was not on the inventory he made separate notes on the blank sheets of paper he had brought with him specifically for this purpose.

Each painting was inspected, some with more detail than others, some with the torch close to and sometimes with the use of one of the magnifying glasses. Occasionally Ian wiped dust or dirt with a damp or dry cloth.

It was just after 3 pm when Ian and Dimitri had finished in the first chamber and they began to move their equipment through to the next chamber. Suddenly Ivan made a "Sshh" noise. Ian and Dimitri immediately stood still. Ivan listened intently at the door. He could hear voices at the top of the stairs. Ian could feel an increase in his heart beating and looked around the chamber. He soon remembered the pile of cloths and pointed to them. Both Dimitri and Ivan nodded and acknowledged that the cloths might be used as their hiding place – if necessary.

The three men waited. Gradually the Russian voices faded and all seemed to be quiet once more. Ivan gave the thumbs up sign and Ian and Dimitri set to work on the second chamber's contents.

By 10 pm Ian had completed all his investigations and made his last note. The three men collected all their equipment and headed for the old oak door. Dimitri pulled the door open and he was immediately hit with the familiar musty, cold air. Ian quickly followed and finally Ivan, who had to first make sure that he would be able to reach through a slit and ease the frames and cloths back roughly into their original position. He also had to make sure the broken lock could not be seen from the chamber. After two minor rearrangements he finally pulled the door into its closed position.

The three men made their way back through the tunnels and Ivan quietly closed the doors behind them. Once they were back in Harvey's shop Dimitri pointed to a different wooden door at the far end of the shop. Ian had not spotted this before. The three men eased themselves along the back of two counters and past racks of clothes until they had arrived at the door. Dimitri slowly opened it and checked all was clear. They all then stepped into a corridor. Despite the darkness Ian could make out the Russian "Fire Exit" sign at the far end. Dimitri slowly pushed on the escape bar and the door opened, letting them out of the building and into a small courtyard. Ian immediately spotted a green van parked on the far side. He began to shiver against the chilled night air, Ivan gently closed the exit door and Dimitri opened the rear van doors. He beckoned for the other two to follow him. The three men all climbed in and the driver switched on the van's ignition and they all drove away and into the night.

# Chapter 11

The van dropped Ian off about 50 metres from the hotel and he walked towards the hotel's main entrance carrying his rucksack. As he moved he kept stretching his legs and neck against the stiffness from the tunnels and the cramped rear of the van.

Before entering the hotel Ian brushed himself down and tried to tidy his hair. He wiped his face and hands and then walked into reception. It was very quiet and only the night porter was on duty. He collected his key and ordered soup and sandwiches to be delivered to his room. He had just realised he hadn't eaten since breakfast and was certainly hungry now.

Entering the room, he put the rucksack on the bed and went into the bathroom. Two minutes later he removed a can of beer from the mini bar and poured half the contents into a glass. Next he changed out of his clothes and put on the hotel's bath robe. There was a knock on the door and Ian collected his tray of food and put it all on to the desk. He then had a hot bath.

Once he was dry and wrapped in the robe once again, Ian attacked his meal with relish.

After he put the food tray outside his door and into the corridor, he suddenly felt very tired. He checked the time on his watch. It was just before 1am but he wanted to unpack his rucksack first before getting into bed. Out came the somewhat dog-eared inventory, the new written notes, pens and unused sheets of paper. Finally, he removed a small oil painting! During a short period when the three men were having a break from their work, Ian had decided to stretch his back and legs. Dimitri had found an old newspaper next to the old picture frames and he and Ivan were reading some of the old news. Ian had wandered through to the first chamber and then over to a group of the smaller pictures that he had already examined earlier. He picked up a small William Nicholson still life oil painting entitled, *Rose in a Glass Vase*. He examined it again and despite the poor light, he could still admire the quality of the work. Finally, he made a decision. When he looked around he noticed he was completely out of view of both Dimitri and Ivan. Quietly he slipped the picture into his rucksack and put the bag back on the ground. He then re-joined the others and suggested they all carry on with their work again.

Now back in his hotel room he looked once more at the painting. The room's lighting was not brilliant but sufficient for a more detailed examination. He'd always enjoyed looking at Nicholson's paintings and decided that this was a quality piece of work. Smiling to himself and thinking of his audacity, he gently pushed the picture under the bed. He looked at his watch again. It was just after 1.30 am and within minutes of climbing into bed he was fast asleep.

Ian had agreed to meet with Dimitri early in the evening at 6 pm in reception. He needed most of the day to prepare his report, pulling together all the information from the old inventory plus the previous night's findings. The next day he would be travelling back to Domodedovo Moscow airport, so there was not much time left to complete his task. Over breakfast he considered how he was going to get his report to Andrei. He was not sure of the security, or indeed the reliability, of the Russian postal system. He had heard different stories about interceptions by the Russian authorities and really didn't know what to believe. After all the work he, Dimitri and Ivan had done, he certainly didn't want his report to get into the wrong hands, or if it did, he wanted to make sure that it was sufficiently vague so as not to be connected with the collection in the Kremlin chambers. Finally he decided he would have a 'belt and braces' plan of action. After leaving the breakfast room he visited the hotel's shop and purchased five 16GB USB memory storage sticks, three overseas postage paid thick envelopes, a small roll of sticky tape and a map of Russia, which was supplied in a heavy-duty cardboard tube.

For most of the day, he processed all the information onto his computer in a spreadsheet format report. He listed 212 paintings by 32 different artists and against each painting he put his comments and thoughts under the columns of: 'Artist', 'Description', 'Condition', 'Commission for Looted Art in Europe Listing', 'Fake or Real' and 'Potential Value'. Once finished he copied the report onto the five USB memory sticks. He placed two on the bed and with the remaining three, he tucked each one between a separate sheet of the hotel's stationery paper and slotted into one of the three pre-paid envelopes. When all three were completed he addressed one to himself at Sotheby's, London, one was addressed to himself at his parent's home in Hampshire and the third was addressed to a Nice post office box number, given to him by Andrei. Of the two remaining memory sticks he would give one to Dimitri and keep the last one about his person. Ian was aware that the international post from Russia was also notoriously slow, but he hoped at least one of the posted copies would arrive at their final destination.

Later that afternoon he gave the sealed envelope addressed to his parents to the hotel's reception for them to post. For the one addressed to Sotheby's he walked along a number of streets before arriving in Teatralnaya Square, opposite the world-famous Bolshoi Theatre. Here he posted the second letter into a blue coloured post box. The third letter he decided, he would post at the airport in the morning before his flight.

At 6 pm, Ian walked into the reception area carrying the inventory folder. Dimitri was already waiting for him and the two men shook hands. Ian suggested they go to the Alexandrovsky Bar for a drink. The waiter showed them to a table in the bar area and the two men both ordered Baltika lager beers. The Alexandrovsky Bar was popular with business people and already there was a buzz and chatter.

Ian passed over the inventory file and said to Dimitri, "Here is the original inventory file. I do not need it anymore. You will also find a USB memory stick in the folder. The stick contains a copy of my report. I am sure you must have a way for an encrypted version to be delivered to Andrei." Ian did not tell Dimitri about the other USB copy files. He just hoped at least one would eventually arrive in Andrei's possession.

Dimitri smiled and said, "Thank you. Yes, I will make sure Andrei gets his copy. Do you want to tell me what the report says?"

Ian wondered how much he should tell Dimitri, but decided he would probably read the report on the memory stick in any case. "It covers all the paintings we saw, with my comments and thoughts of each picture, whether I thought it was a fake, real or needed further forensic investigations and of course my estimate of market value. I have also changed the names of some of the paintings because if the authorities somehow pick up the report then hopefully, they will not connect it with the paintings collection in the Kremlin chambers."

"Excellent. I think this certainly calls for a bottle of champagne." Dimitri put the file on a chair next to him and called over a waiter.

When Ian returned to his room just after 10.30 pm, he decided to do some preliminary packing for the journey home. After firstly dealing with his dirty clothes and spare shoes, he then set about the cardboard tube. He firstly took the metal caps off both ends and removed the rolled up map of Russia. He then pulled out from under his bed, the Nicholson painting. Placing it face down on the bed, he gently removed the picture's hard backing and then the canvas painting from the frame.

After applying two small strips of the sticky tape to the bottom rear of the picture, he gently rolled it up and inserted it into the tube, with the ends of the two sticky tapes protruding out the bottom. The bottom metal cap was then secured to the protruding tapes and pushed back onto the end of the tube. He then tipped the tube upside down making sure the picture was secure and didn't fall out.

When he was happy that all was secure, he then slid the rolled up map of Russia gently back into the top of the tube. After slight adjustments, he looked inside and decided he could not see anything of the painting as the map was larger and now covered the inside walls of the tube. The top metal cap was then secured into position and he stuck a small piece of tape on the top of the metal cap. This would remind Ian which end was the top cap. He sat back and decided he was pleased with his effort and hoped it would thwart any casual Russian investigation at the airport. Finally he put the picture's frame and the hard backing into a plastic bag and planned to put it into the lower basement rubbish bin on the way to breakfast in a few hours' time.

That evening Ian struggled to sleep comfortably. Twice he was awakened by strange dreams. One he remembered involved him being pursued by the Russian Mafia across Red Square! Finally he decided to get up. It was 5.30 am. He shaved and showered and completed the rest of his packing. At 6.30 am he picked up the plastic bag containing the picture frame and backing and headed towards the elevator. When the elevator arrived he pressed the lower basement button. The elevator descended without stopping until it arrived at the lower basement floor. The doors opened and he walked the short distance to a bank of large rubbish containers. Ian looked around and satisfied himself that there was nobody else in the area. The first bin he opened was empty so he quietly closed the lid and opened the next one. This one was nearly full so he pulled some of the rubbish aside and pushed his bag as deep as he could reach. He then covered it with other rubbish until he was satisfied that the bag was not showing. He then returned to the elevator and pressed the button for Ground Floor. When the doors opened, he walked to the lavatory where he thoroughly washed his hands and face and cleaned some marks off his clothes. He checked himself in the mirror, brushed his hair with his hands and headed towards the breakfast room.

After a leisurely meal he returned to his room, checked everything was packed and then departed, closing the door securely behind him. He pulled his suitcase along the corridor to the bank of elevators. One of the elevators had just arrived and he joined a family group also heading for the ground floor. There he walked across to reception and checked out.

At 9 am Dimitri arrived and they both set off in Dimitri's car. During the journey the two men discussed the events of the last five days. Both agreed that it had all gone very well. Despite the heavy Moscow traffic, Ian arrived at the

'Departures' terminal of Domodedovo Moscow airport, in good time for his 12.30 pm flight to London Heathrow. The two men shook hands and Dimitri wished Ian a safe journey. Ian thanked him for all his help and also asked him to pass on his thanks to Ivan as well. Ian got out of the car and retrieved his suitcase and cabin bag from the car's boot. He headed towards the flight indicator board to find out which number BA's check-in desk was. As he walked across the concourse he spotted a small collection of post boxes. He removed the envelope addressed to Andrei from his cabin bag and inserted it into the 'International' post box. He wondered if any of the three postings would eventually arrive at their final destinations. He then headed for the 'Flight Departures' board and noted the check-in desk number.

Thirty minutes later Ian had dropped his suitcase at the BA check-in desk and had advanced through passport control and security, without any delay or problems. He then walked for about another ten minutes towards Gate 24. He was certainly a little more relaxed now that he had not been challenged at security. At Gate 24 the First Class and Business Class passengers were already boarding. Ian joined a short queue, showed his passport and boarding card and proceeded to the plane's front entrance doorway. He immediately found his seat, unpacked some of the contents of his hand luggage and put the remainder in the overhead storage area. When he sat down a stewardess approached and offered him a glass of champagne from a small silver tray. He took a glass, thanked her and sat back, exhaling a relaxing sigh. He closed his eyes for a few moments and then looked around his cabin at his fellow passengers. Deciding there were no familiar faces, he gazed out of the window and watched the activity of loading the last of the bags and suitcases on to the plane.

Earlier that morning the hotel's weather forecast guide had suggested Moscow might get its first snow flurry of the season and Ian was sure he had just spotted a few white flakes drifting past the window. He was happy to be going home. The last five days had certainly been an adventure and hopefully a very profitable one too. He sipped his champagne and thought of Emma. He wondered what he was going to say to her!

# Chapter 12

The flight was uneventful and although Ian had tried to read the *Times* newspaper, which had been given to him earlier in the flight, his broken night's sleep was slowly catching up on him and several times he awoke to find the newspaper crumpled on the floor. Finally he sat up as the stewardess arrived with his meal on a tray. After he had eaten and drank a nice half bottle of Chablis, his mind began to wander again. He kept thinking about the last few days and indeed pondered on what could be happening over the next few weeks, or even the next few months. Was this going to be a 'one-off' experience with Andrei or could there be more exciting adventures? But, then there was Emma and his work at Sotheby's to consider. His thinking was suddenly interrupted when the pilot announced that the plane would shortly be commencing its descent and could all passengers return to their seats and secure their seat belts. Ian fastened his, and glanced out of the window. When he looked down he saw the English coastline slowly coming into view. Nearly home, he thought.

Ian was one of the first passengers off the plane and was therefore able to join just a short queue for passport control. After about a five-minute wait he was called forward and he presented his passport to a female officer. The officer processed the passport through her computer and then asked where Ian had arrived from. Ian explained that he had been on holiday in Moscow for five days, seeing the sights. The officer smiled, gave Ian his passport back and wished him a safe journey home.

Ian now headed for the baggage reclaim area to collect his suitcase. However, when he arrived none of his flight's hold bags and suitcases had yet been delivered to the carousel. He decided to take the opportunity to telephone Emma on his mobile. After several rings Emma's answerphone clicked in and so he left a message, "Hi darling, arrived at Heathrow. Baggage has not yet arrived. Will get a taxi and hopefully be home by eight o'clock. See you soon. Love you." After switching off his call, he then checked through his incoming emails and finally sent one out to Andrei. Just as he finished typing, the carousel began to stir into action and the first bags appeared. His suitcase was the fourth in the queue.

After collecting his case, he headed for the green 'Nothing to Declare" exit route. He passed several empty desks but then saw two uniformed Customs officials standing at the end desk. As he was about to walk by them, the tall, but younger one, spoke to him and asked, "Excuse me sir. Where have you just arrived from?"

Ian was not expecting this and was immediately concerned but also on his guard. He replied, "Russia, Moscow, the BA flight."

"Can I see your passport and boarding pass please sir?"

Ian felt in his inside jacket pocket and pulled out his passport and the paper boarding pass. He handed both documents over.

The official glanced at the boarding pass and then looked in more detail at his passport, checking the photo with Ian's features before passing both documents on to his elder colleague.

"Is there anything wrong?" asked Ian, now really concerned.

The official ignored his question and said, "What were you doing in Moscow?"

"Just a short break. Holiday, sightseeing, visiting some of the art galleries," blustered Ian.

"Can you put your cases on here please sir and open them up." The officer pointed to the tabletop.

Ian took his hand luggage bag off his shoulder and put it on the table. He then lifted his suitcase and placed it next to his hand luggage case.

"Can you open both cases please sir?" repeated the officer.

Both cases were only zipped so Ian was able to open them quite quickly.

A number of travellers were now passing behind Ian and he was feeling a mixture of concern and distinct embarrassment.

"Is there a problem?" repeated Ian. This was the first time he had ever been stopped at customs.

The official ignored his question again and said he would need to look through the bags.

"Are you looking for drugs?" asked Ian, but when the official stopped his search of the hand luggage and looked up at him, he knew he had said the wrong thing.

"Why, do you have some drugs to declare sir?"

"No, no!" exclaimed Ian. "Look, I'm sorry. It's just … well, I do not have any." Ian was now flustered and decided his best policy was to keep quiet and just answer their questions.

The young official resumed his search and started on the main suitcase. After a few seconds the official pulled out the large cardboard tube and gave it a shake. There was no noise, but he asked Ian, "What is in here?"

Ian thought his heart was about to stop, but eventually he

managed to calm himself sufficiently to say, "It's just a map, a map of Russia. A souvenir."

"Can you open it please sir?"

Ian took hold of the tube and made sure he pulled off the marked top metal cap. He inserted two fingers into the opening and pulled out about half of the map, folding back one of the corners to display the map's details to the two officers. The elder officer now seemed to be happy and passed Ian his passport and boarding pass and then walked away.

The younger officer tucked down the contents of Ian's case and said, "Thank you for your patience sir. You can go."

Ian pushed the Russian map back into the cardboard tube and placed it back into his suitcase. He quickly re-zipped the two bags and headed for the exit. He had no intention of waiting to see if they were going to call him back.

When he emerged into the 'Arrivals' hall, he could still feel his heart racing, but he still wanted to get out of there as quickly as possible. He followed the signs for 'taxis' and pushed through the exit door and out into the cold early evening air. He spotted the long queue for the taxis and joined it. The queue moved quite quickly as there seemed to be a continuous flow of arriving taxis which then carried people off into the night. By the time Ian got to the front of the queue he was feeling a lot more relaxed and just wanted to get home.

# Chapter 13

The taxi pulled up in his driveway and Ian paid the fare, including a nice tip. As the car drove away he stood and stared at the front of his house. Such a lot had happened since he had last been here. Now he needed to explain to Emma. A number of the house lights were still switched on so he picked up his suitcases, took a deep breath and headed for the front door. As he arrived under the porch light Emma opened the door and came out throwing her arms around his shoulders and giving him a big kiss.

"What a welcome," said Ian, once he was able to free his mouth to speak. He stared at her for a few seconds. She looked gorgeous and had obviously changed from her office clothes.

"I've missed you. Had a good time?" asked Emma, realising Ian was looking at her admiringly.

"Let's get in and I'll tell you. It's cold out here."

Emma took hold of the hand luggage bag and Ian picked up his main suitcase. They both entered the hallway. The central heating was working and the house felt warm and cosy. He knew he was finally home. He placed the suitcase at the bottom of the stairs next to where Emma had placed his smaller bag. They both then went through to the kitchen. Ian immediately picked up the aroma of Emma's cooking.

"Dinner will be about 20 minutes. it's a casserole I'm afraid. I wasn't sure what time you would arrive home."

"Sounds good … and you have poured the wine too."

Emma picked up both glasses of Chablis, walked over to Ian and handed him one of the glasses. "I heard the taxi pull up. Cheers and welcome home!"

"Cheers to you too. It's so good to be back home again."

They both clinked their glasses and Ian gave Emma a kiss before they both sipped their wine.

"Well, come on then, how was your trip? I got all your vague emails."

"Sorry about that but you cannot be sure who might be listening!"

"Oh Ian, for goodness sake. Who would be interested in our domestic chatter?"

"Even so. Anyway, I'm back now and would have arrived even earlier, but you'll never guess what! I was stopped by UK Customs."

"What! What were you doing?"

"I think it must have been just a random stop because after a few questions and a flick through my luggage they let me go."

"How odd. Maybe they thought you looked like an international drug smuggler!"

"Oh very funny. It's the first time I've ever been stopped," he said, but then thought … and the first time that I've ever tried to smuggle anything into the UK! "I must go to the loo and clean myself up a bit before dinner."

"Okay, dinner will be ready when you come back down."

Ian went through to the hallway, collected his cases and took them upstairs to the main bedroom. After his visit to the bathroom, he changed clothes and started to unpack, putting his dirty clothes in a heap on the floor ready to take down to the utility room. He re-hung his unused clean clothes, placed the new jewellery box in his bedside cabinet, a surprise for Emma later, and took his bathroom bag into the en suite. Finally he removed the small USB memory stick from his coat's inner zip pocket and picked up the cardboard tube and his laptop. These three items he took downstairs to the home office and placed them on his desk. He bent down, leaned under his desk and opened the safe. Firstly he placed the memory stick on the top shelf and then opened both ends of the cardboard tube. Carefully he eased out the small rolled up canvas that was still sticking to the bottom metal lid. He gently unrolled it and looked admiringly at the Nicholson painting once again. He was particularly captivated by the artist's ability to be able to capture the many reflections in the glass vase. Also he loved the pure simplicity of just one single red rose standing proudly and alone, in the vase.

"I'm just about to dish up." It was Emma calling from the kitchen.

"Coming," replied Ian. He then gently rolled the painting up again and placed it, slightly at an angle, on to the bottom shelf on the safe. He closed and locked the safe door, stood up and with a large grin on his face, thought how lucky he'd been after the Customs officers had not made a more thorough search of the cardboard tube.

When Ian appeared in the kitchen the food was already on the breakfast bar and Emma sat waiting.

"So," said Ian, as he joined Emma, "What have you been up to whilst I've been away?"

Emma picked up her fork and started to eat. "Why are you being evasive?"

"What? I'm not. I was just asking about your week whilst I was away."

"Mmmm. So what happened in Moscow?"

"It all went well. I had to look at a collection of 19th and

20<sup>th</sup> century paintings and I think we will be asked to auction some later this year. A few, I think, I can find a private buyer for. Could be interesting. They were mostly by Van Gogh, Cezanne, Monet, Renoir, Whistler, Nicholson and a few others. We will need to check the provenances more thoroughly and maybe carry out some forensic work, but all in all, it could prove to be a very profitable trip."

"And that took five days?"

"Well, no, not exactly, but the air tickets meant the five day stay. I took the opportunity to visit some of the art galleries and museums too whilst I was there."

"So if I'd been with you we would have had some time together to see some of the sights."

"Emma," replied Ian, a little bit more forcefully, "You know that you needed a visa. We will go to Moscow together soon." He hoped he had said enough. Emma became quiet and concentrated on eating her food. Ian picked up his glass of wine and sipped it slowly. He looked across to Emma and wondered what she was really thinking.

Later that evening, as they both lay in bed, Ian asked Emma, again, about her week.

"Nothing special. Mostly routine at work really. Mother telephoned Wednesday evening. Apparently they have discovered some damp problems in the dining room and conservatory."

"Oh," said Ian, only half listening, at which point he leant over to his bedside cabinet and retrieved the jewellery box he had placed there earlier that evening. Turning towards his wife he kissed her on the cheek and said, "I also found some time to do a little bit of shopping." He gave her the box and sat back.

Emma was surprised, but her eyes suddenly lit up. "What's this?"

"Open it."

Emma looked at Ian, smiled and slowly lifted the box's lid. "Oh, they are fabulous!"

She gently pulled out a row of lustrous, yellow-gold pearls. She quickly put them down on the duvet cover and pushed back her blonde hair, tucking it behind her ears. She wanted to inspect the pearls closer to her neck.

"I saw them in the GUM building next to Red Square. I thought the colour would suit you."

"They are really lovely. Thank you." Emma looked again at the necklace against her neck. She then leaned over and kissed Ian passionately. Ian responded likewise and they embraced and caressed each other. Breaking away and leaning back for just a few brief seconds, Emma placed her pearls on her bedside table and switched off the bedside lamp. She then resumed her previous position in Ian's arms.

# Chapter 14

Next morning Emma was up and out of the house just after 7 am. Ian told her he was not due back in at work until the following day so he would try and get rid of his jet lag by having a lie in. By 9 am, however, he was in the home office and had his computer switched on. After checking his emails, he decided to update his Kremlin spreadsheet. Using various internet websites and checking through several of his reference books, he gradually amended some of his comments and opinions. Once satisfied that this was a more accurate report, he then copied it on to two new USB memory sticks. These he placed in his safe next to the original one.

At 1 pm Ian telephoned Sergei and updated him with the details of the Moscow visit. Sergei congratulated him and advised that Andrei was due in London in two days' time and would like to meet with him. Ian checked his diary and Sergei agreed he would book a table at the Cipriani for 7.30 pm on Friday.

The next day, at just after 8 am, Ian was sitting at his desk at Sotheby's. Very few people had arrived at this time. He checked through the messages Penny had left for him and he then started to read the letter received the previous day from Sir Paul Broadway, CEO at Baxter's. In summary,

Sir Paul was pleased with the report and had suggested Ian progress with the report's recommendations. Excellent, thought Ian. Everything is beginning to fall into place.

"Good morning Ian." It was Penny standing at the door. "Did you have a nice holiday?"

"Oh hello Penny, you caught me in my thoughts. Yes I went to Moscow. A bit cold but a nice few days moseying around some of the galleries and museums. So, what have I missed?"

"It's really been very quiet. However, Mr Hopkins said the upcoming auction of the Constable and Turner paintings and sketches you discussed with him, is really generating worldwide interest, both with catalogues and hits on the website."

"Good. I thought it would. Good result from Baxter's too."

"Yes. Do you have any thoughts on the private buyers?"

"Possibly. Sir George Gamble is always interested in Cezanne paintings. Can you give him a call? We need to have a meeting to discuss other possibilities. Can you ask Vic to put on his thinking cap too? Oh and can you also ask him to find out everything about William Nicholson and, in particular, I want a list of every picture he has ever painted."

It was just before 7.30 pm when Ian entered the Cipriani restaurant. After mentioning Andrei Petrov's name, he was taken to a quiet corner where Andrei and Sergei were already seated. He noticed they were already enjoying a glass of red wine and deep in conversation.

When Ian was spotted by Andrei, their conversation stopped and both men stood up and shook his hand. It was Andrei who was the first to speak. "Welcome my friend, the happy traveller returns. Please sit down. I gather you had a successful time."

"Thank you." Ian sat down and put a brown folder on the floor leaning against his chair. "Moscow was a very interesting time."

The two Russians smiled and Andrei said, "I got your little parcel in the post. It came quite quickly. The Russian postal system must be improving. I was a little intrigued by the names of some of the paintings but I guessed you were just trying to be cautious."

"Yes. The last thing I wanted was for the report to get into the wrong hands and then people put two and two together about the Kremlin chambers collection. I've now amended that file. The names are now correct and the valuations have been updated." Ian leaned over slightly to his left-hand side and picked up the file resting at the side of his chair. He handed it over to Andrei. "Here's the updated paper copy, there's also a new updated memory stick. I've had more time since arriving back in England to research the collection more fully. I hope you will be pleased with some of my new valuations."

Andrei took the file and put it on the empty chair next to him. "I'll read that later. You have done an excellent job, don't you think so Sergei?"

Sergei hadn't spoken until this point. "Yes. Dimitri was also very impressed with your professionalism. I received an email from him the day after you left Moscow."

Andrei nodded and said, "Now then, my friend, what would you like to drink?"

"That claret looks nice," said Ian. He hadn't drunk claret for quite some time and assumed Andrei's choice would be both expensive and exceptional.

The three men ate their meals and consumed two bottles of claret. Ian gave a summary of his time in Moscow and the experience of being stopped by UK customs. However, he deliberately avoided mentioning the Nicholson painting.

He thought about asking Andrei what his plans were for the paintings in the Kremlin chambers, but decided it might be better not to know, at least for the time being. Ian did, however, raise the subject of the Baxter paintings. "Did you have time to look at the list of paintings I gave you at Nice airport?"

"Ah yes," replied Andrei, "Very interesting collection, but your prices seem high."

"All 25 are by major artists and they do have good provenances," Ian replied, hoping these factors would influence Andrei.

"My regular customers, let's say, are not mainstream buyers, so the provenances do not matter quite so much. They mainly want to know that they are not buying a fake and that the price is a good one. The painting's history is less of an issue. If any are fakes, well, I still have a market for those … as long as they are good fakes!"

"None of Baxter's paintings are fakes," said Ian. He was hoping Andrei was not questioning his professionalism.

"I'm sure they are not, my friend. Leave it with me to consider. I'll let you know shortly. I need to talk to some of my more wealthy clients."

Ian was disappointed with Andrei's comments. He had been sure that Andrei would have been keener, but then again, Andrei had previously said his main customers 'activities' were in a different art market.

"Anyway, my friend," continued Andrei, "You will be pleased to know that I have opened a Swiss bank account in your name, but I have used my Monaco address for any correspondence. I am sure you do not want it connected to your home address here in the UK. I have already deposited 100,000 Swiss francs and there will be more going into it in the future. Sergei will tell you all the details, how to access the money, passwords and the like."

Ian had wondered what and how he was going to be paid, but he had not expected a Swiss bank account, or a correspondence address in Monaco!

It was Sergei who broke the silence. "If you call at my home on Monday evening I will give you all the details."

Ian was still stunned, but managed to say to Andrei, "Thank you" and to Sergei, "What time do you want me to call?"

"Should we say seven o'clock? Viktor can bring you to my house."

# Chapter 15

Late Saturday morning Ian received a telephone call from his father. Fortunately for Ian, Emma had already left the house to go shopping. After pleasantries were exchanged his father told him a small parcel had arrived from Russia. It was addressed to Ian and intriguingly, the hand writing seemed somewhat familiar!

Ian had forgotten he had sent one of the memory sticks to his parents address and tried to quickly think of an explanation. "I've just been to Moscow on business and I put some hotel details, excursion trips, art galleries, etc. from my computer on to a memory stick. I have been planning to take Emma to Moscow and want it to be a surprise. I forgot I'd sent it to your address. Can you hang on to it until the next time I pop down?"

"Seems all a bit odd." replied his father. Ian quietly agreed! "We'll put it in the guest bedroom. Anyway, when are you two next coming down to visit us?"

"It's all a bit hectic at the moment dad. I'll speak to Emma and check our diaries."

"Don't leave it too long. Your mother's been talking!"

"Okay dad. Send mum my love. Bye." By 'talking', Ian knew that this was his father's word to summarise his mother's grumbling about not seeing her only child on a more regular basis.

On the following Monday morning Viktor telephoned Penny. He said he had a report for Ian and could he see him sometime during the day? Penny checked Ian's diary and told Viktor he would be back in his office at 4.30 pm.

Viktor put down the phone and picked up the William Nicholson file that he had put together over the weekend. He scanned through the background details and the list of 923 known paintings he had managed to identify from either the internet or from Sotheby's own reference books. When he had finished he put the folder down on his desk and leaned back in his chair and wondered why his boss had taken such a sudden interest in William Nicholson's paintings.

Just before 4.30 pm Viktor arrived at Ian's office. Penny, however, told him that Ian had been held up and would be a few minutes late. Viktor decided to take the opportunity to quiz Penny. "Any idea why Ian has taken a sudden interest in William Nicholson?"

"He's not mentioned anything to me. I've been looking at possible buyers for the Baxter's paintings, but as you know, there are no Nicholson's in that collection."

Suddenly Penny and Viktor heard footsteps coming towards the outer office and Ian entered. "Hello Vic, sorry I'm late. Come on in. Penny, any chance you can organise a pot of tea for us please?"

Penny nodded and picked up her telephone. The two men went into Ian's room and sat down. "So," said Ian, "What have you managed to find out about Nicholson? Have you come across him before?"

"He was one of the artists mentioned on the Commission for Looted Art in Europe."

"Okay, so what have you found out?"

Viktor opened his file and started to explain that William Nicholson was born in 1872 and was one of the leading

British artists of his generation. He started as a graphic artist but then, over his 50-year career, established himself as a successful painter. He painted portraits, landscapes and still life pictures and today many of his paintings exchange hands for well over £100,000. Due to the style of his paintings, however, especially in his still life work, a number of fakes have been produced over the years. Skilled forgers have been able to successfully copy or produce work with many of the typical Nicholson characteristics. A lot of his work involves thick layers of paint and scratching back. Obviously a style easy to copy, especially by some of the modern day forgery teams that we know about that are based in Panama. Establishing that a painting is a 'real Nicholson' is therefore not quite so straightforward. Excellent provenances are key, but even then modern day forensic investigations can reveal issues that could not have been identified in the past. Even the experts can, and have, been fooled. Once a painting is deemed a fake by the experts and despite more obvious, up to date, contrary evidence coming to light, they rarely want to be seen changing their opinion. To do so could tarnish their standing and reputations in a very fickle art world."

Whilst Viktor had been talking, Penny had put the two cups of tea on Ian's desk. Ian smiled at her and then mouthed a quiet 'thank you.

Viktor took this opportunity to have a drink and Ian waited for him to continue.

Viktor put down his half empty cup and then handed over to Ian the list of paintings he'd discovered, totalling 923 entries. He explained, "Nicholson was a prolific painter and the number of his paintings I have recorded is certainly not the complete figure. Nobody really knows. The list I have given you is from official records, but there are definitely more."

Ian flicked through the pages Viktor had produced.

Halfway through he saw the title *Rose in a Glass Vase*. Viktor's notes at the side gave a website and Ian made a mental note.

"This is a thorough piece of work Vic. What do you think of Nicholson?"

"There are a couple of acknowledged authorities on Nicholson's work. They both seem to agree that he painted from the heart. For him painting was a sensuous experience. He had a unique touch and a talent to be able to manipulate the paint to capture the mood and texture of the subject. Fakes, I suppose, do not have the same heart input."

"Do you think you would be able to see deep into any painting? Truly 'feel' the heart of the artist? Be able to sense yourself, whether an alleged painting was a true Nicholson or a fake?"

"I don't know. I guess it comes with experience. Some fakes are so good."

After the meeting Viktor said to Ian that he understood he had a meeting with his father at seven o'clock. Ian nodded and Viktor said he would take him to the Kuznetsov home. The two men left the office and hailed a taxi to Belgravia. A taxi home for Viktor was a novelty as he usually walked, whatever, the weather. The traffic was slow and gave Ian time to ponder on the meeting with Sergei. He wondered what it was like to have a Swiss bank account. Surely it was only the rich, and those people who had money to hide, that had such an account.

When the taxi eventually arrived in the Belgravia area Ian looked along the passing streets, particularly at the large properties. He wondered what their market value might be. Finally the taxi turned into Eaton Square and pulled up outside a row of four storey houses. Ian and Viktor got out and Ian paid the driver. As the taxi departed Ian stood back and looked up at the row of properties both to his left and right. Although it was now early evening and partially dark, Ian decided he could see why people wanted to live in this area. This was the life, he thought.

Viktor had already walked to the front door and stood under the white painted portico entrance. Ian joined him and Viktor led them in. The hallway was brightly lit from three crystal chandeliers hanging from the high ceiling. A number of expensive oil paintings covered the walls. Ian stood and stared in awe. This was obviously a very wealthy family.

"Ah, Mr Caxton. Good to see you again." It was Sergei who had appeared through the right-hand doorway. He marched over and shook Ian's hand. "Come into my study. Would you like a drink? Whisky?"

"A whisky would be fine, thank you."

"Viktor can you bring some glasses and a bottle of the Glenfarclas malt?"

Ian had expected to be offered vodka, which he also liked, but a whisky would be a nice change.

Viktor walked off down the hall and Ian followed Sergei into his study.

"Put your coat over there." Sergei pointed to a green, leather, studied armchair behind the door. "Come and sit here."

Ian sat down on another matching leather chair facing Sergei. He looked around the room and quickly spotted two small Gainsborough pictures and a large bookcase. The books, he noticed, predominantly featured the works of English history, art and antique furniture.

Sergei opened his desk side drawer and pulled out a brown folder. "Here are all the documents Andrei was talking about. The instructions should be clear, but if you have any queries give me a ring."

Ian took the folder and glanced inside at the contents.

Sergei continued, "The bank will need your signature so if you sign the special form before you leave we will do the rest."

Ian opened the folder again and removed the relevant form. Sergei handed him his fountain pen and Ian duly signed.

"Good ... and as the American's say, you are now good and set to go! I think that is the phrase?"

Ian smiled and said, "Yes, I think it is. Thank you and pass on my thanks onto Andrei as well please."

Viktor entered the study with a silver tray containing two crystal glasses, a bottle of Glenfarclas whisky and a small glass jug of water. He placed the tray on his father's desk, smiled at Ian and left the study, closing the door behind him.

Sergei stood up and poured two large glasses of the 40-year-old malt, passing one to Ian. "Cheers!" said Sergei, to which Ian replied, "Na Zdorovie!" and both men drank from their glasses. This was Ian's first taste of a 40-year-old malt. It felt much smoother than the whiskies he was used to. He decided he could quite get used to this lifestyle!

"You can thank Andrei yourself this coming weekend. He would like you and your wife to join him in Monaco. You will be staying at his apartment if, of course, you are free and able to travel at such short notice?"

Ian was astonished by the invitation and after a few seconds said, "Er, yes, well I think it would be fine, but I will need to discuss it with Emma first." His mind was racing and trying to remember if they had any arrangements already planned.

"Of course, of course. Here are your flight documents to Nice ... just in case."

Ian accepted the flight e-tickets from Sergei and noticed they were BA, First Class.

"If you cannot make the trip can you give the tickets to Viktor to bring back?"

"Yes of course." Ian took another sip of his whisky and repeated "Na Zdorovie!" Wow, he thought, what is Emma going to say to this!

The taxi dropped Ian home just after 10.30 pm. An extravagant journey from Sergei's house, but after the whiskies, he really didn't fancy the train journey and then the 20 minutes' walk.

A number of the house lights were still switched on so he assumed Emma was at home and not yet in bed. He entered through the front door and called out Emma's name.

"I'm in the bath." Came the response from upstairs. "There's some lasagne in the microwave if you've not eaten. I've already had mine."

"Okay."

Ian went into the kitchen and checked their domestic calendar on the wall. Just as he thought, nothing booked in for the coming weekend. He opened the microwave, checked the lasagne and heated it up. Whilst the machine was whirring he went to the fridge and removed the already opened bottle of chardonnay and poured himself a glass. When the microwave had finished he took the dish out and helped himself to about half the contents. As he sat down to eat, Emma appeared in her bathrobe, with a separate towel wrapped around her head.

"Hi. Do you want some wine?" asked Ian, waving the bottle gently towards her.

Emma walked over and gave him her glass. She then kissed him. "Please. I've just finished my first whilst I was in the bath."

Ian topped up her existing glass and said, "We have nothing planned for this weekend do we? There's nothing on the calendar."

"Mummy was asking when we would be going to see them."

"So has my dad when we chatted on Saturday. Did you agree to anything?"

"No. I told her you had been away on business so we had things to catch up on."

"Okay then, how would you like a weekend in Monaco?"

"Seriously! What's suddenly brought that on?"

"One of the Russians I dealt with in Moscow has an apartment in Monaco and he has invited us over to stay."

"Oh wow. Monaco!"

"If you want to go then we fly from Heathrow to Nice at 4.30 pm on Friday. Back late Sunday night."

"The question is, do I need to buy some new clothes?" Emma left the kitchen with her glass of wine and Ian resumed eating his meal.

# Chapter 16

Next morning, when Ian entered his office, Penny told him that Sir George Gamble had telephoned to say he was interested in Baxter's Cezanne paintings. But he wanted to know the 'real' prices.

"Okay. I'll give him a ring. I might have a buyer for some of the others, but he's playing it a bit cagey. I'm hopeful, however, that I will get a more positive answer this coming weekend."

"Do you want me to speak to Martin Shaw about the Monet and Renoir pictures?"

"Yes please. Good idea. Can you also check up on the Constable and Turner auction preparations as well? Oh, also, I shall be out of the office after lunch on Friday. Taking Emma to Monaco for the weekend. Trying to make up for her not being able to go to Moscow."

"Lucky Emma!" said Penny. She wished she could be whisked off to Monaco for the weekend.

Later that evening Ian was working on his computer at home. He had just opened the website which Viktor had mentioned in his report about *Rose in a Glass Vase*. He eventually found the entry and jotted down the details on his notepad. The historical record was quite sketchy but it did mention the names of two previous owners. That, at least, confirmed the provenance up until 1931. At that point there was no further information, just the note 'whereabouts unknown'. So how, wondered Ian, did this picture finish up in the cellars of the Kremlin? Was it just one of the many thousands of paintings looted by the Nazi's?

Ian continued to investigate further the website's contents, trying to find similar still life paintings to his own. Eventually he found two small still life Nicholson pictures with the common subject of flowers and objects on a table. One had sold for £165,000 in 2006! Well, well, he thought. So mine could be worth £200,000 plus! He smiled and continued to stare at the screen, but suddenly reality kicked in. To get that sort of money, he knew, my picture would need to have a believable provenance since 1931, and of course, how do I explain my current possession?

The BA flight to Nice landed five minutes early. As Ian and Emma were flying First Class, they were two of the first passengers to disembark. However, although Ian only had hand luggage, Emma had told him that she had to come properly prepared. So once through passport control they had to make their way to the baggage reclaim area to collect a large suitcase! Fortunately, when they arrived at baggage reclaim, Ian spotted that the suitcase was already on the carousel waiting to be collected. One of the benefits of travelling First Class, he thought.

Ian lifted the case from the moving belt and as he put it down on the floor, he commented to Emma, "What have you got in here, it weighs a ton!?"

"A girl needs to be prepared."

"But we are only here for two nights."

Emma ignored the jibe and they walked towards the red and green exit corridors. Suddenly Ian stopped and Emma turned and asked "What's the matter?"

"The last time I went through 'Nothing to Declare' I was stopped," replied Ian, slightly concerned.

"Well you won't be this time, you are with me. I don't look like a drug smuggler!"

They both smiled and walked through the green labelled channel. No Customs officer was to be seen and they walked through the final exit doors and into 'Arrivals'.

Immediately Ian spotted the familiar figure of Andrei and they walked towards him.

"Ah, my good friend, it's so good of you to come."

"Hello Andrei. Let me introduce you to my wife, Emma."

Andrei immediately gave Emma a big smile and a hug and then stood back and stared at her. "But my friend, this lady is even more beautiful than you described."

Emma looked from Andrei to Ian with questioning eyes. Ian shrugged his shoulders and all three of them laughed.

"Come, my car is just outside. Did you have a good flight?"

"Yes it was very good, thank you," said Ian. Not only was he carrying his cabin bag, but was pulling Emma's suitcase too. Andrei and Emma walked ahead and Andrei told Emma about some of the sights they would be seeing in Monaco.

The three of them walked across the concourse and out into the warm sunshine. Ian spotted Andrei's dark green Rolls Royce. Emma was impressed and very surprised when the chauffeur got out of the driver's door and took charge of the large suitcase. He then opened the rear door for Emma and Ian to get in. Andrei opened and entered through the front passenger door.

Emma thought this must be how Royalty is treated. She looked at Ian and smiled.

"Once the car was moving, Andrei turned in his seat and spoke to his two guests. "Did you manage to eat on the plane?" Both Ian and Emma nodded. "Good. I know it's a little late but there is a light supper waiting for you in my little apartment if you are peckish when we arrive."

"That sounds good Andrei. Thank you."

"My friend, you do not need to keep saying so many thank yous. We are friends."

"Thank you," said Ian and they all laughed.

It had been some years since Emma had been to Monaco and Monte Carlo and she was glued to the views from the car. She was particularly impressed with the street lighting and the illumination of many of the buildings. Both Emma and Ian pointed to familiar buildings and landmarks on their route. Eventually the car pulled up at a security barrier at the rear of a tall block of apartments. The chauffeur wound down his window, spoke in French to a security guard and then inserted a plastic key card into the security post. The barrier slowly lifted and the Rolls Royce proceeded on to the property. One further security check and the car slowly glided down a slope and into the basement parking area under the building. Ian could not believe his eyes. Parked in some of the large parking bays were Bentleys, Ferraris, Lamborghinis and two further Rolls Royces! Emma and Ian looked at each other with their eyes wide open.

Andrei's Rolls Royce stopped next to the entrance doors to the elevators and the chauffeur let his three passengers out. Ian went to the boot to collect the suitcases, but Andrei said Julian would bring the cases up to the apartment, after he had parked the car.

Andrei inserted a card into a security slot next to the double doors and slowly the doors opened. They all walked into a lobby area and then over to two elevators. Andrei pushed a yellow button and within just a few seconds the elevator door opened and a uniformed lady stepped forward and said, "Good evening Mr Petrov."

"Good evening Louise. Have you had a good day? These people are my guests for the weekend." Andrei casually waved his hand in the direction of Emma and Ian.

Louise escorted her three passengers into the mirror lined compartment and replied, "Yes thank you Mr Petrov." She then said good evening to Emma and Ian.

Ian nodded to Louise and his eyes moved to her side, to the plate which showed the floor numbers. He immediately noticed that the numbers went up to 28 and then a separate entry for 'Penthouse'. His eyebrows shot up in astonishment when he saw Louise press the button next to the 'Penthouse' name!

The elevator climbed quickly and silently and within, what seemed like just a few seconds, arrived at the Penthouse floor level. When the elevator door opened, Louise stepped outside, giving her passengers room to exit easily. Ian and Emma saw a small corridor containing just two other doors. One at the far end had a green illuminated sign saying 'Fire Exit'. The other was a mahogany double door with just a stainless-steel plate at the left hand side of the door. Andrei placed the palm of his left hand on to the plate and after two seconds, the door slowly opened with a low swish sound.

"Come into my little home." Andrei waved his two guests to come through and into one of the largest open plan apartment rooms either Ian and Emma had ever seen in their lives.

"Oh wow," exclaimed Emma. "And you call this a little home! It's fabulous!"

Ian was slowly moving around the room gazing at Andrei's art collection on the walls. He quickly identified the work of Picasso, Renoir, Moreau, Gris and, to his surprise, William Nicholson!

"Ian! Quick, look at this view!" Emma was standing against a large set of patio doors. When Ian joined her, his immediate reaction was "Wow." Even at night-time the view was stunning. He looked down through the balcony railings to the harbour area and then further out into the vastness of the dark Mediterranean Sea. The lights of the huge yachts, harbour-side cafes, bars and the palace of Monaco, over to the right, were spectacular. Emma and Ian were like children in wonderland.

Andrei stood quietly whilst his guests explored. After a short while he reminded them of his presence by saying, "Not bad for a poor Muscovite is it?"

"You are the master of the understatement, Andrei. This is all fabulous," replied Ian. He had been inside some of his client's spectacular properties in the past, but this was still exceptional.

"Come my friends, there is some food in the kitchen and champagne in the fridge. Ah here's Julian. He's brought your bags up."

Julian quietly pulled Emma's suitcase and Ian's small hold-all bag through to the main guest suite. A few seconds later he reappeared and exited into another room.

Ian and Emma were overwhelmed. They slowly walked over to the kitchen area where Andrei was opening a bottle of champagne. The apartment, Emma concluded to herself, had such modern opulence. There was certainly no sign of a woman's touch, but it was still fabulous nonetheless.

Andrei poured three glasses of champagne and passed two to his guests. "I think at this point we ought to have a toast. My toast is to 'Art and all the famous artists that have helped to make this world such a special place'."

All three clinked their crystal glasses and then Ian said, "Na Zdorovie!"

Emma looked at Ian with a querying look. Andrei just smiled and said, "Thank you, my friend."

Andrei opened a second bottle of champagne and the

three of them sat drinking, talking and just looking out at the most stunning of views. Andrei told them that he'd been living in Monaco for over 20 years and in this apartment for the last five. When Ian asked him whether any of the yachts in the harbour below were his, Andrei said he did not own a yacht. He had discovered many years ago that he was not comfortable on water and tried to avoid travelling on ships and boats as far as he could, but he might try a cruise one day. He told them that he much preferred travelling by car and aeroplane. The questions and discussions went on until just before 1am when the host and guests finally decided it was time to go to bed.

Over breakfast the next morning, prepared by Julian, Andrei announced that his good friend Marie would be joining them later that morning. He explained that Marie knew every retail shop in Monte Carlo and La Condamine and would thoroughly enjoy introducing Emma to 'retail therapy' Monaco style! This comment brought a big smile to Emma's face. "For the two men," he continued, "we have business to discuss."

Marie arrived at 11.30 am. Andrei had arranged for her to pass through the security systems and Louise escorted her up in the elevator.

When Andrei introduced Emma and Ian to Marie, Emma estimated she was about 55 years of age. She was still very attractive, slim and appeared to have a very cheerful personality. Andrei had earlier explained that Marie was a very wealthy widow. Her husband had formerly owned a large import/export company in Nice, which she had inherited, and subsequently sold, two years ago.

Over cups of coffee the two ladies chatted away and Ian and Andrei just listened! Eventually Marie decided they were wasting precious shopping time. Emma double checked that she had all her credit cards and the two ladies left the apartment. Before leaving, however, Andrei reminded Marie that dinner would be ready at 7 pm.

"Now then my friend," said Andrei, when the door was finally closed. "I have lots to talk to you about. Let's go and sit at the table."

# Chapter 17

Whilst Ian walked over towards the oval dining table, Andrei disappeared into his study and re-emerged with a large red folder. He joined Ian at the table and sat down.

"You will be interested to learn I'm sure, my friend, that I have put a further 50,000 Swiss francs into your account."

"Thank you Andrei, but why?"

"Two days after you left Russia, my colleagues in Moscow advised me that they had found two buyers for six of the paintings stored in the Kremlin chambers. Dimitri and Ivan returned there last weekend and removed the six paintings from the chambers. The pictures were then detached from their frames and many photos were taken. We have three excellent art copyists contacts and they will reproduce copies of these six paintings. These copies will then be placed in the original painting's discarded frames. When we have buyers for more of the pictures on your spreadsheet, we will return to the chambers with our six copies and replace them back exactly where the original paintings were found. We will then collect our next ordered group of paintings."

Ian was stunned by this information and asked Andrei, "But how did you get these six paintings out of Russia?"

"Ah, there, my friend, it now gets interesting. We have many rich Russians still living in Russia. They have not all moved abroad – not yet anyway. They like to collect objects of value, especially paintings by the masters … as a long-term investment. They otherwise have much difficulty in being able to hide their roubles away from prying government eyes."

"So the six paintings are still in Russia. That's very clever."

"We are clever people, my friend. We have to be. That is why we are rich!" Andrei laughed at his joke before continuing, "We will make you rich too!"

Ian sat back in his chair trying to analyse all that he had heard. After a few seconds he smiled and asked Andrei, "How am I going to be rich then Andrei?"

"All in good time, my friend, all in good time. Firstly, I want you to value all of my paintings here in my little home! I warn you, two are fakes!" Andrei spread out his arms and pointed to his collection on the walls.

"I see. You are still testing me?"

"No, no, my friend. I know you will produce another one of your excellent valuation reports! I have had some of these pictures for many years and I think now might be a good time to sell and take my profit. They are part of my future pension!"

Ian looked around the room. He then got up and walked over to the nearest wall and started inspecting each picture more closely. After a few minutes he asked, "Are there any more paintings in the apartment?"

Andrei smiled. "Oh yes, my friend, and there are some more in my secret vault!" Andrei got up from the table, picked up the red folder and joined Ian in front of a Picasso.

"Here, you will need this information." He passed Ian the red folder.

"I suppose I had better get started."

When the ladies arrived back in the apartment just after 6 pm, Julian accompanied them carrying several boxes and bags. Ian and Andrei were sitting outside on the balcony drinking champagne, talking and watching the activity in the harbour and the sun slowly go down. When they heard the ladies' chatter both men looked back into the apartment. They both got up to join them. Ian immediately noticed that each of the bags, Julian was carrying, seemed to have a very expensive brand name.

Emma quickly read Ian's mind, "Only two are mine. Marie could shop for France!"

"What does that mean?" enquired Andrei.

"Marie obviously enjoys her shopping!" translated Ian. "You both obviously had a good time."

"Oh yes, but I'm desperate for a bath and a change of clothes," replied Emma, who turned and started to walk towards their guest bedroom.

"Do you want to take a glass of champagne with you?" asked Andrei, pointing to the champagne bottle, which was standing in a wine cooler on the kitchen breakfast bar.

"No thank you. Maybe after I've tidied up."

"Marie. I'm sure you are ready," offered Andrei, "I will go and get you a glass."

Marie walked out on the balcony and sat down watching the sun setting. "Fabulous view isn't it?" she said to Ian.

Ian thought her English was good but some words still had a little hint of the usual French accent, which, he decided, in this case, only added to her charm and attractiveness.

"Yes indeed," he responded. "Fabulous. There cannot be many city views with such a fabulous backdrop."

"Do you know I've offered this man millions of euros to buy this apartment from him, but he still will not sell to me. I suppose I might just have to move in instead!"

Andrei arrived with Marie's glass of champagne. He

had heard Marie's comment and wondered what all his other lady friends would say to that. "I would not sell my little home for one hundred million euros!" was his only comment.

Ian sat down again, sipped his own champagne and stared down over the harbour area and then far out into the Mediterranean. The sea was currently a deep golden colour, just holding the reflection of the last of the sun's rays. This is just all so unreal, he thought. If this is what true wealth can buy, then no, I don't think I would sell either!

When Andrei was entertaining guests in his 'little home', he employed the services of Claude Bernhard and his team. Claude, a retired chef formerly with the 2* Michelin restaurant, Les Cinq Sens, was responsible for providing all the meal's ingredients, cooking, serving and clearing up after the evening's meal. Since retirement from full time work, Claude could afford to be very selective and have just a few special clients. He knew that his services were heavily in demand and he could, quite easily, double or even treble his client base, but he only wanted to work for 'his special clients'. Fortunately Andrei was one of those. In return Andrei was very generous to Claude. He dearly wanted to remain part of this small, elite group.

This evening's meal was certainly up to Claude's usual standards and the host and all three guests, thanked Claude and his team profusely, for such a wonderful dinner and experience.

Finally, after coffee and brandy, Marie announced the day had finally caught up with her and she left and entered Andrei's bedroom. Emma too soon followed to the guest's room. The two men remained sitting on the two white leather sofas in the lounge area. Ian leaned back into his seat, relaxed and looked admiringly around the room. He gently swirled the last drops of the remaining brandy in his glass. "Do you know Andrei ... I think I could get used to living like this!"

"Well, my friend, maybe one day you will."

Ian smiled back at Andrei. In his wildest dreams, he could not remotely see how he could ever afford such a fabulous and so expensive a property.

# Chapter 18

After breakfast Marie suggested she take Emma to the Sunday leather market. It was a small street market within walking distance of the apartment block. When Emma queried whether it was just things like leather belts, Marie took it as an affront and explained, "Oh no my dear. It is a special little street market, just in the mornings, on the first Sunday of each month. Every conceivable item made from leather is on sale. It's good fun and you can sometimes get lovely designer shoes and handbags for nearly half price!"

Ian listened to Marie's proposal. His immediate thought was that 50% of Monaco's normal retail price was still quite a lot of money!

"Sounds interesting Marie. Are you coming Ian?" asked Emma, already collecting her handbag.

"No, we fly home later this afternoon and Andrei would like me to look at some paintings before we leave."

After the ladies had left, Andrei said to Ian, "Come, my friend, I will show you my vault."

Ian collected his pens, writing paper and a small torch. When the two men got into the elevator, Andrei said, "Good morning, Louise. Lower basement please." Louise pressed the 'lower basement' button, but as she did so, Ian heard a low, brief buzzing sound. He turned to Andrei with a queried look on his face.

"Do not worry, my friend, it is just part of the security. When anybody wants to go to the vaults, security is informed."

"I see," said Ian, wondering what this extra security entailed.

The 'lower basement' Ian noticed was, according to the list on the elevator wall, the lowest floor within the building, It was two floors below the car parking area. When the elevator arrived the doors opened and Louise stepped out and aside, allowing the two men to follow her. The first thing Ian noticed was a long corridor with about 12, he guessed, strongroom doors along each side. There were no windows, but the air was cool and fresh. Two large, uniformed guards blocked their way. Whilst Ian was still taking in the surroundings and saying goodbye to Louise, Andrei had spoken to the guards in French. He had shown them a pass card, which contained his photograph. He then explained the presence of Ian. Although the guards knew Andrei and indeed, all of the vault key holders, this procedure had to be followed, every time! It was all being recorded on several hidden cameras.

The elder of the two guards led Andrei and Ian along the corridor. They stopped outside no 14. There were no handles on the door, just a metal plate and a small horizontal slot. As Andrei inserted his card into the slot, a green light flashed above the door. Andrei then removed the card and put his left palm on the metal plate. The green light flashed again. Finally the guard placed his left palm on the metal plate. The green light flashed for a third time and the guard walked away and back along the corridor. After about ten seconds the door clicked and slowly began to move inwards. As the door opened three internal lights automatically came on. Ian was amazed at the level of security, but then again, he concluded, we are in Monaco!

Once inside Andrei pressed a yellow button next to the door. Gradually the thick metal door quietly and slowly closed, but there was no click. The vault was about 4 x 4 x 3 metres in size. At the far end there was a group of individual safes of varying sizes. Against the bare side walls were stacked, Ian counted, 24 framed paintings.

"I hope you know how to get out of here." exclaimed Ian. He'd noticed that there was no handle on the inside of the door and whilst he was not claustrophobic, he did not want to remain in this tomb for too long.

As Ian stopped talking he heard a slight hissing noise.

"The guards check the vault every ten minutes. When they put a hand on the door plate that white light flashes." Andrei pointed to a LED light bulb near the door. "I have to press the blue button, over there, within 20 seconds." he pointed again. "The guards will then go away for another ten minutes. If I do not press the blue button within 20 seconds, they enter to investigate. By the way, that noise is the air supply. It automatically comes on after 30 seconds when someone is in here. We don't want you to suffocate!" Andrei laughed.

"Okay." Ian shook his head in disbelief. "We had better get started."

For the next two and a half hours, Ian scrutinised each one of the 24 paintings in great detail. Andrei answered Ian's questions and he made copious amounts of notes. After about the twelfth painting, he was no longer surprised each time he looked at the next picture. Andrei's hidden collection was truly fabulous. When Ian was finally finished, Andrei announced that this collection was the rest of his 'pension fund'!

My goodness, thought Ian, I would accept just two of these paintings for my pension fund!

Finally, after leaving the vault, the two men went back to Andrei's apartment. The ladies had not yet returned. Ian told Andrei that Emma was not aware of any of his real activities in Moscow or indeed, the main reason they were both in Monaco. Andrei agreed that this was probably the best policy ... at this stage!

Ian promised he would complete his evaluation and report back within the week. Andrei smiled and shook Ian's hand. "Thank you, my friend. I am sure it will make very interesting reading."

Ian decided to take this opportunity, before the ladies returned, to ask Andrei, "Have you had any further thoughts about the list of the Baxter paintings I gave you?"

"I have been doing some work, my friend, and I think I may have lined up some interest, here in Monaco." For the right price I would be interested in the three Picassos and the four Monets."

"Okay. So what do you think you would offer?"

"Your valuation minus 20%!"

Ian was a little disappointed, but not surprised. "I'll let the seller know your offers and get back to you."

When the ladies returned Julian had already prepared a light lunch. All four chatted away whilst eating until Ian reminded everyone that they had a plane to catch and must pack their bags. Forty minutes later Emma and Ian were ready to leave. Julian collected their bags and left the apartment.

Emma and Ian said their goodbyes to Marie and Andrei escorted them both to the car parking area where Julian was now waiting at the side of the Rolls Royce. Andrei and his two guests got into the car and Julian closed the doors before getting into the driver's side himself. They again passed the selection of high valued cars, up the ramp and out into the daylight once more.

When Andrei dropped Ian and Emma off at Nice airport, both guests said what a wonderful two days they had experienced. Emma added to Andrei that he was a fabulous host and Marie a super retail guide of Monaco! Andrei laughed and said, "It has also been a wonderful time for me too, my friends, I am sure we will do it again ... some time! I hope you have a good journey home."

Once settled in their seats on the aeroplane and with a glass of champagne in their hands, Ian proposed a toast, "To Andrei ... to our future and to our mutual good fortune!" Both Ian and Emma clinked their glasses and sipped their drinks.

"I'm not exactly sure what you mean?" said Emma, putting her glass down on the shelf next to her seat.

"I've just got a feeling," replied Ian, "that Andrei and I will be doing a lot of business together in the future."

Emma was quiet now. She sipped her champagne and looked out of the window. In her thoughts, however, she was wondering what exactly Ian had meant!

# Chapter 19

When Ian arrived at his office on Monday morning, Penny was already sitting at her desk.

"Good morning Penny. Did you have a good weekend?" announced Ian, as he passed Penny's desk and walked towards his office.

"Not as good a weekend as you and Emma must have had," she replied, following Ian into his office.

Whilst he hung up his coat he said. "It was fabulous, thank you Penny. We stayed with a friend in his apartment and it had a great view overlooking the Mediterranean. It is really amazing the amount of wealth in such a small country. The weather was still warm too." Ian sat down at his desk and Penny followed suit, sitting opposite him.

"Sir George Gamble telephoned on Friday afternoon about Baxter's Cezanne paintings. He said he could be interested in all four, but would be looking for a discount on the valuations."

"Okay. I will speak to him," replied Ian. He knew Sir George always liked to think he was getting a 'good deal'.

"I have also spoken to Martin Shaw about the Monet and Renoir pictures. He's a bit noncommittal at the moment, but says he might be interested in the three Renoirs." Ian nodded his head and Penny continued. "You also said you thought you might have a buyer for some of the others."

"Yes, the friend we stayed with in Monaco. He has offered the full valuation minus 20% for the three Picassos and the four Monets. I don't think Baxter's will take that, but I'll speak to Sir Paul and get his thoughts. Let me think a little more about the other 11 and we can then decide who next to approach."

"Alright. By the way, the preparations for the Constable and Turner auction are well on track. Vic is just finalising the dates when all the pictures will arrive. There might be a minor hitch with the three Constable sketches coming from America, but Vic's chasing the carriers. Apparently there seems to be a problem with obtaining the correct paper-work. Vic knows the details."

"Okay, let me know if there continues to be a problem. We don't want any hiccups to the catalogue at this late stage."

"What do you want me to do about the other Baxter paintings? The ones you thought might be best sold at auction."

"Unless we can show Sir Paul a quicker, more positive result from the private sales, I'm not sure he will use us for any future sales or auction. It really was my idea. He was much keener to have private sales for all the paintings. It's always a tricky issue when the seller prefers a private sale. Professionally you know you are more likely to get a better price at auction for the best paintings, but it is not guaranteed."

"Mmm. Okay, I'll leave that with you for the moment. Do you want me to talk to any of the gallery contacts?"

"No, leave that with me too please. I think I will give Oscar a ring in Hong Kong. The Chinese are getting more and more interested. They are the money people nowadays."

Much later that evening Ian telephoned Oscar. It was early morning Hong Kong local time.

When Ian worked in Hong Kong, he often used Oscar Ding's influence with the Chinese to some success. Oscar was born in mainland China, but his parents managed to smuggle the family into Hong Kong before the changeover of rule in 1997. Therefore Oscar grew up in a very competitive environment and believed strongly in the capitalist structure and the opportunities it gave to people who were prepared to work hard. After updating each other about their recent lives and the changing politics in Hong Kong, Ian told Oscar the problem he had with Baxter's paintings. Oscar asked Ian to email the full details of each painting and he would see what he could do. He also asked if he would get his usual 10% commission for full valuation sales. 10%, thought Ian, would be a better deal for Baxter's than Andrei's offer, but not so good for me!

For the next few evenings, Ian slowly put together his report on Andrei's paintings in Monaco. He was amazed that Andrei had been able to build up such a valuable collection. He decided he would love the opportunity to be able to auction such a prize collection. It certainly would be one of the major auctions of the year!

By the end of the week he was ready to email Andrei the results. However, he had one major problem. Andrei had said he had two fake pictures amongst his collection, but Ian was sure there were three! The question was, should he be honest with Andrei or, fingers crossed, just state the obvious two that he thought were fakes and bluff his way through the third! He examined his notes on the three paintings in question again. He then tried different websites and his catalogue collection, for any additional information. Finally, by Sunday evening, he had made up his mind and emailed Andrei his report. Once the 'sent' message appeared on his computer, he sat back in his chair and stared at the screen. Mmm, he thought, I really hope that I have made the correct decision!

By Wednesday of the following week, he had not heard from Andrei or indeed Sergei. Vic too gave no sign of knowing anything, but then again, why should he?! By Friday Ian became increasingly worried. Had he blown his relationship with Andrei?

The next Thursday was the date for the Constable and Turner auction sale. Ian had managed to refocus on his salaried job and Sotheby's auction proved to be an even better result than he had originally estimated to his boss. The total of all the sales grossed £163 million! This was a fabulous result. Michael Hopkins was ecstatic and marched into Ian's office to personally congratulate him. Ian explained that Vic and Penny had done most of the legwork, but Michael responded by saying that it was an excellent example of perfect teamwork. To celebrate Michael announced that Sotheby's would pay for a staff party on the following Friday night.

Ian was not over keen on this decision as he readily admitted he was not a party animal. However, he did recognise that such a celebration would do no harm whatsoever to Vic and Penny's careers.

At the party, Ian tried to put Andrei out of his mind and just enjoy the celebrations. However, it was just after 9.30 pm when Viktor came over and handed him an envelope. "My father asked me to give you this letter. I think it is from Andrei."

Ian looked at the blank envelope and his heart suddenly began to pump at a much higher rate. "Thanks Vic." he said, deciding to read the contents later.

He tucked the envelope into his inside jacket pocket. His mind began to whirl and as Viktor walked away, Penny came over and asked, "Are you okay? Your face has gone ever so white!"

"Mmm? Oh hello Penny. Yes, yes, I'm fine … Just the excitement … I expect."

# Chapter 20

Ian arrived home just after midnight. Emma had already gone to bed. Ian had told her not to wait up, as he was not sure how long the party would go on till.

Andrei's letter remained unopened in his jacket pocket. During the whole taxi ride he wondered whether to open it or leave it until he arrived home. Finally he decided, if it was bad news, he would far sooner find out the answer, in private at home.

After entering his house, Ian gently closed and locked the door. He listened. He could not hear any noises from his bedroom, so he quietly crept through the hallway and into his home office. Once he'd sat down, he pulled out the envelope. With a paper knife, he sliced open the top and removed the letter. He then started to read.

"Ian? Is that you?" Emma had not been asleep, just reading a book and she now wondered why Ian had not come straight up to bed. When she got to the bottom of the stairs, she turned and headed to the office, where the light was on. She stood in the doorway and saw Ian engrossed, reading a sheet of paper. "Ian?" she repeated.

Ian looked up with a huge smile on his face. "I thought you were asleep."

"What are you reading?"

"It's an invitation. To Hong Kong!"

"When are we going!?"

Two days later, on Sunday evening, Ian received a telephone call from Oscar in Hong Kong. "I have been circulating the details you sent me of the Baxter paintings. They have generated quite a bit of interest, both on the mainland and in Hong Kong. What I need to know is, have any been sold?"

"We have received some offers, but it is a buyer's market in the UK. Prospective buyers are looking for discounts on valuations."

"Okay. I've just arrived at my office, so I'll just get a coffee and then start phoning my contacts."

After Ian put down the telephone receiver, he was just about to leave the home office and get ready for bed, when the telephone rang again. What's Oscar forgotten to mention this time, he thought. However, when he answered the call he got a surprise.

"Hello, my friend, and how are you and your lovely wife, Emma?"

"Andrei! Long time no speak."

"Did you get my note from Sergei?"

"Yes ... and thank you for the invitation."

"Good. I have been very busy and it's been very difficult to speak with you. I have been to Brazil, Columbia, Argentina and Hong Kong. Much too hectic and busy for an old man!"

Ian laughed and Andrei continued. "I am in London later this week. Can you meet Sergei and me on Thursday evening for dinner?"

"I think that is okay. Where and what time?"

"Sergei has booked our usual table at the Cipriani for 7.30."

"I shall be there." replied Ian, making a mental note to book it in his diary.

"Excellent, my friend. Lots to talk about. Must go."

When Ian arrived at his outer office on Monday morning, Penny was sitting at her desk. She was the first to speak. "Are you okay now after Friday night?"

"Good morning, Penny. Yes I'm fine. I think it was maybe a mixture of the end of the auction pressure and the party. All okay now, but thanks for asking."

Penny was not convinced, but she decided that Ian did seem to be better now.

As Ian entered his office he called back, "Oscar telephoned from Hong Kong last night. He thinks he may have found some buyers in China for the Baxter paintings."

"China!" exclaimed Penny. She got up from her chair and followed Ian into his office.

"Mmm, and Hong Kong. Look out for an email from him will you?"

"Of course," said Penny. She sat down opposite Ian and looked at her notebook. "Mr Hopkins's PA telephoned, just before you arrived. Mr Hopkins would like to discuss the Constable and Turner auction results."

"Okay. Can you find out when he is free and book me in please? By the way did you have a good time on Friday, at the party?"

"Yes it was fine. Parties are not really my scene, but it's nice to celebrate success."

"Yes it is. During your career, one thing you will learn is that success usually only happens after a great deal of personal hard work, team effort, connections and lots of good luck! However, never forget, you are always in charge of your own destiny."

Penny was not too sure what Ian was hinting at. Wise

words but was he really talking about her or ... himself? She smiled, nodded and got up from her chair. She walked towards the door where she stopped and turned around. She was just about to speak again to Ian but decided it could wait for a more appropriate time.

# Chapter 21

On Thursday, just before 7.30 pm, Ian arrived at the Cipriani and was shown to the 'usual' table. Andrei and Sergei were already drinking claret and chatting. As Ian approached, both men got up and shook his hand. As usual, it was Andrei who was the first to speak. "My friend, it's so good to see you again. It's been such a busy time. Come, sit down. A glass of our finest claret?"

"Thank you Andrei. Yes please."

Sergei poured Ian a glass and topped up Andrei's and his own.

"So, my friend, I was intrigued to receive your report on my Monaco collection. Very interesting. You obviously spotted the two fakes I told you about, but you also suggested my Picasso, *Five Bathers on the Beach*, is also a fake. Why did you come to that conclusion when I told you there were only two fakes?"

"I could not find any reference to that picture. The provenance you provided didn't really stack up! I have studied a lot of Picasso's work and decided it was too similar to his painting, *Three Bathers*, which is housed in the Guggenheim. When I looked at your painting close to, it seemed to lack his unique touch. Some of the brushstrokes were not quite his style. I felt it was just a poor copy."

"What do you mean?"

"It's hard to describe. Sometimes a picture just feels right. Other times, and despite previous judgements, sometimes a painting just doesn't feel right at all. That is what I felt about your Picasso. If you remember, I did say in my report that you should get other opinions and maybe approach the Courtauld Institute of Forensic Science to investigate more deeply, if you disagreed with my verdict." Ian was worried now that he had made a serious mistake, but deep down he knew he hadn't.

"I paid 300,000 euros for that painting."

Ian shrugged his shoulders and said, "Of course I might be wrong."

"No, my friend, you are not wrong." Andrei's face suddenly changed from a very serious scowl into a more relaxed smile. "I have taken two further opinions and they both say it is unlikely to have been painted by Picasso."

Ian suddenly felt his heart rate begin to slow down, back towards it's normal beat. He smiled inwardly and breathed a sigh of relief. His decision to tell Andrei the truth had paid off. It was a lesson, he decided, that was well learned. Always be professional and honest about your thoughts, judgements and ... gut-feeling! Some people might not like the opinion, but at least you would be seen to be doing your job properly and honest to yourself.

"So, my friend, you will find a further 50,000 Swiss francs have been deposited into your account."

"But you have lost money on the picture."

"No, no I have not, my friend." Andrei smiled and continued, "The man who I purchased the painting from lives in Buenos Aires, he has purchased the painting back from me for 400,000 euros! He has also 'donated' the 50,000 Swiss francs ... for, shall we say, your professional services."

Ian smiled, shook his head and looked from Andrei to

Sergei. Sergei just raised his eyebrows a little and smiled. Ian took this as a message to say 'as you can see Andrei is not the sort of man you should try to bluff or double cross!'

Sergei finally said his first words in Ian's presence, "Shall we order our meal?"

Ian sat back in his chair, sipped his wine and stared at the menu. His mind was still spinning. After about 30 seconds, his eyes were finally able to focus on the meal options! He also temporarily glanced up in Andrei's direction. Andrei was looking straight at him. He gave Ian a smile.

After the men had finished eating, Andrei said, "Incidentally Ian, when I was in Hong Kong last week, it was mentioned to me that a number of 19th and 20th century European paintings would shortly be available from a collection in the UK. When my colleague investigated further, imagine my surprise when it transpired that I had seen this list of paintings before. It was the same list as you gave me of the Baxter collection."

Ian put down his coffee cup and began to explain, "I used to work for Sotheby's in Hong Kong and had an excellent working relationship with several agents and galleries there. As Baxter's were very keen to obtain full valuation prices we felt the Chinese market may be able to pay those sorts of prices."

"That's fine, my friend," said Andrei. "Just remember the three Picassos and four Monets are mine … for valuation minus 20%!"

Ian swallowed the lump in his throat. Sergei leaned back in his seat and smiled at Ian. He understood Ian's dilemma. He could remember similar deals and negotiations with Andrei from their days in Russia.

Andrei continued. "Now my friend, I would like you and Emma to join me in Hong Kong in two weeks' time. I have an opportunity to buy a collection of 20 paintings that I saw when I was there last week. They are all by Gauguin and Whistler. Their provenances are unsure, but I do have four buyers interested already. I need your expert eyes to look at them. I'm not interested in your valuation this time. Just tell me whether you think they are fakes or not."

"Alright," said Ian. "When are we talking about?"

"A week on Friday. I am flying to Hong Kong, arriving late on Wednesday. I have a couple of clients to see first and then I have to be in Singapore on the following Monday."

"You are the globetrotter!"

"Yes, my friend, but I'm getting far too old for this work. It really is a young man's game. If only I was your age again! But, I still enjoy the thrill, the challenge … and of course the money is always very useful!"

All three men laughed. Sergei said he would get Viktor to let Ian have the tickets and full details early next week.

As the men got up to leave the restaurant, Ian thought, I must telephone Oscar. Maybe we can do some extra business whilst I'm out there at the same time.

# Chapter 22

When Ian arrived at his office on Tuesday morning, Viktor was waiting for him and sitting at Penny's desk. Ian said good morning to him. Viktor stood up and said, "Good morning ... my father asked me to give you this envelope."

"Ah, okay. Thank you. Have you seen Penny?" Ian took the envelope and walked towards his office.

"Yes, she's gone to get a coffee. She asked me to hold the fort," said Viktor following his boss into his room.

"Okay." Ian dropped the envelope on his desk and sat down. "Sit down Vic. I've not had a chance to thank you properly for all your hard work tidying up all the loose ends for the Constable and Turner auction. A big part of the auction success was due to all your personal efforts. You and Penny did really well."

"Thank you. I was pleased it was such a success."

"I had a review meeting with Mr Hopkins yesterday. I also took the opportunity to mention what a good job you had done."

"Thank you," said Viktor, he could feel himself beginning to blush, so decided it was now time to leave Ian's office.

Once Victor had departed, Ian opened the envelope. The contents consisted of the flight, hotel and travel details, plus an extra HK$150,000! A little note, written by Sergei, was also enclosed, it said, 'Andrei asked me to give you this money as he thought you might need some cash for taxi fares!' Ian smiled and could imagine Andrei laughing at his own little joke.

When Ian got home later that evening Emma was in the kitchen just finishing preparing their meal. As soon as he walked in he felt something was not quite right. Emma was not her usual cheerful self and she explained that she would not be joining him in Hong Kong after all. There was a bit of a crisis at the office and as it was only a short break they would not have time to enjoy all the opportunities properly, especially as Ian also had business meetings planned.

"That's okay. Another time." Ian and Emma hugged and Ian suggested a glass of wine.

Later that evening Ian emailed Sergei and told him to cancel Emma's flight ticket, but reconfirmed he would still be travelling to Hong Kong. He then telephoned Oscar. They discussed the Baxter paintings and Ian told Oscar of his travel plans. Oscar said he would 'meet and greet' him at Chek Lap Kok airport on his arrival.

Next morning Ian emailed Penny. Although she had been told by Ian of his short trip to Hong Kong, he updated her on his new planned meetings with Oscar. He reminded her of the possible potential buyers of the Baxter paintings in Hong Kong and maybe China and was hopeful that Oscar would have some good news. He also told her that he wanted to know immediately, if she received any new, or revised, offers from any potential UK buyers.

Ian closed down his computer and started to pack a small suitcase of clothes and his carry-on hand luggage. Included, for reading on the plane, were two reference books, one on Gauguin and the other on Whistler. At 4 pm the taxi arrived to take him to Heathrow for his overnight flight to Hong Kong. As the car slowly proceeded through the 'rush hour' traffic, Ian stared out of the window, but his mind was focused on Hong Kong. This was his first trip back to the former British colony since he had worked there several years ago. He had mixed emotions. He thought it would be great to go back to the place where he once called home, to meet Oscar, maybe some of his other ex-colleagues, and also to feel the buzz and vibrancy of the territory once again. He only hoped that going back would not be a disappointment. He knew that often when people have fond memories of someone or somewhere, meeting up again can sometimes be such a disappointment.

The M4 was typically slow progress this time in the early evening. Ian however, was relaxed and calm. He knew he had plenty of time before his flight was due to depart. His mind wandered again and his thoughts moved on to Andrei. He wondered if he was getting in far too deep with him. He enjoyed Andrei's company and envied the man's abilities, connections and wealthy lifestyle, but he was also thinking of how his own life was slowly changing too. He tried to think of why it was changing. He certainly felt more excited working with Andrei, yes that was true. It was all less strict and fewer formalities … much more of an adventure! He was definitely becoming wealthier and happier with the thought of financial security. Also he was definitely enjoying having the chance to experience new challenges and a freer involvement in the art world. But the downside? He thought deeply. Andrei's demands were subtle, but precise, very rewarding and difficult to turn down, well organised but some of his methods were sometimes unlawful! He concluded that he was having a good time working with Andrei, but he also knew that he really didn't want to get on the wrong side of him!

Consequences? Yes thought Ian, there are definitely consequences. Emma! He knew he was slowly becoming deceitful! White lies, black lies, whatever … he was worried. These were the consequences which he didn't like to think about at the moment. Maybe in time things would settle and … well … what? Only time would tell.

Ian's flight landed at Chek Lap Kok, Thursday afternoon. Oscar met him in 'Arrivals' and the two men greeted each other like long lost friends. Ian suggested Oscar had put on weight, to which Oscar retorted that Ian was looking older than he remembered. Both men laughed and headed to the taxi queue. Five minutes later Ian was giving the taxi driver the hotel's name and address details of where he was staying. The driver nodded and the car headed off for the waterfront area of Kowloon. The two men settled back in their seats and started to chat.

Oscar started by saying, "I think I've got 15 possible buyers for the 25 Baxter paintings." Oscar pulled out a paper copy of Ian's original email listing and pointed to each painting in turn. He had written comments at the end of each entry and the price the buyer was likely to pay.

Ian removed a copy of his latest list from his hand luggage bag to compare details. They compared the two sheets. Ian thought it looked as though Sir George and Martin Shaw might lose out on their Cezanne and Renoir paintings, unless they increased their offers. Whilst only one of the Picasso paintings appearing on Oscar's list had an offer price, all the four Monets did! Oscar's comments also indicated that he thought possibly three of these could be purchased for the full valuation. Shit, thought Ian. That causes me a big problem with Andrei.

"Do I know any of your prospective buyers?" Ian asked.

"Only one," replied Oscar. "Andrew Lee of Global Shipping and Export." Ian nodded. "He wants the three Renoirs."

"And the others?"

"One is a new buyer in Hong Kong. The three others are in Beijing."

"I see."

"The market has changed so quickly since you were here last, especially on the mainland."

Ian nodded. "Yes, so I understand. It's amazing isn't it. China is supposed to be a Communist country yet some of the wealthiest people in the world live there."

Two minutes later the taxi stopped outside the Intercontinental Hong Kong hotel on Salisbury Road in the East Tsim Sha Tsui district. As Ian was getting out of the taxi, Oscar suggested he take Ian out for a meal later and they agreed to meet in the hotel lobby area at 7.30 pm. Oscar said he had someone interesting for Ian to meet.

Ian said goodbye, gave the taxi driver HK$2000 and followed the porter, carrying his bags to reception. Fifteen minutes later he was standing in his room and looking out of the large bedroom window. The view was over Victoria Harbour and out towards Hong Kong Island. He quickly identified Causeway Bay, Wan Chai and Chung Wan, the Central District. The harbour seemed so much quieter now. The famous Star Ferries still seemed to be zigzagging to and fro, but the days of the busy commercial activity, he knew, had long been relocated to other areas. The size of Victoria Harbour had changed too. The distance between Hong Kong Island and Kowloon was gradually reducing. More and more land was being reclaimed and developed on. On both sides new skyscrapers had either recently been built or were in progress. It was still a great view, but certainly different now to the picture he had on his office wall back in the UK.

Ian removed a can of Tsingtao beer from the mini bar and unpacked his two cases. After shaving and a hot shower, he put on a clean set of smart casual clothes. Finishing his beer whilst sitting at the room's desk, he opened his laptop and sent emails to both Emma and Penny. At 7.15 pm he left the room to meet with Oscar in the hotel lobby. Who, he wondered, was Oscar going to introduce him to and more importantly ... why?

# Chapter 23

Ian arrived in the lobby area and saw Oscar standing next to the reception desk with his back towards him. He was talking to a petite, Chinese lady. She was smartly dressed in a grey business suit and matching high heel shoes. As Ian walked up he could hear and recognised some of the Cantonese language being spoken. He could only translate the odd word being said. When he arrived next to Oscar, he tapped him on the shoulder and said, "Good evening."

"Ah, Ian. I have just been talking about you. Let me introduce you to my colleague and friend, May Ling."

Ian and May Ling shook hands and May bowed slightly towards him. Ian guessed May would be about 30 years of age. She had dark brown eyes and jet black, medium length, hair. Quite an attractive combination, he thought.

"Good evening Mr Caxton, Oscar has been telling me all about you."

"I hope just the good bits," replied Ian, smiling.

May Ling smiled back and said, "I'm sure there are no bad bits." All three of them then laughed briefly.

Oscar interrupted the conversation. "I hope you are both hungry. I thought we would go over to Hong Kong Island to the Yung Kee," and he led the group towards the main exit doors. The early evening air was still warm and a little fresher after the afternoon shower.

"It's been a long time since I last ate there. I hope the Cantonese food is still up to their usual standard," replied Ian. Yes indeed, he thought, it does seem like a very long time ago!

As they exited through the open large glass doors, a porter hailed a waiting taxi and they all got in. Oscar gave the driver the restaurant's name and the car headed off towards the road tunnel which connects Kowloon with Hong Kong Island. Twenty-five minutes later they walked through the large, glamorous, shopfront-like entrance of the Yung Kee restaurant. As they were escorted to their table, Ian looked at the fellow diners and remembered that this was a long-standing favourite eatery among the local people. It had also won many prestigious awards over the years.

After ordering their food, their drinks quickly arrived. Oscar now came to the point of the meeting. "May works in both Hong Kong and Beijing and she represents a number of art buyers in that city. She has been asked to negotiate with you a price for the list of paintings you sent to me."

May then continued the conversation. "I represent three potential cash buyers, Mr Caxton. If we can agree on the right price, then there is a lot of business we can do together."

"I see," said Ian, a little noncommittal. "You have seen the valuations?" May nodded. "They are the prices I have been asked to achieve by my client."

"What if we want to buy 20 of your paintings, Mr Caxton? Will that make a difference?"

"I already have strong bids for 14 of the paintings in the UK. Which paintings are you interested in?"

May Ling removed a sheet of paper from her handbag. "The three Van Goghs, four Monets, four Cezannes, four Gauguins, four Moreaus and one of the Picassos. Plus I might have an interest in the three Renoirs."

"And your offer price?"

"Valuation less 10%."

"Okay. Well I have no authority to agree to any price less than full valuation, so I will have to put your offers to my client."

"Will we be able to see the paintings?"

"Of course, but they are currently in the UK."

"We have a colleague in London who could view them for us."

"Fine," replied Ian. "However, I think your buyers will need to be closer to the valuation prices first."

"My clients, maybe, can go a little higher, but only after we have seen the paintings and, of course, all documentation."

"A viewing can be arranged."

Oscar had been quiet up until this point. As there was now a lull in the conversation, he decided to intervene. "Ian and I can sort out the details, May. We will arrange for your colleague in London to see the paintings."

May looked directly at Oscar for a few seconds and then she slowly nodded her head.

"Good," said Oscar. "Ah, here comes our food."

The meal was up to the standard Ian remembered from the past. His Cantonese duck was better than anything he remembered eating in the UK. He decided, not for the first time, that he really did miss Hong Kong.

As Oscar lived on Hong Kong Island and May's apartment was not far from the restaurant, Ian travelled back to Kowloon in a taxi on his own. During the journey he digested all of May's comments. He felt frustrated that he was not obtaining full valuation offers, but worst of all, how was he going to square Andrei's offers with Sir Paul?

When Ian arrived back in his hotel room, he saw the flashing red light on the bedside telephone. He picked up the receiver and dialled 123 for message services. After a few seconds he heard the familiar voice of Andrei. "Hello, my friend. I'm staying in your hotel. Breakfast at 8.30. Lots to talk about." The line went dead.

Next morning at 8.25 am, Ian stood next to the entrance to the hotel's breakfast room. Two minutes later he recognised the familiar features of Andrei leaving the elevator.

When Andrei recognised Ian, his face lit up and he bellowed from about ten metres away. "Ah Ian! So good to see you again. Sorry to hear Emma will not be joining us this time. She's not ill I hope?"

"Hello Andrei," said Ian, grasping Andrei's hand. "No, no, she's very busy at work at the moment and I guess we are going to be busy too?"

"Come, my friend. Let's have a hearty breakfast, we have two very busy days ahead of us!"

The two men were shown to a quiet table and after ordering their food and drinks, Andrei pulled out a sheet of paper from his inside jacket pocket. He unfolded it and handed it across for Ian to read. Ian saw it was a list of 20 paintings all painted by Gauguin and Whistler. He immediately recognised a number of the titles from his homework on the plane.

"What do you think?" asked Andrei, once Ian had stopped reading.

Ian had a little thinking time when the waitress delivered the two orange juices and a large pot of coffee. Once she had walked away, Ian answered, "I recognise a number of these paintings. I need to investigate the provenances further. What do you know about them?"

"I was introduced to a Hong Kong man, Alex Fong, two weeks ago, at a dinner party. He apparently owns several successful electrical outlets in Hong Kong. When I mentioned I was interested in buying art, he told me he had inherited 20 paintings, after his father had died. His father had inherited them much earlier from his own father. There is no real provenance proving this, however."

"I see. But you say you have already lined up some possible buyers?"

"Yes. If these paintings are all real, then I can probably make about six million euros profit. I just need to know none of them are fakes! If any are, then that changes the price I'm prepared to pay."

# Chapter 24

After breakfast Ian said he wanted to do more research into the 20 paintings and headed back to his room. For the next three hours he referred back to the two reference books he had brought from the UK and looked at several websites on the Internet. At one o'clock he ordered sandwiches and coffee from room service. He finished writing up all his notes just before 2 pm.

Andrei had suggested to Mr Fong that he wanted Ian to see his painting collection. Mr Fong agreed and an appointment was made for 4 pm, later that same day, at his home. The address was close to Pok Fu Lam Country Park. The house was formerly Mr Fong's parents' home but he and his family had moved in to look after his mother following the death of his father.

At 3 pm Ian met Andrei in the hotel lobby and they arranged for a porter to hail a taxi.

Five minutes later, they were heading for the road tunnel and to Hong Kong Island. During the journey Ian gave Andrei a summary of his findings.

Once the taxi arrived on the island it followed a route gradually climbing up the hillside and along numerous twisting roads. On both sides of the roads Ian observed various sizes of tall modern apartment buildings. Eventually the taxi stopped in Mr Fong's driveway. Gone were the high-rise apartments. Here were the detached houses with their own gardens and the multimillion-dollar market value. Andrei paid the fare and the two men got out. Both stood and stared at the view back down and over the skyscrapers of the Central District. In the distance was Victoria Harbour, across the water, Kowloon and the New Territories. Finally, to the left, part of Lantau Island.

"Good afternoon gentlemen. Magnificent view isn't it?" said a voice from behind them.

Andrei and Ian turned around to see a man standing outside the front door. "Mr Fong," whispered Andrei.

Ian thought Mr Fong looked about 40 years of age. He was well built and a similar height to himself. The two men walked over to the doorway and onto the step.

"Mr Fong, this is the colleague I told you about, Ian Caxton. He is from the UK and works for Sotheby's, the auction house."

Mr Fong gave Ian a big smile and shook his hand. Ian noted a very firm grip. "Come in gentlemen. Would you like some tea?"

Both guests agreed they would like tea. As the three men walked towards the lounge, Mr Fong gave orders to a maid for the tea. When they entered the lounge, Andrei was immediately captivated by the huge picture window. It replicated almost exactly, the view they had first witnessed from the driveway.

"Fabulous," said Andrei. Ian was briefly surveying the paintings on the room's walls, before joining his colleague.

"My wife is still getting used to seeing it each morning. We moved here ten months ago. It was my parent's house and my grandparents' before them. My grandfather was an avid collector, especially paintings. Until now, all those who inherited the house, inherited the paintings too."

Ian took the opportunity to speak for the first time. "You said, 'until now'?"

Just as Mr Fong was about to reply, the maid brought in the tea on a silver tray and placed it on a small table.

After the maid left Mr Fong poured tea and continued with his explanation, "During the last few years of his life, my father did not spend too much time, or money, on the upkeep of this property. It now requires many repairs, maintenance and some updating. All very expensive. Whilst my businesses are doing well, we do not have the capital to carry out these more urgent issues, so it's a case of either increasing the mortgage or selling some assets. Mother has never liked some of the paintings so we thought selling them would achieve two positive results."

"I understand that it is the Gauguin and Whistler pictures that you are thinking of selling?" said Ian, He was walking around the lounge and looking at the paintings again.

"Yes. The main collection is in the dining room. Four are in the study, two on the stairs and six are stored in one of the spare bedrooms."

Andrei kept quiet and decided to leave the discussion to Ian.

"What documentation do you have relating to these paintings?"

"Very little. We have never been able to find any paperwork relating to grandfather's purchases. However, a full inventory was made when my father took over the house and we did the same when we moved in. In both cases, full details of all the paintings are listed."

"You have no idea how, or where, your grandfather purchased these pictures?"

"Mother recalls, from when she was first married to my father, that his father, my grandfather, was a very keen gambler, mainly playing cards. She says that father told her that several of the paintings were obtained to clear some old gambling debts. However, she has no idea which paintings were involved."

"I see. Can we look at the paintings please?"

Of course. Please drink your tea first, gentlemen and I will then give you the guided tour."

Both Andrei and Ian picked up their cups and saucers and helped themselves to milk. Mr Fong had his tea black. Andrei walked back towards the huge picture window sipping his tea and briefly watched as a helicopter came into view and then disappeared behind the trees of the Country Park.

"That will be Mr Lam," suggested Mr Fong. "He lives just down the road and commutes to his business on Lantau island each day by helicopter. He says it saves him about three hours commuting time each day."

"I see," acknowledged Andrei.

"You have finished your tea gentlemen. Come, I will show you the rest of the paintings. The three men exited the lounge and headed for the stairs.

Over the next hour Mr Fong gave a guided tour to the places where the 20 paintings were either hanging or stored. Ian inspected each one carefully and made copious notes as he proceeded. At the end of the tour Ian told Andrei he had sufficient information at this stage.

The group reconvened in the lounge and this time it was Andrei who said, "We need to discuss the paintings together this evening. Can I telephone you tomorrow?

"Of course," replied Mr Fong, "but it is only fair to say that I have had two previous offers."

"I would not expect anything less," said Ian.

Mr Fong shook hands with both men and led them towards the front door. As he opened the door, he announced that his eldest son, Li, would take them both in his car across to The Peak. It would be very easy to obtain a taxi from there.

When the men arrived on the front driveway, a young Chinese man, in tee-shirt and jeans, was standing next to a scarlet red BMW 3 series car. Ian looked at Andrei's alarmed expression. A wry smile appeared on his own face.

During the ten-minute journey to The Peak, neither Andrei or Ian discussed the paintings. It was not until later when they were in a taxi and on their way back to the hotel, that Andrei asked Ian, "So, my friend, what are your thoughts?"

"As far as I can tell, none appear to be fakes. They are all good quality paintings. I have been able to trace records of 12 of them but without proper provenance and authentication, it's still a bit of a gamble."

Andrei sat quietly and looked out of the window and after a few moments said, "You know, my friend, life is … all a bit of a gamble. It was a gamble for grandfather Fong to accept paintings in lieu of debts. It will be a gamble for my buyers to pay my prices!"

Over breakfast the next morning, Andrei announced to Ian that he was flying to Singapore that afternoon. One of his business meetings had been brought forward. He also said he was going to telephone Mr Fong that morning and confirm his previous estimate. He had been in contact with his buyers and they had all confirmed they still wanted to buy. He said he was very satisfied with Ian's opinion and was prepared to pay him 10% of the gross profit when the deal was completed.

This was extremely generous, Ian thought, but he decided to make Andrei a different proposition.

"That is very generous of you Andrei, but can I make a different suggestion?"

"Of course, my friend, what do you want?"

"The seven Baxter paintings. You said you wanted to pay the valuation minus 20%." Andrei nodded and Ian continued. "Could you not pay full valuation instead? It would help me immensely with Baxter's."

Andrei was quiet for a few minutes and then a smile appeared on his face and he said, "Valuation minus 5%! How is that, my friend? Will that help?"

Ian smiled and shook his head from side to side. Andrei just laughed.

# Chapter 25

Ian and Andrei said their goodbyes to each other after they had finished their breakfasts. Andrei had also promised that he would contact Ian again after he had completed his discussions with Mr Fong. On returning to his room Ian resumed his packing but then stopped and decided to telephone Oscar.

They both discussed their meeting with May Ling once again. Ian emphasised that he was keen to get his full valuation prices for the Baxter paintings ... or as close as possible! Oscar agreed he would be pressing for the same result, after all, the higher the sale prices, the larger the commission he would get. Ian then suggested they meet for lunch. It would be the last opportunity for Ian to just have a friendly chat with his old friend. Oscar was similarly keen and agreed to pick Ian up from his hotel at 12.30. He also promised that after lunch, he would take Ian back to the airport for his evening flight back to the UK.

Ian now had some time on his hands before he needed to check out of the hotel, so he sat at the desk and reviewed all his notes from the meeting with Oscar and May Ling. He then updated his Baxter spreadsheet to include Andrei's revised offer. Once satisfied that everything was now up to date, he emailed a copy to Penny. Finally, and before closing his computer down, he sent a quick catch-up email to Emma.

Just before 12.30 pm Ian had all his bags packed. He took one final look out of his window at the view across Victoria Harbour towards Hong Kong Island. His eyes focussed on a lone Star Ferry as it slowly sailed towards Wan Chai Ferry Pier. A tear appeared in his left eye and after he brushed it away with his left hand, he hoped there would still be a lot more opportunities to return to this wonderful country. He knew this panorama picture would continue to slowly evolve and change, as would the politics of the country, but he also hoped that despite these factors, it would always remain such a very special view.

When Ian arrived on the ground floor, Oscar was waiting for him in the hotel lobby. He handed his room key to a receptionist and joined his colleague. Oscar had arrived in his own car, a silver Audi Q5. After the two men had climbed on board, Oscar explained he was taking Ian to a small, but a relatively new, restaurant on Lantau Island. One of his favourites. He also explained that the restaurant was not too far from the airport.

Ian remembered weekends on Lantau Island. Despite the building of the huge Chek Lap Kok airport, the island was still one of the greenest areas in Hong Kong. Many Buddhist monasteries and tiny temples were still tucked away in the more remote areas.

Driving from the hotel car park, it was not too long before they had joined the motorway heading towards Lantau Island. Oscar said that he had spoken again with Andrew Lee. Andrew had confirmed that he was still keen to buy the three Renoirs … and he was now prepared to pay the full valuation.

"At last," exclaimed Ian. "We have finally got a buyer agreeing to pay the full valuation price!"

"I have another possible buyer, David Lai, but I cannot get hold of him at the moment."

"What about May Ling? Have you been able to speak with her again since we chatted earlier this morning?"

"No, I tried to call her, but all I got was her answerphone. I think valuation minus 5% is probably the best there, at the moment. It's not bad, if she confirms all 20 paintings. But I will chase her up."

The conversation went quiet for a few minutes. Ian considered the problem of the four Monets and the one Picasso, which were wanted by both May Ling's buyers and Andrei. However, at this very moment, he did not have an answer to that dilemma. Whilst he was pondering on this issue, his mobile phone pinged to indicate a text message. Ian opened it up and saw it was from Andrei. The message simply read:

*'Hello, my friend. Deal done. Have a safe journey.'*

Ian smiled and texted straight back:

*'Congratulations! Have a safe journey yourself.'*

"Good news?" enquired Oscar, pleased to see the smile reappear on his friend's face.

"Yes. One of my clients, confirming a big deal!" A big deal indeed thought Ian.

"Let's hope it is a sign of things to come!" replied Oscar. He wanted a big success with this one too.

"Yes ... indeed." Ian sat back in his seat and watched the passing countryside. He was amazed at the volume of new large buildings, mostly apartments, that had been built in just the brief time he'd been away.

Ian asked Oscar, "All these new buildings. Who can afford Hong Kong prices nowadays?"

Oscar smiled. "Most buyers now are mainland Chinese. They want to get their money out of Shanghai and Beijing. Some of the whole buildings you can see are sold out, but nowhere near fully occupied. It is seen by the wealthy mainland Chinese as safe long-term investments."

After another five minutes Oscar turned off the motorway and headed towards a small fishing village which could just be seen in the distance. On top of the hill, to Ian's left-hand side, Oscar pointed to the huge statue of the Po Lin Buddha.

"I saw that when we landed in the aeroplane," said Ian, looking at the statue for a few seconds.

Oscar decided to regale Ian with the Buddha's vital statistics, "Largest sitting outdoor Buddha in Asia! Made of bronze, 34 metres in height and allegedly weighing about 250 tons … what one would call a big lad!"

Ian smiled. "Yes indeed … a very big lad! You would make a good tour guide!"

Oscar smiled, "I think I'll stick with the day job."

"Good decision," replied Ian. The last thing he wanted was to lose his best art contact in Southeast Asia.

Oscar finally arrived in the tiny fishing hamlet. There were only about 12 buildings in the hamlet and it was extremely quiet. When Oscar parked his car there was only one other vehicle in the immediate vicinity. Oscar had parked directly in front of what looked like an old, rustic, wooden shack! From the passenger seat Ian had the view which looked out to the sea. When he finally got out of the car, he just stood and stared at the many tiny islands, seemingly just floating on the sun-dazed South China Sea. It was just a fabulous view and all so quiet and serene. Just the gentle lapping of waves breaking on the shore was all that could be heard.

Ian turned around and pointed to the shack. "What's this? This is hardly a new restaurant. One puff of wind and the whole thing will collapse!" Ian was seriously wondering what his friend had brought him to.

"Probably the best local fish restaurant in Hong Kong! Despite appearances the restaurant was only opened six months ago. All the seafood is caught locally and is kept alive in tanks at the back! You just select your own fish and they will cook it!"

An hour later the two men were still sitting on the veranda, drinking two beers and staring out to sea. Ian had followed Oscar's recommendation, so both had enjoyed the 'Flower crab with razor clam and prawn seafood mix', a house speciality! Ian had been told that each different shellfish was cooked separately and then blended together with light spices, oil, vegetables and rice. Simple, but Ian had to agree, it tasted wonderful.

It was Oscar who broke the silence. "Do you miss Hong Kong, Ian?"

An interesting question, thought Ian. He had been pondering on this conundrum for the last two days. "Mostly, yes. London is okay, but really Hong Kong is where the excitement is. At least it was."

"What do you mean ... was?"

"The trouble is we always look back with rose-tinted glasses, don't we? Think of all the good times, the fun and excitement we all used to have. For most of the time I lived here, I was a bachelor and, apart from my work, I had hardly any responsibilities. Now I'm married and have many responsibilities. If I did ever come back it would all be so different ... and not necessarily as good. Never go back, someone once said, and maybe they were right. Besides, Emma never wanted to live here."

"Interesting observation. Yes, it's quite a challenge for expats' wives. I see lots of western divorces. I must admit. If and when I finally settle down with someone, I will probably want to move on too."

"Mmm. I know ... and of course, I would hate to lose Emma."

"Come on, let's get you back to the airport … and back to your responsibilities."

The two men finished their beers and Oscar went into the bar area to pay the bill. Ian took one last look at the lovely view. The sun was now lower in the western sky and beginning to lose its earlier yellow intensity. It was now gradually turning a softer golden hue. Soon it will be sunset, he thought. Such a pity he was leaving.

Oscar came out of the restaurant and the two men walked to the car and climbed in. Ian thanked Oscar for a super lunch and they headed off for the airport.

A few minutes later Ian spotted the outskirts of Chek Lap Kok airport. When Ian first arrived in Hong Kong several years ago, he'd landed at the same airport. At that time it was brand new. However, he always felt a little cheated as he would have loved to have landed at the old airport of Kai Tak. Older colleagues in the office would tell him tales about the history of Kai Tak and the excitement when planes came in to land and had to fly through a narrow gap between the Hong Kong skyscrapers. Window seat passengers in the planes had the unique view of people hanging out their washing on their balconies as the planes dropped lower and lower to hit the runway at the right point. He was told of incidents where planes had overshot their landing point and had to accelerate and climb again, before turning and having another go. One colleague showed Ian photographs of a plane that had landed but could not stop in time before it finished up in the sea! Ian knew that Kai Tak airport had now been converted into a port for the major cruise ships. A practical use, but certainly nowhere near as exciting!

Oscar flicked the car's indicators and followed the sign for 'Departures'. When Oscar stopped at the terminal, Ian thanked him for the lift and for the lovely entertaining day.

They both promised to keep each other informed on the progress of the Baxter pictures and also to keep in touch more generally as friends as well.

Four hours later Ian was on his way back to the UK. His flight had left about 20 minutes late, but he now prepared himself for a long night flight. About 13 hours of darkness, he calculated. He had already converted his Business Class seat into a bed and hoped he would be able to spend most of the journey asleep.

When the aeroplane cabin lights dimmed Ian was lying down and trying to go to sleep. The last thing he remembered was that he had enjoyed the last few days back in Hong Kong but was pleased to be going home. Pleased to be going home to Emma ... and back to his responsibilities!

When he awoke, it was still dark outside and the cabin lights were still dimmed. He looked at his watch and calculated about another three hours before the plane landed. He got out of bed and pressed the electronic buttons that rebuilt his seat, after which he picked up his bathroom bag and set off to the washroom. When he returned the full internal cabin lights had been restored and there was generally more activity in the cabin. He repacked his hand luggage and retrieved his laptop. He decided to update his files for Penny and Vic and decided the coming week was going to be a very busy time.

Ian arrived at work just after 7.30 am the next day. He wanted to make sure he was up to date when Penny and Vic arrived. Once he had sat down at his desk and sipped his coffee, he read through several messages that Penny had left. One immediately caught his eye. Sir Paul Broadway, the CEO at Baxter's, wanted an 'update' meeting! Penny had checked Ian's diary and had arranged an appointment for the coming Thursday. Okay, he thought, no pressure then!

Penny arrived just after 8.15 am and was surprised to find her boss working at his desk and surrounded by papers and two open computers. "Good morning," she announced. "How was Hong Kong?"

"Hello Penny. It was great to be back there once again, but the results of the offers for the Baxter paintings were not as good as I had hoped for. Can you telephone Vic. I would like a meeting with you both later this morning."

"Did you see my note about the meeting with Sir Paul next Thursday?"

"Yes. We need to get our skates on before then."

Later that morning, Ian, Penny and Viktor sat around Ian's table in his office. Ian had produced his spreadsheet and read out the current state of play of each of the Baxter paintings. At the end, he concluded by stating, "We are now in a very testing position. There is no way that I can go to a meeting with Sir Paul, with this level of offers. So … any suggestions?"

Ideas were suggested and discussed. The meeting finished with Penny and Viktor agreeing to try and firm up on the earlier tentative offers and also approach two specialist galleries. All three had then debated possible new extra names to approach. Finally, Ian said that he would speak with Oscar, Martin Shaw and Sir George Gamble. A further team meeting was agreed for 10 am on Wednesday to review progress.

At 4.15 pm Ian's mobile phone rang. To his surprise it was Sergei. Ian was certainly not expecting this caller. "Hello Sergei, and how are you?"

"Very well, thank you. I gather you and Andrei were successful in Hong Kong."

"Yes. Andrei completed his deal."

"Yes, I was speaking with Andrei earlier and he told me about Mr Fong's paintings. He has also given me some information to pass on to you. Can we meet later this evening?"

"Of course. Where and when?"

"I have some business in Bond Street to attend at five o'clock, so should we say six o'clock in The Grapes?"

"That's fine with me."

"Good," replied Sergei. The line went dead.

Mmm, thought Ian, I wonder what Andrei is up to this time!

# Chapter 26

Ian left Sotheby's at ten minutes to six. It had been a cold day, with the odd snow flurry. Now the temperature was below freezing and the pavements were slippery in places. This was definitely the time of year when Ian wished he was living in a warmer climate. He arrived at The Grapes just before six o'clock. There were a few early evening drinkers, but it was not overly busy. Ian was able to quickly look around the bar area but he couldn't see Sergei. He decided to buy a pint of beer while he waited, and walked over to the bar and gave his order. Whilst the beer was being poured Ian looked around the bar area again, but didn't notice any one he knew. He paid the barman, sipped his drink and looked for an empty table. It was at this point that Sergei entered through the main door. He walked over to join Ian and the two men shook hands.

"Hello Sergei, what would you like to drink?" Ian was fairly sure that Sergei was not a beer drinker.

Sergei looked at Ian's glass but decided he would prefer a glass of claret. "Do you know if they sell claret?"

Ian asked the barman, who confirmed they did. Once the wine was poured and Sergei had collected his glass, the two men found a quiet corner of the room and sat down.

Sergei sipped his wine and announced. "It is surprisingly good. Cheers!"

"Cheers!" Ian responded, sipping his beer and waiting for Sergei to tell him the reason for the meeting.

"Andrei telephoned me this morning from Singapore. He told me about the deal with Mr Fong and we are now working with the buyers who had previously agreed to Andrei's terms. Two of the buyers, incidentally, are in London." Ian raised his eyebrows in surprise. Sergei continued, "He also mentioned that another seven paintings had been 'acquired' from the Kremlin chambers." Again Ian's eyebrows shot up! Andrei is unbelievable, Ian thought. "He also asked me to tell you that as a result of acquiring these pictures, his offer for the Baxter paintings is now your 'full valuation'."

"Oh wow! That's great news Sergei. That makes my life so much easier. It looks like everyone's a winner now!"

"Probably not the Russian Government though," whispered Sergei and both men laughed. "Andrei will be in London in two weeks' time. He would like to meet up again, with both you and Emma."

"He seems to be visiting London a lot more at the moment. But yes, that would be nice. Do you know any details?" Once again Ian was excited about the possibility of working with Andrei once more.

"No, but I will be speaking to him again next weekend. I am sure he will then be in a position to tell me of his plans."

Later that evening Ian was sitting in the home office and typing on his laptop computer. A glass of Chablis was also in reach on the desk. He was very pleased to be updating his Baxter spreadsheet with more positive news. He just hoped that Penny and Vic were also being more successful.

In the end column of his spreadsheet, against the four Monet and three Picasso paintings, he deleted the '-5%' so that it now just read 'Andrei, full valuation'. After he had inserted all the new details, he closed the laptop down, picked up his glass of wine and leaned back in his chair, "Cheers my friend ... and thank you!" he said out loud. He took great pleasure in toasting Andrei.

On Wednesday morning at 10 am, Ian, Penny and Viktor all sat around Ian's table in his office. Ian laid a paper version of his spreadsheet in front of the group. It had now been updated with all the latest offers that Ian had achieved. He went through each painting individually and when he came to a painting where Penny and Viktor had obtained recently updated offers, he manually amended both the comments and revised offer details. At the end of the meeting, Ian summarised that now there were 12 paintings which had 'full valuation' offers, ten had 'valuation minus 5%' and three had 'valuation minus 10%'.

"This is much better," concluded Ian, "at least now I've got a good starting point to discuss the pictures with Sir Paul, tomorrow. Hopefully we might now get a commitment to auction the other 28 paintings as well. Thank you both, for your hard work."

Penny and Viktor sat back in their chairs, looked at each other and smiled. They both thought they had earned Ian's praise. However, all three of them still knew that the challenge was not over, not yet, but maybe, just maybe, the winning post was now in sight.

On Thursday morning at 9.45 am Ian arrived in Baxter's visitors' car parking area. He double checked the contents of his briefcase and took a quick check on his emails, using his mobile phone. He got out of the car, locked it and headed towards reception. When he arrived at the reception desk he announced his name and stated he had a 10 am meeting with Sir Paul Broadway. The receptionist picked up her telephone receiver and telephoned John

Chambers, Sir Paul's PA. She then asked Ian to take a seat. Ian thanked her and wandered over to the seating area. He remained standing and thought about the forthcoming meeting. He now felt comfortable and far more confident than he had done just a few days earlier. He hoped that all the increased offers would give him some extra time ... some breathing space, to obtain further improved offers. Five minutes later, John Chambers arrived in reception and walked over to where Ian was standing. The two men shook hands.

"Did you have a good journey?" asked John, leading Ian back towards the elevator.

"It was not too bad coming my way. The traffic on the M4, going in towards London had come to a standstill at the M25 junction, but it was okay for me."

When they arrived at the elevator John pressed the request button. "Sir Paul will be meeting you in the boardroom again, but this time the Chairman and two other Directors will also be present."

"Is that good news?" said Ian. He was hoping it would have been just Sir Paul making the final decision. He didn't like trying to persuade a committee to agree.

The elevator door opened and both men got in. John pressed the sixth floor button and the doors closed. He then answered Ian's question. "I suppose it depends on what you have got to tell us!"

Ian smiled and thought, I hope they take what I have to say as very good news!

They arrived outside the boardroom, John knocked on the door and walked straight in. Ian followed directly behind. John introduced Ian to the Chairman and the two directors, who, with Sir Paul, were already seated around the boardroom table. The Chairman nodded and the two directors said "Good morning" to him. Ian responded likewise.

Sir Paul then welcomed him back and said he hoped Ian had some good news to tell them.

Ian sat down on the chair allocated to him, next to John. He unclicked his briefcase and retrieved a brown folder from which he removed an updated, and more personalised, paper copy of his spreadsheet. He unfolded the sheet and placed it on the table directly in front of him. Now that he was ready, he was asked by John to speak.

"The art market," said Ian, largely focussing his attention towards Sir Paul, "is currently a buyers' market and prices being achieved from recent sales, were reflecting this. For the very top paintings, prices were still holding firm and in some very exceptional cases, above market expectations are still being attained. Your company's collection is a very good collection, but it does not include any of these very top value paintings. Nevertheless, we have still managed to obtain serious offers against the valuations we originally presented to Sir Paul."

Ian now turned his spreadsheet around so everyone could see the details. He then explained the latest offer position for each painting. Sir Paul and the fellow senior management team all leaned forward to see the report more closely. Ian concluded by saying that Sotheby's were still hopeful of achieving the original full valuation prices on each painting, but he would be interested to hear their initial thoughts.

Sir Paul looked around the table and then said, "Based on your initial presentation, we thought you might already be achieving the valuation prices you set."

Whilst Ian tried to keep a straight face, he was definitely feeling a little deflated.

Sir Paul continued, "However, John here," Sir Paul waved his hand in his PA's direction, "from his own research, confirms your opinion that it is not currently a sellers' market. His view is that overall, we might have to accept discounts in the range of 5–10% if we decided to sell now. Your report today is slightly higher than his view, which is obviously good news. We therefore have three options. One, to do nothing further until the market picks up; two, sell all 25 paintings at the prices you have stated; or three, ask you to complete your investigations and report back in, say, ten days' time."

Whilst Sir Paul was talking, Ian glanced slightly sideways towards John Chambers and he gave him the briefest smile of thanks. John's expression did not change.

Sir Paul continued. "We therefore anticipated this situation and have already agreed that you should be given the extra ten days to try and get the best possible prices you can for us."

Ian's deflation suddenly evaporated.

"As for the other 28 paintings," continued Sir Paul, "the board is in full agreement that they should be sold at auction. Can you start the ball rolling on that too?"

Ian smiled at Sir Paul. "Yes certainly, Sir Paul. We will get on with both tasks immediately. Thank you."

"Good. I don't think there is anything else, is there?" Sir Paul looked around the table. "Chairman?"

The Chairman spoke for the first time. "No, let's just hope Mr Caxton can achieve the full valuations within the ten days."

Nobody else made a comment and so Sir Paul thanked Ian for his time and comprehensive presentation and asked John to see him back to reception.

In the elevator Ian thanked John for his support.

John looked at Ian and said, "I thought you were optimistic with your original valuations. My brother works in the art industry and he thought your valuations were, let's just say, a little cheeky! Mind, you still have ten days to prove you were right!"

The doors opened and Ian stepped out. John stayed in the elevator and pressed the button to the sixth floor again. Ian turned around and as the doors began to close, John said to him, "See you in ten days' time, good luck!"

When Ian got back into his car, he cheered to himself! He then telephoned Penny and told her he wanted to have a meeting with her and Viktor at 4pm later that afternoon.

# Chapter 27

At 4 pm Ian, Penny and Viktor were once again assembled around Ian's office table. Penny had arranged for a pot of tea to be delivered and as she and Viktor took their first sips, whilst they waited for Ian to speak.

Ian summarised how the meeting with the board at Baxter's had gone and then listed the tasks for the next ten days. "Vic, I want you to get the preparation work started for the proposed auction of the extra 28 paintings. It's not urgent, but let's get the basics started. Penny, we really need to get the -5% and -10% offers eliminated. We have 13 paintings to attack. Have we had any feedback from the two galleries or the extra buyers we identified?"

"Nothing substantial," replied Penny, "the Craig & Co gallery have said they could be interested but were not prepared to commit to our timescales. I'll keep chasing them."

Viktor then commented. "Martin Shaw has confirmed, following your conversation with him, that he will now support full valuation and Burton Galleries could be interested in the four Moreaus, but they want to speak to you first."

Penny then announced that Oscar had telephoned and wanted Ian to ring him back urgently. Ian nodded. "Okay," he said. "If we get all the right answers from Oscar then we should be very close to our goal."

Later that evening Ian telephoned Oscar, but just got his answerphone. He left a message which was short and simple:

*"Hi Oscar, returning your call. Hope all is going well with May Ling. Give me a ring when you are free."*

It was just before midnight and Ian was about to switch off the light in the home office and get ready to go upstairs to bed, when his mobile phone rang.

"Ian!?" It was Oscar. He sounded a bit harassed and rushed.

"Hi Oscar, how's things?"

"May Ling has gone back to her buyers and it looks as though we might be getting full valuation now on about 15 paintings."

"What! Which ones are we talking about?"

Oscar reeled off the list and Ian grabbed his paper spreadsheet and updated the details recorded on the two end columns.

"Okay," said Ian, excitedly. "This gives us a problem, but at least, this time, it's a good one to have!"

"What do you mean?" Oscar thought he'd now solved Ian's problems.

"Well we now have several paintings where more than one potential buyer has offered the full valuation price."

"Okay. So what are you going to do?"

"Leave it with me for 24 hours. I'll get back to you tomorrow evening. It should be about 11 pm UK time."

"Okay. By the way, remember Andrew Lee? Well he has offered full valuation for the Renoirs and I have finally been able to speak with David Lai. He is prepared to pay full valuation for the four Cezannes."

Ian again updated his spreadsheet. "Okay. Well done. I'll speak to you again tomorrow."

When Ian put down the phone, he put both of his hands over his eyes and whispered, "Oh shit!"

Next morning when Ian arrived at his office, Penny was already sitting and working at her desk.

"Good morning Penny. Can you get hold of Vic? I want the three of us to meet in ten minutes time. There have been quite a few developments last night so we need to get together and bring the spreadsheet together." Ian went into his office and Penny telephoned Viktor.

Ten minutes later they were all sitting around Ian's table. Ian was explaining the details of his conversation with Oscar. He then pointed to his paper spreadsheet and in particular, the various crossed out names, updated offers and the resulting implications.

"Oh, okay" said Penny summarising the current position. "So now we have just four paintings at -5% and the rest 'full valuation' and ..." Penny counted down one of the spreadsheet columns,

" ... 14 where we have at least duplicate full valuation offers. How are we going to decide who is going to have which picture?"

"Vic, you have been quiet so far. Do you have any suggestions?" asked Ian.

Viktor leaned over to the spreadsheet and pointed to the three Renoirs. "Martin Shaw did indicate that he would have to raise the money first for these, so that could take some time."

"Okay, let's go through each offer again and this time identify which buyer is in the best position to immediately proceed," concluded Ian. "We will then be in a far better position to make a final judgement."

For the next two hours the group discussed the pros and cons of each of the potential buyers and whether they knew the buyer's ability to be able to raise the purchase funds immediately. At the end of the meeting, they had agreed on a strategy.

As promised, Ian telephoned Oscar later that evening and he explained the situation. Ian wanted to know how strong the offers from Andrew Lee and David Lai were and how readily the money would be available from them. He also asked the same questions of May Ling and her clients. In summary, Oscar said only David Lai was the unknown, he could vouch for Andrew Lee and May Ling's funds being immediately available.

Ian then remarked. "May Ling's buyers might not get all their pictures. Do you think that is going to be a problem?"

"How many paintings are you saying?" Oscar was now a little worried.

"Eleven. The three Van Goghs, four Moreaus and four Gauguins. Plus, Andrew Lee can have the three Renoirs, unless you decide to offer those to May Ling instead?"

"I'm not sure May Ling expected to get all 20 paintings and as Andrew Lee is a good client, I think I would prefer him to have the Renoirs."

"Can you find out if this is all okay with May Ling, as soon as possible, please, Oscar? Also, can you establish if Andrew Lee would be prepared to accept May Ling's viewing contact?"

"I will drop you an email with all this information."

"One last thing Oscar, your commission." Ian was concerned that when Sir Paul saw the total invoice, he might query Oscar's 'usual' 10%.

"If Baxter sells to both May Ling and Andrew, I could reduce it to say 5%," said Oscar, he knew that even then the commission would still be substantial.

"What if I need some leeway?"

"Okay ... 3%."

"Thank you. I'll make it up to you." Ian sighed with relief. He owed Oscar one.

"I know you will. Thanks … and good luck."

In his office on Monday morning, Ian updated the Baxter spreadsheet on his computer. He then printed off a new paper copy version. Finally, finally, he thought, it was all coming together. He asked Penny to make an appointment for him to meet with Sir Paul. However, he warned Penny that she will be put through to Sir Paul's PA, John Chambers. "Make sure he is aware that we have achieved improved offers, but," he emphasised, "don't give him the specific details. Can you also ask Vic to let me know the outline plans for the auction?"

Ten minutes later, Penny appeared at Ian's door. "I have spoken with Sir Paul's PA. Bit of an obnoxious character isn't he?" Ian smiled. "You have an appointment for next Monday, at 10 am. Vic says you will have his draft suggested details for the auction, for your approval, tomorrow."

"Excellent. We've now got Sir George Gamble definitely on board for the Cezanne's, so we are just waiting on Oscar's email."

Late Wednesday evening, Ian and Emma were enjoying a rare evening of just the two of them together. They were cuddled on the sofa, watching a recorded film on the tv. In the background Ian heard the familiar 'ping' sound of his mobile phone announcing an incoming email. When the film had finished, he moved from Emma's side and picked up the mobile phone. After pressing several buttons, he discovered what he was waiting for. It was the email from Oscar. He quickly scanned through the contents of the message. Suddenly he exclaimed, "Yes!".

It made Emma jump and say, "So you've finally won the lottery?"

"Much better than that. Oscar has been a hero!"

Emma was half asleep and still lying on the sofa. However,

she did decide to find out why Oscar was a hero. "So what's he been doing?"

"He's completed the final pieces of the Baxter jigsaw!"

"Oh," said Emma, none the wiser. "Difficult jigsaw was it?"

# Chapter 28

Oscar's email gave the contact details of a Mr Joseph Zhang, the person May Ling had informed Oscar, she wanted to view the Baxter paintings. Oscar additionally confirmed that Andrew Lee was also happy for Mr Zhang to view the three Renoirs on his behalf.

Ian immediately sent an email to both Penny and Victor, so they could pick it up first thing in the morning. He also attached a copy of Oscar's email details and asked Penny to arrange a viewing appointment for Mr Zhang with John Chambers, but only after he had been to the next meeting with Sir Paul set for next Monday. When you have made that appointment, tell Viktor the date and time. Ian then gave Viktor the task of contacting Mr Zhang and to advise him of the appointment details and to arrange and transport him to and from the Baxter premises.

On the following Monday, at 10 am, Ian was once again in the Baxter & Co's boardroom. This time the meeting was only attended by Sir Paul and John Chambers.

Ian produced yet another updated paper spreadsheet and he explained the recent developments.

"Since our last meeting, we have been able to firm up on a number of offers for the 25 paintings. I am pleased to say that we now have 'full valuation' offers on 21 paintings and 'valuation minus 5%' on the remaining four." Ian looked up and saw John Chambers had a wry smile on his face and Sir Paul was nodding … with approval, he hoped.

Ian continued to advise the gross and nett sale prices, after deducting Sotheby's costs and Oscar's commission of 3%. He then explained how the sale proceeds would be collected from the various buyers and how the money would be paid to Baxter's. He concluded by explaining the standard procedure for packing, collecting and delivering the paintings to the new owners.

When Ian had finished the room went temporarily quiet. Finally Sir Paul said, "So it looks as though we will now have to redecorate our bare walls!" Both Ian and John laughed.

Inside, Ian was jumping up and down with joy. He continued and explained what he was proposing for the auction of the remaining pictures. He suggested three possible options for presentations, marketing, advertising and timescales. When he had finished, Sir Paul said. "That all sounds very good. John will liaise with you to agree all the final details."

Ian was escorted back towards reception. As they waited for the elevator to arrive, John said, "Well done. I did not think you would achieve those figures. Incidentally, neither did the board! You certainly surprised Sir Paul too!"

Ian left Baxter's office with a huge smile on his face. When he got into his car, he immediately telephoned Penny and told her what had happened. He then asked her to inform Vic and also Michael Hopkins of the good news.

The appointment for Mr Zhang to visit Baxter's premises was agreed by all parties for two days' time. Fortunately for Viktor, Mr Zhang's office was only ten minutes away from Junction 3 on the M4 motorway, so he was able to collect him and arrive at Baxter's premises in good time and without any traffic problems.

When Viktor arrived back at Sotheby's later that afternoon after taking Mr Zhang back to his office, he immediately went to Ian's office, collecting Penny on the way.

"So how did it go?" asked Ian. Although he was comfortable that Mr Zhang would not find any problems. Nevertheless, he was still a bit nervous as he certainly didn't want anything to go wrong at this late stage.

"I think it went okay, replied Viktor, slightly hesitantly. "He was very thorough and took quite a few notes and photos. I find it difficult to read these Orientals, but he did a lot of smiling and nodding. His English is not very good, but obviously, a lot better than my Cantonese!"

"Thank you Vic," said Ian, smiling at Viktor's comment. "I am fairly confident there will not be a problem, but I'm certain Oscar will confirm all is okay as soon as he knows the answer."

Ian and his team had to wait another 24 anxious hours before Oscar confirmed all was well, and the group of buyers still wanted to proceed … and, just as important, at the previously agreed prices!

Sergei had arranged for the dinner meeting for Andrei, Ian and Emma to be held at the Cipriani. The Russian's usual table had been reserved for 7.30 pm. It would be the first time Emma had been to the Cipriani and she was a little anxious. Ian had told her about his previous experience and said she would be fine, there's nothing to worry about. Emma, however, was still not sure.

During the late afternoon, as she was getting ready for the dinner meeting, Emma felt a mixture of apprehension and excitement. She thought about the famous restaurant and having to eat in the same room as possible celebrities. It all seemed just a little bit … unreal. Despite living in outer London for the last two years, she was still a Cotswold girl at heart and not comfortable with the more glitzy offerings in London. Still she knew it was important to Ian and wanted to show support where she could. Nevertheless, she was still not sure about Andrei and had become increasingly concerned about his ever-increasing influence in Ian's life.

Ian had arranged for a taxi to collect them at 6 pm. It was now 5.55 pm and Ian and Emma were standing in their hallway, putting on their thick overcoats.

"Are you still worried?" asked Ian. Emma was very quiet, which he knew was not a good sign.

"I shall be okay," she replied, but inside she knew this dinner date could well be an ordeal.

Ian saw headlights from a car arriving in their driveway and they both headed out into the cold night air.

The taxi arrived outside the restaurant at 7.15 pm. Ian paid the fare and they entered the building. After stating who they were and that they were meeting Mr Petrov, the maître d' welcomed them and led Ian and Emma into the main seating area. Emma hesitantly looked at some of the other customers as she passed their tables. However, she was sure she didn't recognise any celebrities. Ian immediately spotted Andrei sitting at his usual table. Andrei was reading the menu, he had a glass of red wine in his hand and in the middle of the table, there was an open bottle of his favourite claret.

When Andrei spotted his guests, he immediately jumped to his feet and gave Emma kisses on both her cheeks and a strong handshake to Ian.

"It's so good to see you again Emma. You are looking radiant my dear," said Andrei, in his usual flirtatious way with the ladies.

Emma was immediately embarrassed and made a quiet reply of, "Thank you."

Ian decided to come to Emma's rescue and asked Andrei how he was.

Andrei smiled and said, "My friend, I am fine, but I do not like this cold, wet, British winter climate." After escaping the long, harsh winters of Moscow, Andrei could never understand how, or why, people in Britain put up with the depressing winter months.

"There are worse places to live in the winter than Britain," retorted Ian.

"Yes, there are my friend. Now then enough about the English's favourite topic of conversation, more important, what would you like to drink?"

Emma said she would like a glass of Chablis and Ian replied that he would be quite happy to share Andrei's excellent claret.

Emma then decided to defend Britain's corner by saying, "The point about the British weather is that it makes you appreciate the different seasons. It would be boring if the climate was the same all year around."

Andrei ordered Emma's wine and poured Ian his claret from his own bottle. "No. Give me the warm weather every time. After spending my first 43 years in Moscow, I do not want to see snow, ice and cold ever again."

"Not everybody is in your fortunate position Andrei, to be able to choose." Emma was trying not to show her annoyance at his comments, but she still wanted to make her point, that some people still had jobs to go to!

Ian sat quietly enjoying the first sips of his wine. He was a little surprised at Emma's apparent attack on Andrei, but decided to let his wife argue her point of view. However, Andrei's next comments did make him sit up and wonder where the conversation was going.

"So," said Andrei with a teasing smile on his face, "would you not swap living in Britain for a life in a much warmer climate ... like Hong Kong or ... Monaco?"

Emma looked at Ian and wondered if there was some sort

of undercover plot going on. "Andrei," Emma continued, "we do not have the money to be able to live your lifestyle. I also enjoy my career, my home and the closeness of my family. I accept, all is not right in Britain, but I do not want to live anywhere else!"

At this point, Emma's wine was delivered and before the conversation continued, Ian decided to try and relax the mood and raised his glass and said "Cheers!" Both Andrei and Emma followed suit and three glasses clinked together.

The conversation went quiet until Ian decided to ask Andrei, "So, Andrei, what brings you back to the UK at this moment? You are becoming a regular visitor."

"Yes I know, but there is much business to be done here currently. I have two particular clients in London and I have several paintings that they want to buy, so I am here to see if we can complete a deal. I then fly off to New York. More business."

"Would you excuse me for a minute?" asked Emma. She rose from her chair and walked away to find the Ladies.

"My friend," announced Andrei, "your life seems to be somewhat predetermined, if that's the correct word?"

Ian looked at Andrei and decided he was right! Is that what I really want? Six months ago he would have said yes, without a doubt, because he already knew Emma's feelings about living abroad. But now? He had now experienced new wealth opportunities, new excitement, new challenges … indeed a whole new world had gradually been opening up!

Andrei seemed to be able to read Ian's mind. "Big choices, my friend, very big choices indeed!"

Ian continued to stare at Andrei. He slowly, but surely, began to nod his head in agreement. He then picked up his glass of claret and took a gentle sip.

When Emma returned and sat down, she looked at Ian with concern. Whilst in the Ladies, she had been thinking about what had been going on recently in Ian's life, especially since he had met Andrei. She had a feeling that he was not being totally straight with her. What was he hiding?

The atmosphere for the rest of the dinner was tense and by the time the meal had finished, all three were pleased it was over. Ian was a little annoyed but mainly disappointed. He'd hoped the evening would have gone far better than it had. He knew that Emma had some concerns about Andrei and was also apprehensive about eating at the Cipriani, but he was very surprised she was quite so aggressive towards Andrei.

Outside the restaurant, all three said their goodbyes and Andrei was driven away in a taxi. Emma suggested they walk for a while. Ian was concerned as to what Emma was going to say. He really did not know why Andrei had raised the subject of the British weather and then compared it with Monaco and Hong Kong. How was he going to convince Emma?

"What was that all about, Ian?" asked Emma, pulling up her coat collar against the chilly breeze. There was a small covering of snow on the pavement and this only added to the frosty atmosphere. She decided that the Hong Kong and Monaco comment was almost like a planted question to see how she reacted. But why would Andrei do that?

"What do you mean? It was just a meal with a friend."

"Since when has Andrei become a friend? I thought he was just a business colleague?"

"Well he is, but he has also become a friend."

"I think there are things you are not telling me."

"I'm not sure what." Ian had both hands tucked deep into his overcoat pocket. Emma could not see his right hand. His fingers were very firmly crossed. He was back with the recurring dilemma between the truth and hiding the full story. He really did not know what to say, or what to do next.

"Why did Andrei ask me about Hong Kong and Monaco?"

"Oh I don't know," replied Ian, and he truly didn't! It was a surprise to him that Andrei had said these things. "Maybe he was using these two places as examples that are warmer than England in the winter. I have been to both places recently and you enjoyed the holiday in Monaco."

"It is not as simple as that and you know it."

Ian knew Emma was right but he still did not have an answer. Why had Andrei seemingly provoked Emma. He knew Andrei did not do anything without a reason and he tried to figure out what this reason could be. Indeed, why had Andrei arranged the meal in the first place? Ian decided he still had a lot to learn about Andrei.

It was one week later when Ian received an email from Andrei. It was written in Andrei's usual wary style. Ian was working in his Sotheby's office at the time. The Russian thanked Ian for all his efforts in enabling him to secure the three Baxter Picassos and the four paintings by Monet. He also informed Ian that he had already sold the Monets for a 'tidy' profit and the Picassos were now hanging in his dining area in Monaco. He signed off by saying he would be in touch again soon. He also hoped Ian had now worked through his issues with Emma. After reading the email, Ian leaned back in his chair and decided he really must come clean with Emma, but what, and how! How was he going to explain? That was going to be the tricky bit.

Penny came to Ian's office door, but she could see Ian was deep in thought, staring out of his window. She decided the message could wait. She was, however, concerned with Ian's recent behaviour. He seemed to be far more troubled lately and not the normal, cheerful boss that she had become used to. The Baxter paintings issue was now largely solved, so she did not really understand why he appeared to be feeling ... depressed!?

Later, when Ian was passing Penny's desk to go to lunch, she stopped him and told him that Oscar had telephoned earlier that morning and he would ring again this evening, at his home.

"Okay," said Ian, "thank you." He then walked out of the room. It's all very odd, she thought. I wonder if Vic knows anything?

Over lunch Penny discussed her thoughts and concerns about her boss with Viktor. They both agreed he did not seem himself. Penny asked if he was aware of any issues that could be troubling Ian. Viktor knew he had to be careful what he told Penny, because the full extent of Ian's dealings with his father and Andrei were none of Sotheby's, or Penny's, business. Nevertheless, he too, could not put his finger on the main problem of why Ian was, well, just different!

The preparations for the Baxter paintings auction were all going smoothly. Viktor was organising it well and had taken delivery of all the 28 paintings. He had checked each one thoroughly and had noticed some minor damage to four frames and one of the pictures. He decided he would mention these issues to Ian. In the meantime he arranged for all 28 paintings to be properly cleaned and stored, ready for viewing in five days' time. Once he had put his phone down to the team specialising in picture cleaning, he thought more about the forthcoming auction. He knew there was a reasonable amount of interest being shown in the pictures, not only in the UK, but also from potential buyers in Asia and the USA as well. He was therefore cautiously optimistic that the paintings would achieve better results than just the sellers' Reserve Prices.

It was just after 11 pm when Oscar telephoned. Ian was in his study. "Hi Ian, how's things?"

Ian's answer was not the usual jovial response that Oscar was expecting.

"Everything okay Ian? You sound a bit down."

"Sorry Oscar, been one of those days." Ian tried to sound a little more upbeat. He therefore asked Oscar in a happier voice, "So what can I do for you?"

"Thought you might like to know, I gave details of the Baxter auction paintings to May Ling. She has advised me that she will have a representative at the auction."

"Okay. So what else is happening in Hong Kong?"

"It's otherwise all a bit quiet at the moment. May Ling's buyers and Andrew Lee have received their pictures and they are all very happy. Also thanks, by the way, I received my commission yesterday."

"That's good news."

"Sure you are okay Ian? Where's the usual banter?"

"Sorry," repeated Ian, "I must get some sleep. Chat again soon." Ian switched off the call.

After Oscar had put down the phone, he was certain something was not right. He thought back to when the two of them were sitting in the sunshine, on the veranda at the seafood restaurant on Lantau Island. He knew he had definitely caught a nerve when he mentioned both Emma and Hong Kong in the same context. Was that the problem?

After Ian had finished his telephone call, he decided he must go and find Emma. He found her in the lounge, curled up on the sofa and reading a book.

"Can we have a chat?" Ian was hating this moment, but he knew it had to be done.

# Chapter 29

Emma was enjoying a quiet evening. Work had been hectic and Ian was still in a strange mood. He had said earlier in the evening that he was expecting a telephone call from Oscar, so he had gone to the home office immediately after dinner. Emma just wanted to relax and read a book. A book she had started some months ago, but was still only half way through. When Ian appeared in the lounge, she was just thinking about going to bed. Ian slowly ambled in and Emma immediately thought there was a problem. Was it from the conversation he had just had with Oscar?

Ian walked towards Emma and stated that he wanted to have a chat. Emma put the bookmark against the current page, placed the book on the side table, unfurled her legs and moved her body into a sitting position on the sofa. She had anticipated Ian would finally get around to telling her what his problem was, now she hoped this was going to be the moment.

"Come and sit here." Emma patted the side of the sofa next to her.

Ian, rather sheepishly, did as he was told and sat down. Emma waited for him to speak.

"I've not been totally honest about all my activities over the last few months." Ian was not looking at Emma, he was focusing on his hands hanging down in his lap. He was trying to put everything into some logical sequence.

Emma remained quiet, but a little frightened about what Ian was about to tell her.

For about the next hour, Ian summarised all the events he had been involved in with Andrei. From his first meeting in The Grapes, through to the Baxter paintings that Andrei had recently purchased. The only bit he did not mention was the Nicholson painting he had 'acquired', which was still residing in the home office safe.

Emma had listened to every word, without interruption or comment. When he had finally finished, for a few seconds, there was complete silence in the room. Emma was partly annoyed and partly relieved with Ian's explanation. She had been worried for the last few weeks. Her imagination had been working overtime. Were there issues at work, another woman or was it all to do with Andrei making demands that Ian could not achieve?

Ian had not dared to look at Emma. He felt a mixture of guilt, shame and relief.

"Why have you waited all this time to tell me?"

"Each time I thought about it, I knew you would not approve … and it was so … well, exhilarating! I looked at Andrei and saw what he had achieved. His wealth, his lifestyle, his exciting times and success. I wanted some of that, for you and me."

"But I did not ask for Andrei's wealth or lifestyle. Yes, he has a fabulous apartment in a lovely country, but it's … all artificial. It's not the real world is it? Here, in our lovely home, you and me, our careers, that is the real world, that is our success!"

"But I want to give you more. I want you to be happy …"

"But I am happy," interrupted Emma, "When have I said I'm not?"

"Your parents are wealthy and, when you were growing up, you never had to want for anything. I just wanted to make sure you could continue with that lifestyle."

"Ian," she retorted firmly, "I did not marry you for your money or my past lifestyle. I married you because I love you and thought we would be so happy together. Working hard at our careers and enjoying the benefits and rewards that our hard work would produce. Look at what we have achieved in such a short period of time."

"I have got about 300,000 Swiss francs in a bank account," pleaded Ian.

Emma laughed. "From what you have said, it sounds as though you have earned it! You have not broken the law … probably, well not the British law, and you have used your skills and experience to help Andrei. Okay, his world might be sometimes, somewhat underhand, but your involvement has been more from a professional involvement, not an illegal one hasn't it?"

Ian was certainly pleased and relieved that he had not mentioned the Nicholson painting. He was also surprised with Emma's comments. He had expected, as a minimum, that he was going to be in for a serious earbashing! "So what about Andrei … and Sergei?"

"Look, if working with Andrei gives you this extra excitement and challenge and you keep within the law, and it doesn't interfere with your work at Sotheby's, then I am not going to stop you. But please promise me one thing …"

Ian finally looked up at Emma, waiting for her to finish her plea.

" … I do not want to hear that you have been crawling around in tunnels under the Kremlin ever again!"

"Agreed." said Ian and he leapt up and on to Emma. He then gave her a long and lingering kiss.

Next morning, when Ian arrived at the office, Penny was sitting at her desk. "Good morning Penny," he said, conveying the cheery mood of the old Ian.

"Good morning to you," said Penny somewhat surprised. "You sound perky!"

"Sorry if I've been a bit of a bore. Had some issues to resolve, but all sorted now!"

"Vic wants to speak to you about the Baxter auction."

"Okay, can you get him to pop up ... in about ten minutes?" Ian disappeared into his office.

Penny rang Viktor's number. When Viktor answered his phone, Penny explained that Ian seemed to be back to his usual self again, and he would like to see you in about ten minutes.

When Viktor entered Ian's outer office, Penny smiled at him, stood up and they both walked into Ian's office together.

Ian looked up from his desk and said, "Ah, Vic, come in, sit down, both of you." Viktor and Penny briefly glanced at each other. Penny was trying to convey the message of 'see, back to his old self!'

As they sat down, Ian asked, "So how are the final preparations going?"

Viktor explained that everything was now in place. "All the pictures had been delivered and are now in the building. I gave them a thorough inspection when they first arrived. I found that there was minor damage to four of the frames and an almost invisible small cut on one of the picture's canvas."

"A small cut?" Ian's attention was suddenly focused. He could not remember any damage when he inspected the paintings at Baxter's. "Whereabouts and on which painting?"

"It's in one of the corners of the Juan Gris painting. It

looks as though it has been there for a long while, but I thought you might like to take a look?"

"Okay. Are all the pictures in the usual pre-auction storage room?"

"Yes. I've had them all cleaned and prepared ready for viewing tomorrow."

"Right. We had better have a look now then." Ian rose from his seat and headed to the door. Viktor and Penny were surprised with Ian's sudden action and followed quickly in his wake, trying to keep up with Ian's urgent pace.

Viktor looked at Penny and whispered. "You are right."

They both hurried to keep up with their boss.

When they arrived at the storage room, Viktor led Ian and Penny to the racks where the Baxter paintings were stored. Viktor removed the temporary covering on the Gris painting and lifted it on to a nearby desk for his boss to make a closer inspection. He then switched on a strong table lamp to help Ian assess the painting's damage more closely.

Ian agreed it was a Juan Gris oil painting and its composition showed a collection of colourful books piled on a table. After a few seconds Ian said out aloud his thoughts for Viktor's and Penny's benefit. "An excellent example of Juan Gris's personal Cubist style. The picture is painted in an abstract form. It depicts the books as if they are being seen from a multitude of viewpoints. A good example of how he sometimes uses mathematics in a painting."

Penny looked over Viktor's shoulder at the painting. She never had really understood or appreciated modern art. Indeed she could not understand how or why other people raved about such paintings. The artist was obviously very talented so why not just paint a good life-like composition?

As Ian continued to look at the quality of the work, Viktor pointed to a slight gash in the top right-hand corner.

It was about two centimetres long and hardly noticeable until it was pointed out.

"Well done Vic. I certainly missed it when I was looking at this picture in Baxter's premises. But as you say, it looks as though it has been there for some time. Can you check to see if it is mentioned on the provenance papers?"

"I've already looked, and it's not."

"Penny," Ian turned towards his PA. "Can you have a word with John Chambers and find out what Baxter's know about the damage?" Penny nodded and went back to her office.

"Let's just keep this to one aside for the moment Vic," said Ian. He looked at the rear of the canvas and gently ran his finger along the small gash.

When Ian had finished, Viktor replaced the painting back in its cover and put it on a separate shelf, away from the others.

"Is this damage likely to affect the value we might get at the auction?" asked Viktor. He was still concerned that if the painting did not achieve the valuation, the blame may be laid on him.

"It is probable that the gash can be invisibly mended. So, in the long term, there shouldn't be any real detrimental effect to the picture, or its value."

"Do we state there is some damage on the exhibition card?"

"Good point. Let's see what Penny finds out. Now then, let's look at the damaged frames."

Viktor uncovered the four paintings where he had identified some damage to the frames. Ian looked at each one in turn, but came to the same general conclusion. They were all old wear and tear nicks and small dents. On their own, they were very unlikely to detract from the value of the paintings.

When Ian and Viktor returned to Ian's office, Penny said she had spoken to John Chambers and he said that he was unaware of the damage, and didn't think it had been done whilst the painting was in their possession.

"Mmm. So is he trying to pin the blame on us?" asked Viktor, a little worried again. "Because I noticed it just after it was unloaded from the lorry. It was then delivered directly to the storage room. It's had its cover on all the time since I inspected it."

Ian sat back behind his desk once again. "I think we all know this damage has been there for many years. I tell you what Vic, get Eric to verify it … as soon as possible. He's been restoring similar minor damages for probably 40 years."

# Chapter 30

Viktor took the Gris painting to Eric Powell. Eric is an expert in restoring minor damage work, particularly on canvas oil paintings. Now officially 'retired' for the last three years, he had since been recruited by Sotheby's on a very part-time basis for his expert opinion and knowledge of minor damage to paintings. Eric just worked for a few hours on Tuesdays and Thursdays. Viktor had first met Eric about a year ago and thoroughly enjoyed chatting with him. He was a mine of information and Viktor never ceased to be amazed at the depth of his knowledge. Eric just loved chatting with anyone who had a serious interest in art restoration.

"So, young Vic, what do you think has happened here then?" Eric was now in his late sixties and his eyesight was not quite as good as it once was, but with the use of a strong magnifying glass, he was still able to appraise most damages and more importantly, how the paintings should be repaired.

"It looks old, the cut fibres are not clean," said Viktor hopefully. He was praying Eric would agree.

"Mmm." Eric kept looking at the damaged area close to. He inspected both the front and the back of the canvas. "Looks like the cut is from the front and probably done some time ago. Might even have been done by the artist."

"Are you serious?" asked Viktor, with possibly just a little too much glee in his voice.

"It's well hidden and not that obvious. Even when you look quite close to. It might have been done by a pallet knife, or more likely, a sharp quill."

"A quill!?"

"If you look through this magnifying glass, you can see some little, almost invisible, dots of blue paint at the edge of the cut. It could be that the artist was trying to scrape off this blue paint – but, unfortunately, he got just a little bit too heavy handed with a quill!"

Viktor took hold of the magnifying glass and looked for himself. "Oh, yes. I see what you mean. Can it be repaired?"

"Oh yes, that's not a problem. However, some might think that the picture could just be worth more with the gash, especially if the artist had accidentally done it himself. A unique feature, one might say!" Both Eric and Viktor laughed.

On the day of the auction, both Sir Paul and John Chambers were keen to be in the audience to witness events. Sir Paul was especially keen to know what price the paintings would finally achieve. He had already in his own mind spent a large proportion of the sale proceeds on supporting the costs of the new company computer system and he certainly didn't want any negative surprises. Two of the directors had already raised concerns about his decision to sell the company's assets and indeed, some of its history. This all had to go right.

When they both walked into the auction room Ian immediately spotted Sir Paul and John Chambers and walked over to greet them. He then took the opportunity to update them both on the findings of the damaged Gris picture and his decision not to have it repaired.

Sir Paul showed his concern when he asked, "Won't that result in less interest and lower offers?"

Ian explained. "When all 28 paintings were displayed for the viewing, an extra note was included in the Gris painting description. The note mentioned the tiny gash, but it also suggested that the gash could have been accidentally caused by the artist himself. Possibly due to rough use of a sharpened quill!"

"Oh," said Sir Paul, somewhat surprised with this comment. John Chambers just smiled and said, "Interesting thought."

The auction started at 11 am. The room was probably 60% occupied, but there was a lot of activity on the telephones. The auctioneer, as a result, seemed to slow the proceedings down slightly, so that the telephone bids could be given adequate time. As the auction progressed, each picture was achieving more than the seller's Reservation Price, but not always Ian's full valuation. Ian and Viktor watched the proceedings with great interest. Ian was particularly keen to see the reactions of Sir Paul and John Chambers as the hammer went down on each lot.

Lot 19 was the Juan Gris painting with the tiny gash. The auctioneer highlighted the slight 'imperfection' and stated that it may have been caused by the artist himself.

The bidding started slowly in the room, but soon a battle ensued between three potential buyers on the telephones. When the bid price went past Ian's valuation, John Chambers looked over at Ian and gave him one of his wry smiles. Ian smiled back. It eventually sold for £70,000 above valuation! The rest of the paintings had achieved mixed results, but all exceeded the seller's Reservation Price.

When all the sales were added up, the average was about 4% below the collection's 'full valuation'. Not a massive success, but not a disaster either … and all 28 paintings were sold.

Sir Paul and John Chambers walked over to where Ian

and Viktor were standing. Sir Paul was the first to speak. "Not a bad result. I found it all quite exciting. Nearly bid a couple of times myself!" All four laughed.

"I think you achieved a good result," said John Chambers. "The Gris painting was a bit of an inspired surprise."

"I'm pleased both of you are happy with the result. It was Vic ..." Ian pointed to his colleague standing at his side, " ... who suggested the extra note about the gash on the picture's description. A bit of a gamble, but it worked."

"Well done my boy, excellent decision." said Sir Paul, tapping Viktor on the shoulder. Viktor wanted to remind Ian that it was Eric's suggestion, but he let it pass, for the time being.

Two days later, Ian telephoned Oscar. It was about midnight UK time, so Ian thought Oscar might have arrived at work. However, when Oscar answered his mobile phone, he told Ian he was still at home.

"Hi Oscar, how are things?"

"Well, well," replied Oscar. "More to the point, how are you?"

"I'm fine."

"You do sound a bit more with it today. So what's happening?"

"The Baxter auction went okay. It could have gone slightly better for the seller, but overall I think they went away happy."

"I told you May Ling was going to be represented there. Well, she acquired four of the paintings for her buyers, so she was happy too. I think we have got a good connection there. She's very active and certainly has some wealthy buyers in and around Beijing."

"Oscar, I have a little proposition for you to consider."

For some time Ian had become more and more

uncomfortable with his Nicholson painting. Taking the picture from the Kremlin chambers was an opportunist moment, but not necessarily one of his brightest ideas. He now realised that it was possibly more of a liability than an asset, after all he had no proof of ownership and no provenance.

"Okay," said Oscar, pleased that his old pal seemed a lot more on the ball today, but still curious as to what this proposition was going to be.

"A little while ago, I acquired a Nicholson painting. There has been no provenance since 1931, but I'm sure it was stolen by the Nazis during the Second World War. Its title is *Rose in a Glass Vase*. Well, I'm now looking to sell it."

"I have a lot of questions."

"I would too if I was in your position. However, I want you to trust me on this one, Oscar. A similar Nicholson painting was sold in 2006 for £165,000. However, that had good provenance. I will accept £30,000 and you can keep whatever excess you achieve over that."

"I see. So are you looking for it to be sold in the Asian market?"

"That's my thinking. Europe and America would be … too difficult and Russia is … well, a no, no. South America might work, but I thought of you first and your Chinese connections."

"Okay, I'm at home today. I'll make a few calls tomorrow."

"That's fine. Let me know what you think in a few days' time. I won't be doing anything else with the picture for the time being. But please, Oscar, the painting should never be connected with me. The owner's name must remain anonymous."

"Okay, I understand, I think! I will get back to you in a few days."

Oscar put down his phone and walked into his small

office-cum-library. He looked along the rows of bookshelves until he found his copy of *William Nicholson: A Catalogue Raisonne of the Oil Paintings* by Patricia Reed. He pulled it off the shelf, sat down at his desk and opened it at the index. He searched for *Rose in a Glass Vase*.

For most of the morning Oscar investigated the history of William Nicholson paintings. Not only did he thoroughly research Patricia Reed's book, but he accessed several websites on the subject too. He found reference to Ian's *Rose in a Glass Vase*, plus other pictures painted about the same time and in a similar style. Like Ian had told him, he could not find any provenance after 1931 for this picture and he wondered where the Nazi connection came in? What had Ian got himself into? he wondered. Still he had a few ideas that he wanted to explore. Also, May Ling's new buyers in Beijing, might just be interested too. Two in particular, he'd discovered, were not overly interested to know where a painting had come from, they were only interested in the painting's quality, the artist's name and that the painting was genuine.

It was just over a week later that Oscar telephoned Ian at his home. When Ian answered the call he listened to a very serious Oscar on the other end of the line.

"Ian, this Nicholson painting. I have been investigating possible buyers both in Hong Kong and on the mainland. Two possible buyers have shown some interest, however, one serious question. Does it have anything to do with the Russians?"

Ian was certainly not expecting this question from Oscar. However, he was quick on his feet to think of an answer.

"I don't know. The guy I bought the painting from said he just thought there was a Nazi connection. Why? What have you found out?"

"One of May Ling's Beijing buyers is quite an aficionado of Nicholson's work. He says your painting has been reported stolen from a collection in Russia."

Oh shit thought Ian! "Does this guy say any more?"

"No. Just that the word 'on the street' is that, before it was stolen, it was probably in the possession of the Russian Mafia!"

Oh shit again thought Ian! "Oscar I didn't know. I don't want us to get involved with them!"

"It looks as though you might already be involved buddy! I would go back to the person you bought it from."

"Nobody can link it back to me though, surely?"

"I only told these people that I had heard from a friend of a friend that this particular Nicholson painting may be for sale."

"Okay. Look Oscar, I think we had better postpone the idea of selling this picture for a while. Sorry if I've dropped you in it." Ian was not only concerned for himself, but also for his pal, Oscar. The last thing he wanted was to be in any potential conflict with the Russian Mafia. He knew for certain who would be the loser! Now he had a new and more serious dilemma!

He sat back in his chair and mulled over exactly what Oscar had just told him. He was now over the initial shock of Oscar's comments and his mind was becoming a little clearer. He realised that two of Oscar's comments didn't quite stack up. Firstly, his Nicholson painting hadn't been in the possession of the Russian Mafia, it was in the Russian government's underground chambers. Secondly, Oscar said he'd been told that the painting had been stolen. Okay, he had stolen it, but, nobody else knew. Not even anyone in Andrei's team!

When Ian eventually went to bed, Emma was just switching off her bedside light. Ian climbed into his side of the bed and lay on his back. Staring into the darkness of the room, he could not get the Nicholson painting out of his mind. Emma snuggled back and Ian turned on to his side and cuddled up. He was convinced, however, that if he did eventually go to sleep, he was bound to have many nightmares about the Russian Mafia!

When he awoke the next morning he was certain he had only been asleep for about two hours. During these two hours he had not been chased, or threatened, by the Russian Mafia, but during the hours awake, he thought about nothing else.

He looked at his bedside clock. It was 5.25 am. He quietly got out of bed, went into the bathroom and shaved and showered. After getting dressed, he went back to the darkness of the bedroom to collect his wristwatch. Emma was still asleep and her alarm clock was not set to ring until 6.30 am. Ian crept quietly downstairs. After only half a cup of coffee, he left the house and started the 20-minute walk towards Esher railway station. The cold drizzle quickly hit him. He pulled up the collar of his overcoat. Although it still felt like the middle of the night to Ian, a few other early commuters were also walking the same route. Several cars and the occasional bus also passed by, but Ian hardly noticed them. His mind was focused back on the *Rose in a Glass Vase*, and the Russian Mafia.

When he arrived at the railway station he checked the indicator board and noticed the next London bound train was running ten minutes late. He decided he had time to pop into the buffet room and collect a cup of coffee. Once obtained, he sipped his warm drink and slowly walked towards the London bound platform. Whilst he waited for the train, he kept thinking about Oscar's comments and wanted to be sure that the information that he'd been given was correct. But if it wasn't how did this contact know the picture had been stolen in Russia? No mention was made of a theft from the Kremlin and where did the Russian Mafia come in? Nobody had mentioned to him that the collection of paintings in the chambers were the property of the Mafia. Surely he had been told they were owned by the Russian government. Andrei would definitely know. Also he was sure Andrei would not put Dimitri, Ivan and himself in such danger. Andrei had said many times that he did not want to have any possible conflict with the Russian Mafia. In conclusion, he decided he did not know who to believe. One thing was certain, however, he had to do something ... and quickly!

At this moment his train arrived at the platform and he climbed aboard. Fortunately he was able to find an unoccupied seat quite quickly. Although it was still very early in the morning, the train seats were nearly all full. At the next station, Ian observed, a number of embarking commuters would have to travel standing up. The joys of London commuting.

The train slowly pulled out of Esher station and Ian leaned back in his seat and closed his eyes. His mind quickly shifted back to his painting and the Mafia issue. He weighed up the pros and cons of several options, but had to admit, he was still not sure what the best course of action was going to be.

A few minutes later he decided it was all down to two possible options. His favourite option was to move the picture to a safety deposit box at his bank. He knew that his home safe was no security against the real professionals. His second, less favoured option, was to fully discuss the matter with Andrei. Surely with all his experience, he was bound to come up with a sensible suggestion.

# Chapter 31

Not surprisingly, Ian was one of the first members of staff to arrive at Sotheby's offices that morning. He had never before arrived so early at the office. The central heating had only just started and there was a definite chilly atmosphere both in the office ... and in Ian's mind! He collected a cup of coffee from the vending machine and headed towards his own office. The corridor lights were on, but most of the rooms he passed were still in darkness. Other than Arthur, the security guard at reception, he did not meet anyone. It was all so quiet. If the Russian Mafia were planning to get him, then now, he decided, was the right time to do it!

As he entered his outer office, he switched on the lights. He was half expecting a Russian welcoming committee, but all was very quiet and normal. He entered his own office and switched on the lights. Again nothing out of the ordinary. He hung his overcoat up on the wall near the back of the door and walked over to his desk. He even thought about looking under it, for what ... bombs!? He realised that he was becoming paranoid ... and probably worse, ridiculous. He sat down, sipped his coffee and switched on his computer. Whilst it was powering up, he went through the paper messages Penny had left for him on his desk. Nothing was urgent.

Whilst consuming another sip of coffee, his computer sprung into life. He immediately accessed his email inbox. Again nothing out of the normal ... except, what was this? One particular email caught his eye. It had the title of *Rose in a Glass Vase*! Ian did not recognise the sender's name and was definitely concerned about opening it! He doubted that it was a scam, but, who ...?

"Good morning Ian. You are in early." said Penny standing at his door. Ian nearly jumped out of his skin with surprise.

"Oh, hi Penny." replied Ian, trying to calm down.

"Are you okay? Sorry if I made you jump."

"I did not hear you come in. My mind was elsewhere."

"Did you see my messages? Nothing urgent though."

"Yes. Thanks." Ian paused. His mind shifted back to his emails. "Do we know anyone called Sokolov?"

"Sokolov? No ... no. I don't recognise the name. Sounds Russian. Somebody you met in Moscow maybe?"

"No." said Ian slowly and looked back at his computer screen. "Okay."

Penny decided to leave Ian to his thoughts and walked back to her own desk.

Ian just stared at the email title, *Rose in a Glass Vase* and the sender's name V. Sokolov. He closed his eyes and wished he was thousands of miles away – back in Hong Kong!

After pondering over the problem, he decided not to open the email. To do so would indicate his email address was live. After all, he thought, it could just be another annoying, 'phishing' email. However ...

At lunchtime, Ian told Penny he might be a little late back from lunch. He left Sotheby's building and turned left along New Bond Street. Ten minutes later he walked into a branch of the HSBC bank. He went up to the enquiries desk and announced his name and that he had an account with

HSBC, but at another branch. He explained that he wanted to know how one could acquire the use of a safety deposit box? The young assistant said she was not sure, but would ask one of her colleagues to come and speak with him. She disappeared and after a couple of minutes, returned with an older female colleague.

"Hello Mr Caxton." The older lady shook Ian's hand and suggested they go somewhere that was more private. "My name is Lucy Bristow," she announced, as they entered a small, glass fronted office. Ian sat down and she closed the door.

Fifteen minutes later, Ian thanked Ms Bristow for her time and said he would call at the HSBC bank address she had advised on Thursday for the 3 pm appointment.

That evening, Ian sat in his study and read through the paperwork Ms Bristow had given to him. He completed the application form and placed all the papers in his briefcase. He then opened his laptop and accessed his email account. The inbox still highlighted the email from a V. Sokolov … and it still remained unopened … and would do for the foreseeable future, he decided! He checked his other inbox emails and was relieved to find no further correspondence from V. Sokolov.

On Thursday, at 2.55 pm, Ian walked in to the HSBC bank Ms Bristow had referred him to. At reception he stated his name and said that Ms Lucy Bristow had made an appointment for him with Mrs Osborn to set up a safety deposit box account. The receptionist picked up her telephone and dialled an internal number. At the same time, she suggested Mr Caxton might like to take a seat and pointed to several sofa chairs.

Ian said thank you and wandered over to the empty seats and sat down. He gazed out of the window and watched the passing pedestrians going about their normal daily business.

He wished he could swap places with any of them at that moment. Not for the first time Ian wondered what he had dropped himself into.

"Hello Mr Caxton, my name is Jenny Osborn."

Ian stood up immediately and clasped Jenny Osborn's outstretched hand and replied with a "Hello."

"Please come with me, Mr Caxton, and we'll deal with your application."

Ian followed Jenny towards the elevators. He estimated she must be about 30, slightly overweight, but nonetheless, quite attractive and with a welcoming smile. When the elevator doors opened, Jenny pressed the button for floor -5. As the elevator slowly descended, it reminded Ian of the security vaults below the apartments where Andrei lived.

Jenny was the first to break the silence by saying, "What we will do first, Mr Caxton, is go through the paperwork." The doors of the elevator opened and they both stepped out into a long, well-lit corridor. "After that I will give you your key and set up your security code."

"Okay," replied Ian. Jenny showed him into a small office, with just a desk and two chairs. The room had just one picture on the walls. Ironically, it was a similar photograph to the one he had in his office of the view from Kowloon across the harbour towards Hong Kong island. Jenny noticed his smile and turned round slightly and looked at the picture behind her, herself.

"Quite appropriate for HSBC," said Ian.

"Yes," replied Jenny. "I have always wanted to go there. It looks like a fascinating place."

"It's my favourite. I worked there for several years."

"Please sit down Mr Caxton." Both of them sat down. "It must have been an exciting place to live and work."

"Oh yes. I do miss it."

After the paperwork was checked, Jenny explained fully

how the security system and all the procedures worked. Ian was then taken out of the office and along the corridor, passing a number of security doors. Jenny stopped outside the door with the number '8' prominently displayed at eye level.

Ian was shown how to open the door using his own keycard plus Jenny's. Once both cards had been inserted, Jenny pushed the door and it opened quite easily. The internal lights immediately lit up the room and Ian saw three walls covered with various sizes of safety deposit boxes. The room was otherwise quite bare, with just a small table and two chairs in the middle. Jenny walked over to the rear wall and pointed to the box numbered '313'. She explained that each security box had its own keypad. The door of 313 was slightly ajar and Ian looked inside. A small LED light bulb lit up the inside space sufficiently for him to see the overall internal dimensions. He decided this was quite adequate for his requirements.

Jenny showed him how to set up his own eight-digit security code. The code could include any combination of numbers, letters and a small range of characters. Whilst Jenny turned away, Ian pushed the security door to and pressed the keys of his chosen code. There was a ping and Jenny turned around and inserted her security code. The keypad pinged again.

"The keypad now recognises your code and only your code," stated Jenny. "It is currently locked on your code and you enter the same code to both open and close it. Please, try to open it." Jenny once again turned away from him and Ian inserted his code. Immediately there was a ping and the door opened a few centimetres. With Jenny still having her back to him, he pushed on the door and inserted his code again. Another ping and a tiny red light lit up next to the number 313. After four seconds the red light switched off and there was a final ping.

"There we are, all secure. All ready for your worldly goods!"

Ian smiled at Jenny's joke. "Thank you," he said. "This all seems to be fine ... and just what I need!"

On Saturday Emma had left home early in her car. She had promised her parents that she and Ian would visit that weekend. This was a last-minute decision on Emma's part and had caught Ian on the hop. However, he told her that he had to pop into Sotheby's office first, to collect some papers in preparation for a meeting on Monday. He would join her later in the afternoon and planned to catch the 1.20 pm train from Paddington. Emma had confirmed she would collect him from Kingham railway station, which was about 20 minutes away from her parents' home.

At 11 am Ian entered the HSBC offices. In his rucksack he had the paper files he had just collected from Sotheby's office, plus the same cardboard tube he had purchased in Moscow. The cardboard tube, once again, contained the *Rose in a Glass Vase*. Ian remembered the procedures outlined by Jenny Osborn earlier, and when he exited floor -5 from the elevator he was met by a uniformed security guard. Ian showed him his keycard and he and the guard walked along the corridor to the door showing number 8. Both the guard and Ian inserted their cards and the door opened. The guard walked away and Ian entered. He walked across to box number 313 and inserted his code. Once the security box door was released he pulled the door wide open. He then bent down to the floor and removed the cardboard tube from his rucksack and placed it into the security box. He then closed the door and inserted his code again. After the red light had extinguished, he heard the final ping. Suddenly he felt a great sense of relief. He smiled with satisfaction that the picture was no longer residing at their Esher home! But what next for the painting? That decision would have to wait for another day!

# Chapter 32

Both Emma and Ian enjoyed their brief stay in the Cotswolds. Ian always enjoyed a bit of banter with his father-in-law. However, he did find Emma's mother more of a trickier proposition. He was convinced that she thought Emma could have done so much better in her choice of a husband! He also felt that no matter what he did to try and change her opinion, he would always have that battle. Nevertheless, he did feel fortunate that his father-in-law did not have the same derogatory view of him.

It was already dark when Emma's car joined the M4 at Junction 15. The traffic was unusually light. Heading towards London, Emma switched the car into cruise control. Ian sat in the front passenger seat and read the papers he had collected from his office the previous day. After making some extra notes, he leaned over and put the folder in his rucksack and placed it on the back seat.

Ian looked out of the window into the darkness. He then said to Emma, "Your dad was in good form. We had quite a chat."

"I'm pleased you get on with him."

"Pity your mum still gives me those frosty looks."

"Mum's like that with most people. Don't worry about it."

"I would still like to get on better with her. After all, she is your mother."

"Children do not select their parents."

"Mmm. Even so."

"I have not heard you speak about Andrei lately."

"No. It's all gone a little quiet on that front. I wonder what he's up to?" Ian was certainly missing the buzz and excitement that surrounded Andrei's lifestyle.

"Are we back to normal now then Ian?"

Ian thought about the painting he'd just stored at the HSBC bank and this mysterious Mr Sokolov. He decided to duck the question. "Maybe Andrei's moved on to other things."

Emma immediately recognised that Ian had not answered her question. However, she herself decided not to probe any further either ... at this stage.

The journey continued in silence. Ian stared out of the window again, but he was not really looking at anything. His mind drifted from Oscar to May Ling, to Andrei and Sergei, to *Rose in a Glass Vase* and a certain Mr Sokolov. He had not received any further emails from him ... and he didn't plan to open the original email either ... at least, not just yet!

Emma wondered what Ian was thinking. Was she missing pieces of Ian's recent life again? She knew once Andrei got back in touch, Ian would want to be off on his adventures once more. Something in the back of her mind reminded her of similar incidents in the past. She thought hard and then suddenly it became much clearer. It was from her child-hood. She remembered reading about Alice's Adventures in Wonderland. There was definitely a similarity, she decided. Was she now just a little bit jealous?

It was on the following Wednesday morning, just after 9.30 am, that Viktor knocked on Ian's office door.

"Hello Vic, come in, sit down. How's things?"

"Fine thank you." replied Viktor, although his response was slightly sheepish. He sat directly opposite Ian and shifted uneasily in his chair.

"So what's on your mind?" Ian thought quickly and tried to guess what Vic was going to say. It was not like Vic to be so cagey.

Viktor had tried to prepare for what he was going to say to Ian, but in the end, he decided just to speak how he felt at that moment. "Do you remember you asked me to research as much information as I could find out about William Nicholson?"

Ian nodded and immediately wondered where this was leading to. He was not surprised Viktor had finally raised the query. Viktor was bright and would certainly have wondered why all of a sudden, and without any explanation, Ian wanted such a detailed report on Nicholson.

"Well my father was asking about him over the weekend. It was all rather strange. I told him all the information I had given to you and, well, he asked quite a lot of questions. He has never shown that level of interest before in any artist and, well, ... I thought maybe you ..."

"What sort of questions?" interrupted Ian, who had suddenly become quite concerned.

"Well, er, he wanted to know about certain specific Nicholson paintings."

"Do you remember which ones?"

Viktor put his hand inside his jacket pocket and pulled out a sheet of folded A4 paper. He leaned over towards Ian and handed him the paper. "After I had finished talking to him, I made a note of all the paintings he was interested in. That's the list as far as I can remember."

Ian scanned down the list of ten picture titles. At the bottom he spotted *Rose in a Glass Vase*! He just stared at the paper. He thought his heart was going to stop. His breathing changed to short, quick intakes. What the hell was going on!?

After a few seconds Viktor interrupted Ian's panicky thoughts. "Why is Nicholson so important, all of a sudden, to everyone?"

Ian handed the paper back to Viktor. He quickly tried to calm himself.

"I don't know. I was interested because a client in Epsom approached us saying he was thinking about selling his collection of Nicholson paintings and I wanted to be up to date. Also, I thought it would be an interesting investigation, and good experience, for you."

"I see."

"Maybe just a coincidence, your father asking too."

"Mmm," mumbled Viktor. He just knew there was something he was missing. Why were Ian and his father both being so evasive?

"Do you want me to speak to your father?"

Viktor got up from his seat. "No ..., no I don't think so." He started to walk towards the door. "Thank you. Sorry for ..."

"No problem," interrupted Ian.

As Viktor exited Ian's office, he felt something was definitely up, he just knew it! But what? He just didn't have a clue. Maybe he should do his own further research and investigations.

After Viktor had disappeared, Ian just sat back and stared at the picture of Hong Kong on his office wall. After a couple of seconds he said under his breath, "shit ... shit! What the hell is going on?"

Ian spent the next 30 minutes trying to figure out why all of a sudden, several people were so interested in his painting. Nobody, but nobody, knew about him taking the *Rose in a Glass Vase* from the Kremlin chambers. So why raise the subject with him now? Where was Andrei? He surely must know something, and Sergei too, he obviously knows a lot more. Ian decided he would try and put the whole matter out of his mind for the time being and concentrate on his day job. However, he found it difficult to focus and concentrate. The picture of the *Rose in a Glass Vase* kept creeping back into his mind. Finally, just before lunch, he made a decision and telephoned Sergei. The number he dialled rang, but after 20 seconds there was no answer and a recorded message cut in to say the family were not available, could you please leave a message. Ian slammed down his phone. No, he did not want to leave a bloody message. He wanted to speak to Sergei!

He left the office just after 1.30 pm. He was not hungry and decided just to walk and get some fresh air. As he strolled from New Bond Street into Old Bond Street, the last thing on his mind was the history of this famous street. As he headed towards Piccadilly, he passed many buildings displaying the blue plaques of famous former residents. Lord Nelson, Jonathan Swift, William Pitt the Elder and many others. In previous times, Ian had been fascinated to know of all the celebrities who had lived along these streets. Now, he just stared at the pavement immediately ahead of him. He just ambled without any thought of where he was actually going ... or indeed why! He was thoroughly fed up with the whole situation and rued the day he had ever met Andrei and the rest of the dam Russians!

Sergei and Ludmilla Kuznetsov returned home to Eaton Square just after 2.30pm. Sergei went into his study and sat down at his desk. He opened up his laptop and waited for his emails to download. Whilst waiting he looked at his answerphone and saw there were no recorded messages. However, he did notice that there had been one new call received, but the caller had obviously not left a message. Sergei clicked the 'calls' button. He looked at the telephone's display panel and was sure he recognised the number that had telephoned. Checking through his list of contacts, he realised it was Ian Caxton's telephone number at Sotheby's. Mmm, he thought. Now that is interesting!

# Chapter 33

After wandering along several streets, Ian entered a small park. It was largely protected by wrought iron railings and various shrubs. London is famous for its parks and open spaces and many were deliberately planned over the centuries to be incorporated into the ever-growing London city. Ian was once told that London was made up of 40% public green space. He found this difficult to believe, but gradually he realised that any short walk within the Greater London area very quickly brought one within touching distance of a park, however large or small. Especially during the summer and also on other warm days, Ian often spent some of his lunch time eating his sandwiches and enjoying a brief break of sunbathing in one of the nearby parks. He was usually surrounded by colourful flowers and shrubs and he liked listening to the occasional bird calls and songs. It was also good thinking time. The fresh air and general quietness often helped him think about issues and his problems more clearly.

Today, however, was not summer. The flowers were long gone and it was just the bare earth areas that remained. The park had been 'put to bed' for the winter and it was not quite spring just yet.

In the centre of the park there was a pond edged by a concrete pathway. Ian sat down on one of the metal benches and stared out in the direction of the pond. In the middle there was a small island and Ian noticed a black stone statue of a lion lying down near the centre. There would normally be a flow of water emerging out of the lion's mouth, but, during the winter months, this was switched off. A pigeon was tentatively trying to land on the lion's head. Ian's mind, however, was still more focused on all the issues surrounding the *Rose in a Glass Vase* and especially what he should do next.

Ten minutes passed and he was feeling increasingly cold. The sun was shining, but lacked the normal summer heat. The cold breeze was the stronger factor today. Ian decided that he really needed to speak to either Andrei or Sergei urgently. Standing up he looked around and realised he was the only person in the park. He pushed his hands deep into his jacket pocket and headed back to the warmth of his office.

When he arrived back at his desk he telephoned Sergei's number again. This time Sergei answered the call on the second ring. "Hello Ian. You telephoned earlier this morning. What can I do for you?"

"Sergei, I have received a strange email from someone called V. Sokolov. Do you have any idea who this person is?"

Sergei laughed to himself. "Oh. So you have been in contact with Comrade Sokolov."

"Well not exactly in contact with him. I have just received an email and wondered who he was and what to do with it?"

"What did the email say?" Ian could not see Sergei's teasing smile on his face as he spoke on the telephone.

"Er, well, I have not opened it. I normally just delete emails from people whose names I do not recognise. They are more often just 'scams'."

"Well Ian, Comrade Vladimir Sokolov is one of the alias names Andrei uses, so it is probably from him."

"Are you sure!?" Ian was staggered. If what Sergei was saying was correct, why hadn't Andrei told him of his alias names?

"Oh yes. When you open it, you will see that I was right."

Ian found this difficult to believe. "But why use an alias in any case?"

"Andrei does not like to use his own name in email correspondence. By using an alias it is more difficult for anyone to trace these names back to him. A lot of Russians use alias names this way."

"I see, but I've received maybe one or two emails previously from him using his own name. He could have told me. Maybe I should set up some alias names myself!" suggested Ian jokingly.

"It might be a good idea, especially in our world." This time Sergei's comment was made with more seriousness.

This was not the comment Ian was expecting. It did make him wonder though.

"Oh, okay. Many thanks Sergei." Ian put down his telephone. He was certainly relieved in one respect, but now both concerned and intrigued. At least now it looked like the email was not from the Russian Mafia, but how did Andrei appear to know all about his connection with the *Rose in a Glass Vase* painting?! He decided he would definitely have to read this email and find out what the contents said. He opened up his laptop and then pressed the keys to get his email inbox. He was just about to access the email details when Penny appeared at the door.

"Ian," she said, "Have you forgotten your meeting with Mr Hopkins in five minutes?"

Ian certainly had. He immediately shut his laptop down and got up from his desk. "Thanks, well done for the reminder." he said to Penny as he passed by her. As he proceeded along the corridor he decided he would open the email tonight when it would be much quieter and more private!

On the train journey home that evening, Ian was still pondering on Sokolov's – or was it Andrei's – email. Did Andrei know of his theft? How was that possible? If he did, what were the consequences and why email me using an alias that he knew I didn't know the existence of? Is Andrei trying to test me, and if so why? Once again this stupid painting was causing him headaches … and not for the first time! Once again, he wished he'd never taken the damn thing in the first place!

When Ian arrived home, he found the house empty. Emma had obviously not returned from work. He quickly decided to take advantage of this opportunity and immediately went to the office and switched on his laptop. Whilst it was powering up he went into the kitchen and removed a can of beer from the fridge. After cracking the seal, he walked back to the office sipping his first beer of the day. He sat down at the desk, accessed his emails and scrolled down to the Sokolov email. Finally he pressed the open button and held his breath. The contents of the email read:

*"Hello my friend!*

*I have a possible buyer of the ten William Nicholson paintings we identified from my original itinerary. Your report shows there are only nine. The one missing from your report is Rose in a Glass Vase. My question is: did you miss this one from your report? Can you email me at this userid, asap.*

*Vladimir Sokolov."*

Ian picked up his can of beer and leaned back in his chair. His heart was beating faster and he stared at the screen. After a few seconds he took several long swallows from the can. Well, well, well, he thought. So now what do I say?

"Hello, Ian?" Emma called from the hallway.

"Hi," replied Ian. "I'm in the office." Ian closed down

his laptop and joined Emma in the hallway and kissed her. "Just having a quick beer. I'll cook tonight. Do you fancy a Chinese?"

"That would be lovely. I'll just get a glass of wine and go up for a quick bath and a change of clothes."

"Okay, dinner should be ready in about half an hour."

For the rest of the evening Ian felt more relaxed than he had done for several days. He still had to reply to Andrei, but he hoped the worst of his problems were now behind him ... or was it just misplaced optimism?!

The following morning Ian had planned to work from home that day. A new client, John McLaren, an investment banker currently living in the Mayfair area, had a collection of recently inherited 18th and 19th century paintings he wanted to sell. The McLaren family were moving to the United States. Mr McLaren had informed Ian that the painting collection would no longer be appropriate, or practicable, in the Florida climate. Ian wanted to spend some quiet time investigating the history of the collection. He was also considering the possibility of handing this client across for Penny to deal with. She had now proved to be very competent and he was confident that she could achieve a good result for both the client and Sotheby's. He made up his mind to speak to her tomorrow morning.

As soon as Emma had left for work, Ian decided he would first reply to Andrei/Vladimir's email. When he heard Emma's car leave their driveway, he finished his coffee in the kitchen and went through to the home office and switched on his laptop. He had been struggling to sleep during the night, but this gave him the opportunity to think of what he was going to say to Andrei. Now he was ready to reply.

He sat down at the desk and pondered as to how best he should compose the email. Andrei obviously liked communications to be written in a nonspecific, vague sort of way, thus avoiding the possibility of other prying eyes understanding the message. But of course, he still wanted to make sure that Andrei knew he was referring to the collection stored in the Kremlin.

After several minutes playing around with two different drafts, he started to type the first possible response.

*"Hello Vladimir,*

*The painting you referred to was not in my report because I did not see it in the collection I viewed. If I remember correctly, there were about 15 paintings listed on the original inventory that were no longer available for me to see and include in my report.*

*Regards, Ian."*

He read through the draft again, but was not sure that this was the right answer. He then typed up the second possible reply.

*"Hello Vladimir,*

*The painting you referred to is in my possession. If you really need it then we can discuss it the next time we speak.*

*Regards, Ian."*

He read and re-read both possible options, weighing up the pros and cons in each case. One was a lie, but the other the truth. Which would be the best answer for Andrei?

Finally he made his mind up and before he could prevaricate any further, he pressed the send button. For about five seconds he could have stopped the communication, but he watched the message on the screen finally state 'message sent'. He hoped and prayed he had made the right decision.

# Chapter 34

When Ian arrived at his office the next morning, he asked Penny to join him to discuss the McLaren collection of paintings. Penny picked up her notepad and followed her boss into his office.

"Sit down at the table Penny," said Ian as he placed his overcoat on the hook behind his door and then walked over to join her with his laptop. As he opened up the lid and waited for the computer to come to life, he continued. "Yesterday I spent quite a bit of time investigating the ten paintings Mr McLaren is looking to sell. I have put together a spreadsheet of my findings and I will email it to you."

Penny listened and nodded to indicate she understood. However, she did wonder what Ian was about to tell her next.

Ian's computer had now come to life and he found the McLaren spreadsheet. Ian turned the computer around so that Penny could see the screen and he pointed to and read down the list of paintings plus his comments against each picture. Penny had leaned forward to get a better view and concentrated on what Ian was saying.

"It's a nice collection and I don't think we should have any problems at an auction," said Ian, after he had finished explaining the list, "so I'm suggesting you deal with this case yourself Penny." He leaned back in his chair and waited for Penny's reaction.

Penny was not expecting this sort of challenge and sat up with alarm on her face. "Are you sure?"

"Oh yes, you are certainly ready to have a go on your own. If there are any problems or areas you are not sure about, you can always talk them through with me first."

Slowly Penny's face changed from mild alarm to a more relaxed pose. She was pleased to hear her boss's flattering words. "Thank you. I would really like the opportunity. It appears to be a straightforward case."

"I knew you would. You are a talented woman and just need your confidence boosting a little more. The best way of doing that is to meet with the client, face to face, and present him with an attractive proposition. John McLaren seemed like a nice man when I spoke to him on the telephone. However, he readily admits he knows little about art so he may need his hands holding. Why don't you get the ball rolling by telephoning him and setting up an appointment to view the collection? His telephone number and address are all on the spreadsheet. After you have met with him we can have a chat about your findings and your valuation suggestions. I'll email the spreadsheet to you in a few minutes and you can get straight on with it."

"Thank you Ian. I'll ring Mr McLaren as soon as I get your spreadsheet."

Penny left Ian's office and went back to her desk and checked her computer. About a minute later the familiar ping of an incoming email caught her attention. It was Ian's spreadsheet arriving. She checked it was all complete and printed off a paper hardcopy. Two minutes later she was ringing the telephone number listed on the spreadsheet.

"Hello?" A female voice, with a definite American accent, answered the call.

"Hello," replied Penny. She was surprised to hear an American accent, "I was wondering if I could speak to Mr McLaren please?"

"I'm afraid he's at work. I'm Mrs McLaren."

"Oh hello Mrs McLaren. My name is Penny Harmer. I work for Sotheby's and understand your husband wants us to look at your painting collection for a possible sale."

"Oh does he? Well I do not know anything about selling the pictures."

Woops thought Penny. What have I gotten myself into? "Do you think I should speak to him or do you want to speak to him first?"

"I've been in Florida for the last two weeks. We are moving there shortly."

"Yes, so I understand," interrupted Penny.

"I just flew back and arrived this morning. Not seen or spoken to my husband for about a week."

"I see," replied Penny, and the conversation went quiet for a few seconds.

"I'll speak to John and get him to ring you back."

"Thank you," said Penny and she gave Mrs McLaren both her telephone number and email address. The line then went dead.

"Huh!" said Penny out loud just as Ian was passing by her desk.

"Not good news?" asked Ian. He stopped and waited for Penny to explain.

Penny summarised the conversation she'd just had with Mrs McLaren.

"Tricky. Let's hope Mr McLaren has not dropped himself in it. I guess there is nothing else to do for the moment until one of them gets back to you."

It was just after 10 am the next morning when Penny's telephone rang. "Hello, Penny Harmer speaking," she answered.

"Hello Ms Harmer, I'm John McLaren. I understand you spoke with my wife yesterday."

Unlike Mrs McLaren, this was certainly a British accent, thought Penny. "Yes, I was trying to contact you, but I was only given your home number. I'm sorry if I caused a problem."

"I see. Why were you calling me?"

This comment somewhat surprised Penny. "I understood you approached Sotheby's to help you to possibly sell your painting collection. I was ringing up to make an appointment to view them."

"I see, but I gave a list of my paintings to Mr Caxton. What else do you need?"

"Mr Caxton is my manager. He's asked me to view the paintings and make a report."

"I see. Do you need to come to our house?"

"Er, well, yes. Unless you want to bring the collection into our office," responded Penny. I thought Ian said he was a nice man, he seems a bit weird!

"I see. Not the most practical solution is it?"

"No," replied Penny, now becoming frustrated. "Mr McLaren, do you want to sell these paintings?"

"What about six o'clock tomorrow evening?"

"At your home or in our office?" Penny felt Mr McLaren deserved that!

"Mmm. You can come to our home. Do you know the address?"

Penny repeated the address written on the file and the line went dead.

After putting the receiver down she got up from her desk and approached Ian's office. "Ian, can I have a word please?"

Ian was sitting behind his desk with two computers open. "Yes Penny. Come in. You look a little flustered."

Penny walked over to the front of Ian's desk and sat down

opposite him. She explained the weird conversation she had just had with John McLaren.

"I've only spoken to him once and he seemed okay then," said Ian, a little concerned. "Following that conversation he emailed me the list of his paintings. Do you still want to go to their house tomorrow?"

"I'm not sure. They both sounded ... well, a bit weird."

Ian smiled. "What about asking Vic to see if he wants to go with you?"

"Yes. I think I will do that."

Later that day Penny discussed the two McLarens and their painting collection with Viktor. Viktor agreed to accompany her, but he also joked that he would escort Penny as her 'bodyguard'! More seriously, he then explained that he knew where Adam's Row, in Mayfair, was and informed her that it was only about a ten minutes' walk from the office. Also it was partly on his way home.

It was just before six o'clock when Penny pressed the front doorbell at the McLaren's house in Adam's Row. She was hoping nobody would answer. Viktor stood just behind her.

Unfortunately for her, however, the door was opened not by either Mr or Mrs McLaren, but by a young child, probably about seven years of age!

"Can I see either your mummy or daddy please," announced Penny, bending down to the child's level.

Suddenly the door closed and they both heard the child shout "Mummy, there's a lady and a man at the door!"

Penny stood back alongside Viktor and they both looked at each other. Penny shook her head from side to side. She wanted to run, but Viktor was more intrigued.

About a minute went by before the front door was opened again. This time a blonde attractive lady with a strong American accent asked "Yes?"

"Mrs McLaren?" enquired Penny.

"Who wants to know?"

Penny now fully recognised the voice from the telephone conversation. "I made an appointment with Mr McLaren for six o'clock to review your collection of paintings."

"I spoke with you on the telephone two days ago, didn't I?"

Penny and Viktor glanced at each other and then Penny said, "Yes you did and your husband telephoned me yesterday morning and made this appointment."

"He's not home from work yet!"

"Oh," said Penny, becoming more exasperated by the minute.

At this point Viktor decided to say something. "Mrs McLaren, we are from Sotheby's and Ms Harmer here, made an appointment with your husband to view your paintings, which we understand you want to sell."

"As I say, he's still at work."

Penny was all for leaving but Viktor was a little more tolerant and persistent. "All we want to do is look at the paintings and make a few notes. Would it be alright if we came in and did this please? It will only take a few minutes."

"I don't know."

That was it as far as Penny was concerned. She stepped back from the side of Viktor and was just about to suggest to him that they leave when a man came up behind her and made her jump.

"Hello. You must be Ms Harmer." Penny turned around and nodded. "I'm John McLaren. Shall we all go inside the house?"

Mrs McLaren opened the door wider and Penny and Viktor followed John McLaren into the hallway. Mrs McLaren held the door open and stared at each of them as they passed by.

"I'm sorry I'm late. There was a big hold up on the Central

line from the City," said Mr McLaren, he was, however, looking at his wife whilst he was talking.

Viktor felt the apology was more towards his wife than them.

Mrs McLaren closed the door and wandered down the passageway towards the kitchen where she closed the door behind her. The hall and passageway were poorly lit and quite cluttered with various children's toys.

"The paintings are in the lounge and dining room. Would you follow me please."

The first room they entered was the lounge. It was a large, cold and dark room. When Mr McLaren switched the light on it only increased the light marginally.

Both Viktor and Penny saw six paintings hanging on two of the walls. Wow, thought Viktor.

What is this?! thought Penny. She opened up her note-book and started to make notes. Viktor made some extra comments quietly to Penny and she jotted them down too. Viktor also took some photographs using his mobile phone.

After about 15 minutes Penny asked if they could see the other pictures. Mr McLaren led them back into the passageway and opened the door directly opposite. Again he switched on the light, but the room had the same dimness and it was also very sparsely furnished. The four remaining paintings were all hanging on the far wall. Penny and Viktor walked over to examine them closer. They then looked at each other with raised eyebrows. Penny once again scribbled notes into her notebook and Viktor took some more photographs. When they had finished Penny asked Mr McLaren whether he had up to date provenances for all the pictures?

"Provenances?"

"Yes, proof of ownership. Also, have you got any other documentation as to who owned the pictures before you?"

asked Penny. She really didn't believe this family could own such a valuable collection!

"No sorry, this was my grandfather's house until he died six months ago. I am the last remaining member of the family, so I've inherited it all."

"I see," said Penny, and then she smiled to herself, remembering that this was the annoying phrase Mr McLaren kept using when they spoke on the telephone.

It was now Viktor's turn to ask a question. "What about any family papers, legal documents, insurance policies? Do you remember if there were any references to these paintings?"

"Sorry, but there were two lots of solicitors that dealt with all that. We just want to sell everything and move to Florida, to be closer to my wife's family. We've sold some of the furniture already, that's why it's rather sparse in here. The house has just been sold as well. We move out in two weeks' time."

"Could you give us the name and address of the solicitors you used please?" asked Penny. Viktor was still looking at the picture at the far end of the room.

Mr McLaren gave Penny the names and addresses of the two firms of solicitors and she jotted the details down in her notepad.

Penny was desperate to get out of this dreary, cold and creepy house.

She announced. "Well thank you Mr McLaren. We have seen enough for our initial inspection. We will be in contact with you again very shortly. We need to do some further investigations and we'll inform you when these have been completed."

"Remember," interrupted Mr McLaren, "we are moving to Florida in two weeks and I want to know what is going to happen to these paintings well before then."

"We will get back to you by the end of the week," said Penny, itching to leave.

She walked into the passageway and onwards towards the hall. Mr McLaren followed and then finally Viktor, who temporarily paused in the dining room doorway and looked back at the four paintings one last time. He finally joined the other two at the front door.

Mr McLaren opened the door and Penny headed down the steps. Viktor stopped at the door and shook Mr McLaren's hand. He then said "Thank you for your time, sir." He then joined Penny in the street. They both heard the door close behind them and they looked straight at each other.

"Do you really believe that?" said Penny.

"Fabulous," replied Viktor, "But it's all wrong! Come on, I need a drink. My treat."

# Chapter 35

It was just after 9 am the next morning, when Ian entered the outer office. Both Penny and Viktor were waiting for him.

"Aha, a welcoming committee. Good morning to you both," said Ian as he started to take off his overcoat.

Penny immediately spoke with some excitement in her voice. "We went to see the McLarens yesterday evening."

"Okay. Good. Come into my room and tell all."

All three walked into Ian's office. Ian hung up his coat, walked over to his desk and sat down. Viktor and Penny sat on their usual seats facing their boss.

For the next 30 minutes Penny and Viktor gave Ian a detailed account of their bizarre appointment.

When they had finished their story, Ian said, "So the list of pictures that Mr McLaren gave to me bore no resemblance to the paintings you saw?"

"Correct," said Penny. "In all that gloom we couldn't really judge if any were fakes, but if they are real, then they must be worth millions!"

"At least!" added Viktor. "So what do we do now?"

"I think that if you are both right, and I don't doubt for a minute you're not, we must get the pictures out of that house and looked at by the experts. And as you say if they are all real … well…"

"I will talk to the two firms of solicitors this morning and see if they have any paperwork relating to the pictures," said Penny. This was her case and she definitely wanted to be in control.

"Good luck," said Ian, "Solicitors nearly always hide behind comments such as 'client confidentiality', but by all means have a go. They may respond to a nice female voice."

"Sexist!" replied Penny, and they all laughed.

Two days later, Ian was in his office with Penny. They were discussing the McLaren collection of paintings. Penny was telling Ian about her conversation with Mr McLaren's grandfather's solicitors. She explained that she eventually got to speak with a male clerk, Peter Overton, who was a little more forthcoming with information and, in particular, with some details of the paintings.

"Peter Overton," said Penny, "told me that the grandfather's affairs were in quite a mess and it had been difficult to find any paperwork. They had a copy of his signed will on file, but were not sure if these were his final wishes. It was dated ten years ago. On this will the solicitors were nominated as the Executors, but the main beneficiary was the grandson, John McLaren. The solicitors contacted John McLaren and asked him for his help. Unfortunately, he didn't seem to know anything about his grandfather's affairs as he had not met with him during the past 15 years! Also Mr McLaren apparently went on to say that he was very busy at work and to contact his own solicitors! So in their capacity as Executors, the solicitors employed a firm of detectives to investigate. About a month later the detectives provided their report and concluded there was probably no other will likely to have been written since the one drafted ten years ago. The detectives had obtained legal permission to enter the house and the only copy of any will they found was exactly the same as the one the solicitors held. There were lots of old files, but little relating to the last ten years. It's almost as though the grandfather died ten years ago!"

"So what about the paintings?" Ian was interested in this background history, but mainly wanted to get to the real story behind the paintings.

"Well, the detectives found an old inventory report dating back about 20 years. This report listed the names of the ten paintings that Mr McLaren emailed to you. Strangely, none of the paintings Vic and I saw that evening appeared on this old inventory! Also Mr McLaren says he has no documentation relating to any of the paintings currently in his home. Peter Overton thinks that John McLaren does not know anything about art and paintings in general and just copied the old inventory listing when he emailed it to you. He probably did not understand that the inventory bore no relationship to the paintings in his possession."

"So, where do the paintings currently hanging on the McLaren walls come from? By the way, what's the grandfather's name?"

"He's Alfred McLaren. Nobody seems to know where the current pictures came from!"

"What about insurance? Has a policy been found?"

"Peter told me that they found a householder's insurance policy and several old renewal papers, but it looks certain that cover lapsed about ten years ago. He said he'd checked with Alfred McLaren's insurance broker, the name that appeared on the last renewal notice, and they confirmed their records showed all the cover lapsed ten years ago. The old insurance policy incidentally just listed the old inventory paintings."

"It all looked like such a straightforward case when John McLaren telephoned me!"

"Please tell me, Ian, they are not all like this, are they?"

"Oh no," replied Ian, "some are really complicated!" They both laughed.

Over the next 24 hours, Penny and Viktor searched the internet for any information relating to the current ten paintings residing at Mr McLaren's home. Although Penny had jotted down in her notebook a description of each picture and, as far as they could ascertain, the name of the artist, they didn't know if they were real, or just fakes. Each of the ten picture frames were devoid of any definite identification. They had a strong idea from the style of each painting, but were struggling to put the picture's name against the possible artist. After further efforts they thought they may have now identified just three strong possibilities. It was mid-afternoon when Viktor suddenly had the brainwave! He quickly changed websites and scrolled down the huge list of paintings that this new website contained. "Yes!" he shouted out loud.

"What's the matter?" enquired Penny. Viktor had made her jump.

Viktor then showed Penny the website and explained his thinking.

"Oh my God! Are you sure?" exclaimed Penny. "Oh wow!"

"I think we ought to have a word with Ian. This is out of our league!" replied Viktor.

Penny and Viktor were working in Penny's office area, so they both got up and went over towards Ian's room, stopping at the open door. Ian was sitting at his desk reviewing a future auction catalogue.

"Ian," said Penny, excitedly, "Vic's come up with an amazing theory. I think you should listen to him."

Ian immediately put down the catalogue, adjusted his seating position and said, "Come in, come in, both of you. I'm all ears!"

It was two days later when John McLaren reluctantly

agreed to meet with Ian and Penny. He suggested meeting in a small cafe in Lime Street, opposite the famous Lloyds of London building. This, apparently, was just a five minutes' walk from his office. It was his only option, and it would also have to be during his lunch break, as he was so busy at work and, he reminded them, he and his family were moving to Florida in a week's time.

Penny and Ian were now sitting at a small table against the far wall of the suggested cafe. They had a perfect view of the entrance door, but John McLaren was already 15 minutes late. Ian and Penny sipped their coffees and Penny was growing more frustrated with Mr McLaren's lack of respect and general disorganisation. Ian was not too pleased either, bearing in mind what he had to say to him.

Two minutes later John McLaren appeared at the entrance and looked around the room. He spotted Penny sitting with someone he did not recognise. Penny stood up and waved him over. Mr McLaren briskly walked over to join them and before either Penny or Ian said a word, he announced that he only had a few minutes and remained standing.

Penny ignored Mr McLaren's comment and said, "May I introduce you to my boss, Ian Caxton. I believe you two have previously spoken on the telephone. Ian stood up and held out his hand. Mr Mclaren looked down at Ian's hand and after a brief moment of doubt, finally decided to complete the handshake.

"Please sit down, Mr McLaren," said Ian, seriously. "What I'm about to tell you is extremely important." Ian sat down and decided not to offer purchasing a drink for Mr McLaren as he wanted to make his point as quick and as succinctly as possible.

Mr McLaren sat down and waited.

"Do you know ANYTHING about the ten paintings you showed Ms Harmer and her colleague the other evening?"

"No, I know nothing about paintings and just want to sell them before we move to Florida. Why?" said Mr McLaren, glancing at his wristwatch.

"You are possibly in very serious trouble. I thought I had better warn you before you have a visit from the police."

Suddenly Mr McLaren's attention shifted from his wristwatch to Ian. "What the hell are you talking about?"

"We are fairly sure all those paintings are stolen."

"What!? What rubbish! Why would my grandfather have stolen pictures?"

"That's exactly what we would like to know, Mr McLaren, and, more specifically, why are YOU trying to get Sotheby's to sell stolen paintings?"

Mr McLaren shifted in his seat and pondered on Ian's comment. "I really do not know what you are talking about. I inherited those paintings from my grandfather and I have no future need, or use, for them. I simply want to sell them. I telephoned Sotheby's in all good faith!"

"Have you ever heard of an organisation called the Commission for Looted Art in Europe?" asked Ian, looking carefully at Mr McLaren's facial reaction.

"What?! No. Never heard of them! Why? What have they got to do with me?"

"It was set up in 1999 with the prime aim of recovering and achieving restitution of lost and stolen artwork. They are mainly looking for artwork stolen by the Nazis."

Mr McLaren's eyes were wide open in surprise. He was also starting to sweat. "The Nazis! This is preposterous, completely ridiculous. I repeat, what's all this got to do with me?"

Ian leaned forward to apply the killer blow. "Mr McLaren, those ten paintings in your house are all listed as stolen by the Nazis in and around the 1930s! If I were you, I would go home immediately because the police are probably at your house as we speak. I assume your wife will be at home!"

Suddenly Mr McLaren leapt up from his chair and ran out of the cafe.

It was about an hour later when Ian and Penny returned to Sotheby's. Ian said he wanted to make a telephone call and Penny went in search of Viktor. She eventually found him by one of the coffee machines talking to a colleague.

Viktor spotted Penny rushing down the corridor towards him. By the time Penny joined him the colleague had walked away.

"So, how did it all go?" asked Viktor, keen to know the outcome of his theory.

"Ian was fabulous. McLaren kept denying any knowledge of the paintings being stolen, but once Ian said the police were probably already at his house, he ran out of the cafe like a scalded cat!"

"Wow. So now what?"

"Ian wants us to meet with him in his office in ten minutes' time. He wanted to make a telephone call first."

"Okay, let's go!" said Viktor, striding behind Penny with an excited smile on his face.

When Penny and Viktor arrived at Penny's desk, they could hear that Ian was still on the telephone. As soon as Penny saw the red light on her extension to Ian's phone go out, she knew the call would be over. "Come on, he's finished the call."

Penny and Viktor entered Ian's office and he waved them over to the two chairs in front of his desk.

"Well done Vic, excellent intuition. I telephoned my friend in the Met Art Squad, Detective Sergeant Paul Davies earlier this morning and tipped him off about the McLaren paintings. I have just spoken to him again and he said they have taken John McLaren into custody and also taken all the paintings from his home."

"Wow," said Viktor, "I just knew there was something dodgy about McLaren."

"Mmm. Apparently it's not that straightforward," replied Ian. "The police think John McLaren is probably totally innocent, but want to try and get as much information as possible from him before he is released. The police have some old records about Alfred McLaren going back up to 12 years ago. Apparently they had a few suspicions about Alfred's illegal art dealings going back some time, but no actual proof. Twelve years ago it all suddenly went very quiet."

"Oh, that's all very disappointing," said Penny. Her earlier enthusiasm had now disappeared.

Ian continued. "It looks like Alfred traded and obtained his last collection of paintings during the period after the last inventory had been completed. The police think that maybe that was up to 12 years ago. It is also likely that once Alfred McLaren found out that the police were watching him he decided to stop trading immediately. Funny though, you would have thought that if he did know the police were watching him, he would have wanted to get rid of all his collection very quickly."

"At least now these ten paintings will hopefully be returned to the correct owners," commented Viktor.

"The police are already talking to the Commission. I'll let you know how it all pans out. They have already asked me to pass on their thanks to you both. Michael Hopkins also wants to thank you too. He would like to see you both in his office at four o'clock later today."

# Chapter 36

It was a week later when Viktor was in Sotheby's reception area and he spotted Ian entering the building. He quickly went over and stopped him as he approached the elevators. "Hello Ian. Can I have a private word?"

"Hello Vic, what can I do for you?"

"It's a message from my father. Andrei is coming to London and he would like you to meet with him on Thursday. He will be staying at the Savoy hotel."

Okay thought Ian. Now we will know if I made the right decision. "I think that's okay. What time and where?"

"Father says Andrei will contact you when he arrives in London."

"Thank you," said Ian, and he carried on walking towards the elevators. Whilst he waited for one of the doors to open, he thought about Andrei and wondered what he was going to say on Thursday. Had he made the correct choice when he'd responded to Andrei's email?

Late on Wednesday afternoon, Viktor and Penny met with Ian in his office. Ian had heard from his friend in the Metropolitan Police Art Squad and now wanted to bring them both up to date.

"The police telephoned earlier this afternoon and have updated me with the latest news on the McLaren case. As expected, the police could not find any evidence that connected John McLaren, directly, with the stolen paintings. They were happy that he didn't even know of the paintings existence until the grandfather had died. As a result, they eventually let him go and the family have now moved on to Florida as planned. All the paintings have been handed over to the Commission for Looted Art in Europe and two of the pictures have already been returned to families of the original Austrian owners."

Both Penny and Viktor felt a little disappointed, but it was Penny who said, "I was hoping they were going to throw the book at him! They are a weird family. I suppose it's all finished now."

"The Commission is still trying to find out all the legal owners of the other eight paintings, but yes, I guess ours, and the police's involvement, is finally finished." Ian sympathised with their disappointment and also felt a little sad himself. However, he also knew that he was hardly in a position to be too judgemental of people who stole paintings!

As Viktor and Penny were leaving the room, Ian's telephone rang. Ian waited until both his colleagues had left before picking up the receiver.

"Hello my friend." It was the familiar voice of Andrei.

"Hello Andrei, or should I say, Vladimir?"

Andrei ignored the joke and replied, "I am staying at the Savoy. Can we meet tomorrow evening in the American Bar at 7.30?"

"Yes, that's fine with me." replied Ian. He was pleased that there was no anger or aggression in Andrei's voice. He just sounded like the usual Andrei. Maybe I made the right decision after all.

"Good. See you then, my friend."

Ian heard the click of Andrei's phone and the line was dead. Although he was surprised with the abrupt finish to the call, he did know that Andrei was not keen on discussing details or, indeed, indulging in any long conversations on the telephone. His early years living in Russia had taught him many lessons and one of them was always to assume a third party was listening to all telephone conversations!

Ian had never been in the American Bar at the Savoy Hotel before. Indeed, he had only been further than the Savoy Hotel's reception area once, and that was to meet with a Sotheby's client in the client's suite some time ago. So now as he entered the famous bar his senses were on full alert. He noticed that the room was decorated in a warm art deco style, with cream and ochre painted walls and blue and gold chairs. The walls were also adorned with many photographs of previous famous guests. A pianist was currently playing classical American jazz on a baby grand piano in the centre of the room. Ian decided it was all very opulent, exquisite and no doubt, very expensive! He spotted Andrei sitting at a table quite close to the bar. He was in conversation with another man. Ian looked closely at the stranger, but decided he didn't recognise him.

He checked his watch. It was 7.31 pm, so he was on time. He pondered on the dilemma, but eventually decided not to interrupt their discussions. He looked around the room for a temporary seat and sat down at a nearby empty table and watched and listened to the pianist. A waitress walked over and asked if he required a drink. Ian explained, and pointed to Andrei, that he would have a drink when his colleague had finished his conversations. The waitress smiled and walked away looking for another potential customer.

After a further few minutes there was little sign of the stranger, still talking to Andrei, getting up to leave. Ian again looked around the room and then to the collection of photographs on the walls. He tried to guess how many of these celebrities he knew. He eventually decided that he could only possibly recognise about 10%. Most of the people, in the black and white photographs, he decided, were probably at the height of their fame and careers, too far back in history for him to recognise. Certainly long before he was even born!

Ten minutes later Andrei and his colleague stood up. They shook hands and the colleague walked out of the bar. Andrei looked around, spotted Ian and waved him over.

"Hello my friend." Andrei shook Ian's hand. "I am so sorry for the delay, but Mr Colbourne is a very important client of mine and, hopefully, he is going to buy two of my pictures."

"It's no problem Andrei. I have been enjoying the music."

"Jazz is not really my music. I prefer Tchaikovsky and Rachmaninoff."

Ian smiled. "Yes, their music is good too, different, but still very good."

"Anyway, thank you for coming. Now then, the reason I like this bar is because my friend, Erik, over here." Andrei pointed his finger towards the bar. "He produces the most fabulous cocktails. Did you know the cocktail menu is just a work of art on its own? It starts with the short and light drinks, then moves through long cocktails before finishing with intense short drinks. All are served in this beautifully crafted glassware." Andrei picked up his half-filled glass to show Ian. "Now my friend, I insist you try 'The Googly'."

"The Googly! That's a type of bowling delivery in cricket. Okay, but what's in it?" It was very rare for Ian to drink cocktails and even rarer still to know the makeup of the drink's recipe.

"I don't know anything about your cricket, but I do know The Googly is a wonderful drink. As to what is in it, I'm not sure, but Erik will tell you if you ask him. I just like to make my way through the menu!" Andrei laughed and waved for the barman to come over. He then ordered two Googlies. For a few minutes the two men talked more about the Savoy and Andrei said it was his favourite London hotel. Just as Ian was wondering when Andrei would get to the point of the meeting, the two drinks were delivered. Ian was suddenly astonished. They were presented to the table on strange looking bespoke coasters.

Andrei noticed that Ian was looking at the coasters with a curious expression on his face. "Erik told me that they are designed to emulate the shutter of a camera! Don't ask me why!"

Ian smiled and wondered what other surprises he would be experiencing this evening.

"Now my friend, to business," said Andrei, after sipping his drink. "So, you say you have the *Rose in a Glass Vase* painting. How, may I ask, did you acquire it?"

"Andrei, can I just say that, yes, I have acquired it and, yes, it is still in my possession."

Andrei smiled for a few seconds and then laughed out loud. "Excellent my friend, excellent! We will make a proper dealer of you yet!"

Ian was pleased and somewhat relieved, but also slightly concerned. "So, Andrei, do you want this picture?"

"I am pleased to say Dimitri has obtained the other nine pictures from the Kremlin and they are now in Monaco, so yes, I would like to put the group of ten back together. Should we say 50,000 Swiss francs?"

Ian quickly did an exchange rate calculation in his head. He knew the painting was certainly worth a lot more, but he'd already decided to get the problem out of his hair once and for all, and he also knew that Andrei would not let him off lightly. "Seventy thousand," replied Ian, although he would have been happy to get £30,000 earlier from Oscar, but he wanted to see how far Andrei would go.

Andrei laughed, sipped his cocktail and said "My friend, 60,000 Swiss francs have already been deposited into your Swiss bank account."

This time it was Ian's turn to laugh. "You are incredible, Andrei," said Ian, with a smile. He was more than happy with Andrei's generosity.

"Yes, I know. You will be too one day." Both men laughed together this time. Andrei then raised his glass and said "Cheers, my friend!"

Ian picked up his glass, raised it to Andrei's and gently caressed it. "Na zdorovie, my friend, na zdorovie!"

"Spasibo, Ian," replied Andrei. "Now I have some work for you, my friend."

Ian's ears suddenly pricked up. He was hoping for a new adventure and a new challenge. He had slowly realised over the last few months that despite feeling as though his life had been turned upside down and inside out, he had missed the excitement of working with Andrei. It was certainly pressurised and sometimes definitely stressful, but always exciting!

"Okay, so what are you proposing?"

# Chapter 37

"Well, my friend, a Russian colleague of mine lives in Edinburgh, in Scotland. He has contacted me to say that a Scottish Lord, that he is friendly with, needs to sell some of his family's collection of paintings. Apparently, because he has some money problems. His name is Richard Forsyth, but is also known as the 'Laird of Baltoun', whatever that means. According to my colleague, the family has fallen on difficult times, but as well as wanting to sell the paintings, he also insists on keeping the sale out of the public eye. Wants a private sale, which is where we both come in."

"If he is a Laird, that does not make him a Lord."

"I do not understand your title system. Lords, Earls, Barons, Knighthood, it's all confusing."

"Do not worry Andrei, it is also confusing for a lot of British people too. What I do know is that anybody with a title, or several titles, will usually only use their highest-ranking title first. So, if this Richard Forsyth was a true Lord he would use the name Lord Richard Forsyth, or just simply Lord Forsyth. The term Laird is a generic name for the owner of a large, long-established Scottish estate. A Laird will often place the title of 'The Much Honoured' before his name. This is a courtesy title used by some of the Scottish gentry who do not have a higher-ranking title. If you therefore received a letter from this Richard Forsyth he would sign his name 'The Much Honoured Richard Forsyth, Laird of Baltoun'."

Andrei just stared at Ian in disbelief, with his mouth slightly open. He was totally baffled. "You are talking in a different language. How do you know all these things?"

"At Sotheby's we deal with many titled people so it is vitally important to know their correct titles. To get it wrong could at best be embarrassing, but much worse, totally unprofessional and potentially, a business disaster! Did you know the Queen's former husband, Prince Philip, has a title that is at least 130 words long!?"

"What!? You are joking, yes?" Andrei sat back in his seat smiling. He then sipped his cocktail and awaited the next English gentry history lesson. "Have you sold any of the Queen's paintings?"

Ian sipped his drink and waited for the taste to hit his tongue. "Mmm, this good."

"Excellent. I will tell Erik."

Ian now answered Andrei's question. "Fortunately the Queen has no need to sell the family paintings ... not yet anyway!" Ian laughed at his own joke, but Andrei just looked at Ian with a surprised and bewildered expression. "So," continued Ian, "what else are you going to tell me about this Scottish Laird and his collection of paintings?"

Andrei tried to recall what exactly he wanted to say to Ian and after a few seconds, said, "Well I would like you to join me when I go to Scotland. I want you to look at this family's painting collection and give me your opinion. Apparently most are quite old and relate mainly to the family's history."

"When are you suggesting we should go?"

"I have two tickets booked on the BA flight to Edinburgh at 7.25 tomorrow evening."

"I see, so you know of my social diary entries for this coming weekend, do you?" said Ian, smiling.

"No, my friend, but I have already put another 100,000 Swiss francs into your bank account."

It was now Ian's turn to sit back in his seat. He looked across at Andrei and smiled and shook his head gently from side to side. "You are incredible, Andrei."

"You have said that before, my friend."

"And I dare say there will be many more times when I say it again!" replied Ian, still shaking his head.

Both men laughed and finished their drinks.

When Ian arrived home later that evening, he gave Emma a summary of his meeting with Andrei.

Fortunately Emma knew she and Ian had no firm plans for the weekend. Not that any plans would have made much difference to Ian, she thought. She knew he would still want to go on this trip with Andrei. "So when will you return?"

"We leave Edinburgh on Sunday on the 12.45 lunchtime flight."

"I hope it doesn't snow for you."

Ian met Andrei late afternoon, at London Heathrow as arranged. They had a small meal and a drink in the First Class Passenger's Lounge before they boarded their early evening flight to Edinburgh. During the journey Andrei decided he wanted to know more about the English system of titles and how one bought a title. He quite liked the idea of being known as an Earl or a Lord.

Ian laughed at Andrei's question and proceeded to inform him that British titles are not bought. They are an honour and are personally presented, usually by the reigning monarch. They are awarded to recognise a person's achievements or service to the country. Additionally titles can be inherited. He then went on to list the various titles and the ranking order. Andrei absorbed all these fascinating details with both interest and enthusiasm. Suddenly the one hour's flight journey had passed very quickly.

When Andrei and Ian exited the aeroplane at Edinburgh airport, they had to descend the steps and walk the short distance across the tarmac to the terminal. There was a bitterly cold breeze which was a shock to their systems after the warm interior of the plane. Fortunately there had not been any recent falls of snow. When they entered the terminal building, they immediately felt the benefit of the increase in temperature.

Not having to go through passport control or collect suitcases from baggage reclaim, they were able to quickly pass into the Arrivals hall where they met a line of people displaying boards with various people's names written on them. Andrei quickly spotted his name and tapped Ian on the shoulder. Ian looked to where Andrei was pointing and they walked towards the person holding the board. Andrei announced his and Ian's name to the board holder and asked if they were going to be heading to Baltoun Castle. The man said something that Andrei didn't understand, but Ian told Andrei that's where they were heading.

The man took hold of Andrei's small cabin case, but Ian said he was quite happy carrying his own. The three men exited the building and walked the short distance to a parked green Range Rover.

The bags were placed in the boot area and the three men climbed aboard. Within minutes the car had been whisked away in a westerly direction. They were told that it was a 25-mile journey to the Laird's estate. Ian and Andrei travelled in silence. Andrei read some emails on his mobile phone and Ian looked out of the window picking out small features of the countryside. There was very little other traffic on the roads and Ian was able to benefit from the car's main beam headlights.

Ian was also thinking about the Laird's collection of paintings. He was worried that most of the paintings were just portraits of family ancestors. Andrei had given him limited information, but Ian had been able to make some initial investigations using the internet. Essentially he was aware that there are 27 pictures to be viewed. All had been in the family, according to the Laird, for at least two centuries. However, Ian could only find independent evidence on three paintings. These three were attributed to the famous Scottish portrait painter Sir Henry Raeburn. They appeared to have been painted before Sir Henry had become the Portrait Painter to King George IV in Scotland at the beginning of the 19$^{th}$ century.

It was about 40 minutes after leaving the airport that the driver announced they were now entering the Baltoun Estate. Both Ian and Andrei stopped what they were doing and from their back seats, leaned forward to see through the driver's windscreen. However, all they could see in the headlights was a long gravel road with trees and fields either side. After several minutes of the same limited night view Ian asked the driver how much further it was to the house.

"Baltoun Castle, sir, is about another five minutes," came the reply from the driver in a very strong Scottish accent. Andrei, again, could not understand one word that he had said.

"How many acres does the Laird own?" asked Ian, still looking into the darkness in front of him.

"It's just over 20,000, sir," replied the driver in a matter-of-fact tone.

Ian sat back in his seat and looked across to Andrei who had a puzzled look on his face. "It's a big estate!" whispered Ian.

"There's the castle, sir," announced the driver.

Both Andrei and Ian leaned forward again and looked

through the front windscreen. In the far distance the silhouette of a very large stone building adorned with several turrets, could just be made out through the darkness. As the car drove closer Ian could make out a little more detail of the castle's facade. The car slowed down and then crossed a drawbridge. Ian noticed the moat below and the reflections of moonlight. The car then passed under a large stone archway before pulling up in an inner courtyard. It stopped outside what appeared to be the huge main entrance door. A smaller door, within the larger entrance door, opened and a man in a red and black check kilt walked towards the car and opened the rear passenger door for Andrei. The driver meanwhile let Ian out his side. Both men stood and looked around at their new surroundings.

"Good evening and welcome to Baltoun Castle gentlemen. I am Jenkins the butler," said the man wearing the red and black check kilt. "The Laird is waiting for you in the library. I will show you the way. Duncan will deal with your luggage."

Before Ian could respond Jenkins strode off towards the castle door. Ian smiled when he noticed that Jenkins walked with a definite air of some importance. Ian tapped Andrei on the shoulder and they both followed Jenkins. Duncan collected the guests' bags from the car boot and followed them into the castle.

Jenkins led Andrei and Ian through the old oak inner door and into the entrance hall of the building. The hall was huge and the stone walls were adorned with an array of swords, muskets and various historical weaponry. Two old iron chandeliers hung down from a vaulted ceiling and produced the only hall lighting, which was not very bright at all. Ian assumed these iron chandeliers once held many wax candles. Now, even if everything else looked very old, there was at least some electrical lighting.

Ian stared around the huge room. It reminded him of a setting to a Harry Potter film!

Andrei had not said a word since exiting Edinburgh airport and was now staring at every feature as the group walked along a similarly low-lit corridor. Jenkins eventually stopped, knocked on another old oak door, entered and announced. "Your guests have arrived, sir."

Andrei and Ian followed Jenkins and entered the library. They were immediately confronted with three bookcase covered walls and several additional freestanding bookcases in the middle of the room. All of the bookshelves seemed to contain a very large collection of books of varying sizes and ages.

"Come in gentlemen," a voice announced from behind one of the bookcases. The Laird then appeared and walked over and shook hands with both Ian and Andrei. "Welcome to my home. Have you eaten?" The Laird was dressed in the same pattern kilt as the butler wore. Ian thought his Scottish accent was less broad than the driver's and he also looked a little younger than the 38 years of age mentioned on the estate's website.

Ian spoke up for both he and Andrei and said, "Yes sir, we had a meal before we left London."

"Fine. Now then gentlemen, first things first. Please call me Richard."

"I'm Ian and this is Andrei," replied Ian, waving his hand towards Andrei.

"I do apologise that my wife is not here to meet you. She has taken my two children to stay with her parents for the weekend in Edinburgh, so the castle will be a little quieter than usual." Richard and Ian gave a small laugh and Richard continued, "Jenkins, can you bring us the whisky." Jenkins, who had remained standing in the doorway, nodded and left the room. "So, gentlemen, did you have a good journey and did you find Duncan waiting for you in Arrivals?"

"Yes, a pleasant flight … and thank you to your driver for collecting us from the airport," said Ian looking at Andrei in the hope he would finally say something. Andrei was still somewhat spellbound by his surroundings.

"1320," announced Richard to Andrei. "That was when the first castle was built by my ancestors, but, in 1557, it was largely destroyed by fire and the present building replaced it. Since then small additions and changes have been made, but most of what you see is 16th century … and it's upkeep, well it costs a small fortune!"

Andrei nodded and continued to look around him. Ian smiled and said, "Yes, I believe it would."

Jenkins returned with a silver tray containing a bottle of malt whisky, three tumblers and a small jug of water. He walked across the room and placed the tray and contents on the tabletop.

"Jenkins," said Richard, as Jenkins started to walk away. "Could you put more logs on the fire, I'm sure these gentlemen are used to warmer properties."

Jenkins walked over to the only wall that was not covered by a bookshelf. In the centre was a large stone fireplace with a substantial, old, black, iron fire basket holding a number of partially burning logs. Jenkins removed three more logs from a large wicker basket sitting next to the stone hearth and placed them on the glowing embers. He then left the room once again, closing the door quietly behind him.

In the meantime, Richard had poured three large measures of whisky and said, "Please help yourself to the water gentlemen. I prefer mine neat." He handed a glass to each of his guests before saying, "Slainte."

Ian responded by wishing the Laird, "Your good health."

All three men sipped their drinks and Richard then said, "Breakfast will be at 9 am and after that I will give you a tour of the castle and show you the paintings. Maybe by then, Andrei, you will have something to say?"

Ian and Richard laughed but Andrei just smiled and sipped his whisky.

It was 8.30 am the next morning when Andrei knocked on Ian's bedroom door. Ian opened it and let Andrei in. Ian's room was similar to that of Andrei's and the rest of the inside of the castle, thick red/grey stone walls, small single pane windows with lead panelling … and no heating!

Andrei's first question was, "How do you switch the heating on? My room is like Siberia!"

Ian laughed and replied. "Andrei, this is Scotland. It is an old castle and there is very little in common with Monaco!"

"But it is freezing. How do people in Scotland keep warm?"

"You have a short memory Andrei. Moscow must have been much colder."

"Yes, it was, but we still had some heating."

Ian laughed again. "After breakfast Richard is going to show us around the castle. Put on your thickest clothing. You will then keep warm."

"I'm glad you are here, my friend. I struggle to understand a word these people are saying. Is it really English they speak?"

Again Ian smiled. "Andrei, it is Scottish. The words are similar but the accent and pronunciation are very different. I sometimes have difficulty in understanding all the words myself."

"What do you think of this Laird Richard?"

"On the face of it he is in a difficult position. Like most of the British aristocracy, their income is probably limited and their costs continue to escalate. Most of the estate's assets are controlled by legal trusts so Richard is largely just a custodian."

"Why can't he just sell up and move on ... to a warmer climate!"

"The whole purpose of the trusts is to avoid many of the British inheritance tax liabilities. However, these trusts come at a price. Richard probably cannot sell land, the castle, furniture and most of the possessions as they are controlled and set down by the various trusts. It all looks like a wonderful life, but in reality there are massive day to day issues and lots of restrictions to any change."

"So that could be why he wants to sell the paintings."

"I'm somewhat surprised that they are not protected by the trusts too. We shall have to see what he has to say about that."

Ten minutes later Ian and Andrei entered the dining room and found Richard sitting at the breakfast table reading a newspaper. "Good morning," announced Richard once he'd heard his guests enter the room. "Did you sleep well?"

"Very well Richard, thank you," said Ian, "but Andrei finds your climate a little chilly."

"I'll get Jenkins to lay a log fire for his room this evening."

Ian smiled and whispered to Andrei. "Richard will arrange heating for your bedroom this evening."

Andrei's eyebrows shot up and he whispered back, "Thank you, my friend."

"Gentlemen, do help yourselves to breakfast." Richard pointed to a number of silver plate covers. "If there is anything else you would like, I will call Jenkins."

After both Andrei and Ian had consumed a hearty breakfast of porridge, kippers, toast and English breakfast tea, Richard suggested they start the promised tour.

They left the dining room and Richard guided his guests to various ground floor rooms, pointing out particular features and showing them the paintings that he was

considering to sell. When they finally reached the drawing room, Richard suggested they sit down and he would
explain a little more about Baltoun Castle.

"The estate is set in more than 20,000 acres. It is in a broad
and fertile lowland valley and in addition to parkland and
gardens, the estate produces cash generating crops as well as
lumber, venison and beef. We also have 12 lodges close to
the two streams that run through the estate. These we try to
rent out. Both the lodges and streams generate a trout and
salmon fishing income. The castle, however, is protected
as a category A listed building and this statutory listing is
maintained by the Historic Environment of Scotland. This
severely limits any alterations we might want to make. We
have to obtain all sorts of special planning permission for
any changes. So, as you can see gentlemen, our income is
somewhat constrained and we have got to the stage where
maintenance and improvements cannot be made without
both substantial investment and approved planning permission. Both are difficult to obtain and very time consuming
to achieve. Essentially my family is now quite poor and we
are only custodians for the next generation. It's all a bit of a
millstone. With maintenance, wages and taxation we need
to generate an income of over two million pounds a year
just to stand still. We have not achieved that level of income
for the last three years."

"Excuse me for asking Richard, but why are the paintings
not covered by the same trusts as all the other property?"

"They probably are, but I cannot find any definitive reference to the paintings in the castle documents. What I want
to do is sell the originals and replace them with copies. In
a perfect world I would not want to sell them at all, but if
we carry on the way we have, there will be no estate for
my family to inherit. I have been in discussions with the
Scottish National Trust and they are interested in taking

over the estate, but to be honest, that is my last resort. My ancestors would turn over in their graves but, of course, they did not have the same running costs as we do."

"I think the best thing now is for Andrei and I to go back and have a second look at the paintings, if you don't mind. We can then discuss our thoughts with you later."

"That's fine. Take your time gentlemen. Lunch will be served at one o'clock."

"Thank you," said Ian and the Laird left Andrei and Ian to their discussions. Once the drawing room door was closed, Ian summarised his thoughts and Richard's comments. Andrei nodded as he now fully understood the situation from Ian's translation. He also understood Richard's predicament.

"What do you think then, my friend?" Andrei queried.

"I'm not sure Andrei. Let's have another look at the pictures. What Richard is proposing is probably outside the regular picture market. I know Sotheby's would not want to be involved with selling paintings that might be protected by a trust. One for your market, I think, Andrei."

"Okay, so now we are in my world, we are now talking about money."

By lunch, Ian and Andrei had viewed all the paintings for a second time. Richard had earlier suggested that they enjoy a business free lunch and then meet and discuss their findings later that afternoon after he had concluded a business meeting about the marketing of his trout and salmon fishing with the Scottish Tourism authorities.

Immediately after lunch, Ian and Andrei took the opportunity to wander around the outside of the castle. As they walked over the drawbridge and looked down and across the moat, a chilly wind suddenly sprang up and both men pulled up the collars of their overcoats and pushed their hands deep into their pockets. Once over the moat, they looked back together at the impressive building.

Andrei was the first to speak. "Do you know, my friend, this is all very confusing. We have this Laird who owns all this land, his businesses and this castle and he says he's poor! It does not make sense."

"That's because Richard owns very little personally. As I said to you earlier, the estate is owned by the various trusts. Richard is just the current CEO, if you like. However, unlike most CEOs, Richard has very little personal power. It is all controlled by the wording of the trusts and the Historic Environment for Scotland."

"I still do not really understand, but what do you think of the paintings?"

"I need to do some more research. They all appear to be originals and the Sir Henry Raeburn portraits are in excellent condition, although they could do with a thorough cleaning."

"Do we offer a price today or do you want more time?"

"I would like more time. Most of the Laird's collection is of excellent quality and I would really like to look a bit deeper into the history of the painters. I'm sure you do not want to overpay and I would not like to embarrass us all with an undervaluation."

"That's good because I would like time to be able to discuss the paintings with possible buyers first. It is a most unusual collection."

"I know, they will not be too easy to value," replied Ian. He knew that there was a limited market for these sorts of pictures. Unless the artist was highly renowned, it was usually just the owning family who saw any worth in them … and that was just largely sentimental!

The two men walked on a little. "You know Ian, I've never been to a place like this before. Just look around you, it is so beautiful. The mountains over there," Andrei pointed to a group of mountains mostly covered in snow, "They are really special, especially against that blue sky. I love those funny cattle as well." Andrei pointed again, this time to a large group of cattle with long horns and long, shaggy, reddy yellow coats.

"They are called Highland cattle, quite famous in these parts," replied Ian.

The two men continued their walk around the castle grounds and through into the gardens before finally deciding it was far too cold to be outside any longer. They retraced their steps back, across the drawbridge, over the moat and into the inner courtyard. When they re-entered the castle building, Jenkins was waiting for them in the hall. He was holding a silver tray containing two glasses of an amber liquid. From each glass a small amount of steam was rising.

Jenkins spoke. "I thought you gentlemen would benefit from one of my 'hot toddies'."

Andrei had never heard of this phrase before, but nodded his head when he heard Ian say, "Yes please, that would be excellent."

Ian took both warm glasses from Jenkins and offered one to Andrei. Andrei initially looked at Ian suspiciously but when he took his first sip, he smiled at Jenkins and said, "Thank you, very good."

Jenkins smiled back and placed the silver tray on a nearby table for the guests to place their empty glasses. He then walked away and left the two men alone in the hall.

"Do you like the hot toddy?" asked Ian, but he already noticed the smile on Andrei's face.

Andrei was using the warm glass to thaw out his hands. "Do you know what we're drinking?"

"As far as I can remember, it's a combination of whisky, honey, lemon and hot water. The brown stick is cinnamon and these are cloves." Ian pointed to two black seeds in his glass. Hot toddies are sometimes known as 'winter warmers'!"

Later that afternoon, Ian and Andrei met up with Richard in the drawing room. Ian explained that Andrei was interested in buying the collection, but they would need more time for research further before making an accurate valuation and a fair offer. Whilst Richard was disappointed, he did understand their position and, after all, he really did want to get the best possible price.

The evening was a relaxed dinner and even Andrei felt he was beginning to understand some of the Scottish language, or was it due to the benefit of the whisky? Either way, he was really enjoying his first experience of Scotland and Laird Richard's home. In so many ways it was all so different to Monaco, but mentally, he was warming to the history and character of the castle, even if it did lack central heating!

When Ian and Andrei finally decided to retire to bed, Ian pointed out and explained about some of the old weaponry on the walls in the hall. As they slowly climbed the oak stairs, he also said that he hoped Andrei's bedroom would be much warmer this evening. When they arrived at Andrei's room, Ian waited whilst Andrei opened the door. He immediately felt the warmer temperature and turned to Ian with a smile. However, he was staggered when he walked further into the room and spotted the source of the heat. He just could not believe that in the 21$^{st}$ century people still had log fires in the bedrooms! Still, he concluded, it was a lot better and certainly a lot warmer than the previous evening.

"More like Monaco now rather than Siberia!" he suggested to Ian.

Ian just smiled and said, "Goodnight Andrei," before walking along the corridor to his own somewhat chillier bedroom.

After a lengthy breakfast, Ian and Andrei said their goodbyes to Richard. They thanked him for his hospitality and promised that they would be in touch within the week. Duncan, Richard's driver, loaded the luggage into the Range Rover and the three men drove away, back along the route they had travelled previously in the dark. There had been a heavy frost overnight and many of the fields and trees had a white tinge to them, but fortunately no snow. Andrei just looked out of his window and thought of the endless possibilities this estate offered … in the right hands!

It was late afternoon when Ian arrived home. His and Andrei's journey had been delayed due to the backlog of flights following the overnight heavy frost. Emma greeted him with her usual hug and kiss before asking him how the weekend had gone. Ian gave her a summary of the events, the problems Richard was encountering and why he needed to sell some of the family's heritage.

"It's so sad," said Emma. "Mummy told me, some time ago, about her friend, Lord Haskings-Smythe. He was in a similar position. He and his family now live in the gatehouse and a middle eastern family rent the main house and grounds!"

"It's all a very different world now for most of the aristocracy," replied Ian, "Sadly history seems to have little relevance today. On its own, it certainly doesn't pay for the 21$^{st}$ century bills. I guess that's why a lot of the old country estates have now been passed on to the National Trust, or where they are still family owned, they have had to open their doors to the general public."

"I hope you are able to help Richard. You say he has a young family and it sounds as though he needs a bit of luck."

The trouble is, Ian thought, Andrei is a very hard businessman and probably does not fully understand the word 'sentimentality'.

# Chapter 38

On the following Monday and Tuesday evenings Ian researched further into the Laird's family paintings. At the end of the Tuesday evening he had completed his usual spreadsheet of comments and valuations. After a final check, he emailed a copy to Andrei's alias email address, V. Sokolov. Andrei was still residing at the Savoy. He had informed Ian that he was still hoping to finish his business dealings with Mr Colbourne before he flew back to Monaco.

On Wednesday, as Ian was about to leave his office for lunch, his laptop pinged to announce an incoming email. It was from V. Sokolov. Andrei wanted to meet with Ian that evening at 7.30 pm in his Savoy suite. He also said he would be checking out of the hotel first thing Thursday morning. Ian quickly replied that he would be there.

At 7.20 pm, Ian arrived at the Savoy hotel and, after announcing himself at reception, he was told to go directly to Mr Petrov's suite, as he was expected. Ian walked over towards the elevators. Three minutes later he was knocking on the door to Andrei's suite. Andrei was quick to respond and invited Ian into the suite. "Come in my friend, come in. Thank you for seeing me at such short notice, but I have to be in Monaco urgently. Mr Colbourne is buying my pictures and I have to get things arranged."

Ian was only half listening to Andrei as he was still taking in the sheer grandeur of the luxurious suite. Not for the first time did Ian feel Andrei's life was in a completely different world to his own!

"Something from the mini bar, my friend? Whisky, wine?"

"No thank you. I'm fine. This is a fabulous suite Andrei. You do live in some style."

"It's what hard earned money can provide, my friend. Maybe one day you will have the same."

Ian smiled. "In my dreams maybe."

"Back to business. Thank you for your usual comprehensive report. The total valuation seems a little high though."

Ian was expecting this comment from Andrei. "I think it is fair Andrei. It still leaves you scope for some profit."

"Ah, my friend," smiled Andrei, "so you are still thinking about me too."

"Andrei, I am always thinking about you, but I also need to believe my valuations are reasonable based on my professional judgement."

"Okay Ian, I'm only joking. Indeed, after achieving a good profit on my picture sales to Mr Colbourne earlier today, I am in a more generous mood. I liked your Laird and have some sympathy for his situation. Maybe I can do some more business and help him in the future. I am prepared to pay the full valuation prices you have put on the paintings."

Ian was stunned. Was it correct what he was hearing? He was sure Andrei would have wanted to offer less, but then again, it also sounded as though Andrei may just have some alternative motives! That, he thought, would not surprise him one bit!

"Alright Andrei, if you are sure, I will telephone Richard first thing in the morning."

"Excellent my friend, excellent. I have possible buyers for three of the pictures already and would not want to let them down!"

"Andrei, you are incredible!" said Ian, and not for the first time he smiled and shook his head from side to side in disbelief.

"Yes I am, my friend … yes I am!" Both men laughed and Andrei suggested a whisky would now be the most appropriate toast. Ian agreed and Andrei went over to the mini bar where he removed a small bottle of malt whisky and two glasses. Whilst Andrei was playing host, Ian took the opportunity to look around the suite a little more. Andrei poured two large measures which nearly emptied the bottle. He picked up the two glasses and carried them over to where Ian was standing. He was looking at the view from the large window.

When Ian received his glass, Andrei said, "Cheers to Laird Richard and Scotland."

Ian smiled at Andrei and simply said, "Cheers … my friend." The two men clinked their glasses.

It was just after 10.30 the next morning when Ian telephoned Richard to explain the research results and his final valuation figures. He also advised that he had spoken with Andrei and that he was prepared to offer the full valuation price for each of the paintings that were for sale. When Ian had finished speaking, there was a short period of silence on the other end of the line and Ian began to wonder if the call had been disconnected.

Suddenly the familiar Scottish brogue apologised for the delay in replying and said he was feeling slightly emotional and also quite guilty. He was wondering what his ancestors would say. Finally, Richard told Ian that the valuations and Andrei's offer both seemed to be very fair. He went on to explain that he had previously received some offers for some of the paintings, but none had come close to Ian's valuations. He thanked Ian for all of his efforts and asked if he could please convey both his acceptance and thanks to Andrei and for his offer. Ian confirmed he'd pass on this message. Ian then explained that one of Andrei's representatives would be contacting him shortly. They would need to obtain Richard's bank account details so that the funds could be transferred to the correct account and also to agree a mutually acceptable date for the packing and collection of the paintings.

When Ian put down the telephone receiver he sat back and wondered how much Andrei was going to make out of both this and Mr Colbourne's transactions. He guessed it must be a lot more than he earned in a year at Sotheby's!

Five minutes later he decided to stretch his legs and get a cup of coffee. As he passed through the outer office, he met Penny, who was entering the office from the corridor. She immediately stopped and asked him, "Did you see the news on the internet this morning?"

Ian shook his head and said he hadn't looked at the news on his computer so far today.

Penny explained, "Well, it appears that a group of men were shot in the chambers and tunnels under the Kremlin on Monday evening. Apparently, they were challenged by guards when trying to steal and carry away some valuable paintings that were stored there."

Ian's blood suddenly seemed to drain from his body. "What!? Oh wow!" he exclaimed. "I didn't know there were paintings being stored under the Kremlin," he said, trying to recover from his initial shock standing in front of Penny.

"Nor did I, but apparently, according to the news report, there is quite a collection stored there. Paintings that the Russian government have purchased over the last few years!"

"Thanks, I'll have to look it up." After this comment Penny sat down at her desk and Ian left the outer office to get his coffee. As he walked along the corridor he suddenly recalled what Penny had just said – the political statement issued by the Russian government saying, 'paintings purchased over the last few years'! Mmm, he thought, the statement should have said, 'stolen from the Nazies at the end of the Second World War'!

Ten minutes later Ian was back, sitting at his desk. He logged on to his laptop and eventually found a report about the theft at the Kremlin, on one of the news websites. The report didn't give too many details and not much extra information to that which Penny had already told him. His thoughts went out to both Dimitri and Ivan and he wondered if they had been amongst the people who had been shot. He suddenly had a cold shiver when he realised it could have been him who had been shot! He wondered if he should speak to Andrei. But then, after further thoughts, he decided to keep as low a profile as possible. After all, Andrei would have already found out about the news and what else could he do at the moment anyway?

For the next few days Ian looked at the internet on a daily basis for any updates on the shooting. However, there was no more extra 'real' information announced and certainly no names issued of the people who had been shot. Rumours on social media suggested the thefts were the work of the Russian mafia and others propounded that it had been an 'inside job', carried out by a group of people working within the Kremlin! Ian wondered if Andrei's people in Moscow were responsible for this propaganda. Wisely trying to divert any attention away from themselves.

After five days the robbery became old news and then it disappeared completely from daily British reporting. Ian was not sure if this was good or bad news. Eventually he decided to just concentrate on his Sotheby's work and obtain more information if and when Andrei next called him.

# Chapter 39

By the time the Moscow news bulletins about the shooting had disappeared from the internet news reporting completely, Ian had still not heard from Andrei. He was getting worried and asked Viktor if his father had spoken to Andrei. However, Sergei's answer was that he had not been in any form of communication with Andrei for some weeks. Viktor also stated that his father had heard about the shootings but unfortunately, he had not been able to find out any more details as to the identity of the people who had been shot.

It was on the following Tuesday that Viktor emailed Ian and asked if he could speak to him about a personal matter. Ian was sure it must be about Andrei and so he suggested they meet in Ian's office later that afternoon after work. When Viktor arrived at Ian's office, Ian noticed immediately that Viktor had a worried look on his face. Although Penny had left at five o'clock, Viktor asked if he could close Ian's office door?

"Of course, Vic, come in and sit down." Ian waited for Viktor to sit down and for him to speak.

"Earlier this morning my father had a telephone call from Dimitri, whom you apparently met in Moscow. It's not totally clear but, according to Dimitri, it was Ivan and two other colleagues who were shot. They were exiting the Kremlin chambers and entering the tunnel with five paintings when they were challenged and then shot by the guards. All three men were killed instantly. Several other people were subsequently arrested, including Dimitri, but as there was no concrete evidence that any of them were involved, they were eventually released. However, in Russia, that is not always the end of the matter and so Dimitri and his wife quickly fled the country. My father says that Dimitri's telephone call was from Austria, but Dimitri had told him that he would not be staying there for long. My father then tried to contact Andrei again, but it appears he is still not responding to any communication. It's not unusual for Andrei to temporarily disappear, but my father is really concerned this time, because of what has happened in Moscow."

"I see," said Ian. "Thanks for telling me. Did your father suggest anything that I should do?" Ian was not sure if he could do anything, but he did feel that at least he should ask.

"No, not at this stage. My father says we will all have to wait and see and … just hope that Andrei is alright. He also asked that if Andrei contacts you first could you tell my father?"

"Of course I will. Thank you, and can you also say thank you to your father for this information, please?"

"Of course."

Viktor rose from his chair and left Ian's office. Ian leaned back in his own chair and pondered on the Kremlin shootings and wondered where the heck Andrei was! Could he be in Moscow? He doubted it, Andrei had told him several times he had no intentions of ever returning to Russia … but of course, Andrei was a law unto himself … and he was not absolutely sure!

After dinner that evening, Ian was in his home office

and catching up on personal accounts and paperwork. He had also promised himself an hour to spend time tidying up a lot of the files and reference books he had been using recently. It was just after 10.30 pm when he decided he was finally finished for the evening and would go upstairs and get ready for bed. As he rose from his chair his mobile phone suddenly rang. He wondered who could be ringing him at this time of night. Checking his watch, he guessed it must be Oscar from Hong Kong. However, when he answered the call he was very surprised ... but also very relieved.

"Hello my friend and how are things?" It was Andrei's voice.

"Andrei!" exclaimed Ian. "Where the devil have you been? Everyone has been trying to get hold of you."

"I've been in Scotland meeting up with your Laird again. We have agreed on lots of business plans together. The broadband and Wi-Fi there, if you remember, is very poor, so I have been out of touch with the internet and with my mobile phone services too. I couldn't receive any text messages either. So, tell me, why has everyone, as you say, been trying to get hold of me?"

"Have you heard about the shootings in Moscow?"

"Shootings? What shootings?"

Conscious that Andrei did not like details to be discussed over the telephone, he tried to explain, in vague terms, what had happened. However, he had not really got started before Andrei cut in and said, "My friend, I am on my way back to London for two nights before I go back to Monaco. Can I meet with you tomorrow evening at the Savoy? We can then discuss this matter in more detail then."

Ian advised Andrei that he could arrive at the hotel for about 7.30 pm, to which Andrei agreed.

As soon as Ian had finished his call with Andrei, he immediately dialled Sergei's number, but got his answerphone.

He assumed Sergei had gone to bed already and just left a simple message:

"I've been in contact with Andrei!"

As Ian was preparing to get into bed his landline telephone rang and he recognised Sergei's number and then his voice. "I received your message. Is there anything else I should know?"

Ian just told Sergei that Andrei had finally contacted him earlier. Apparently he's been in Scotland for a few weeks. Andrei is returning to London tomorrow and we have plans to meet in the evening. He's staying at the Savoy hotel before flying back to Monaco.

Sergei thanked him and said goodnight.

Ian arrived at the Savoy Hotel the next evening, at just before 7.30pm. He announced his name to the woman on the reception desk and was told that Mr Petrov was expecting him and to go straight up to his suite. Ian walked over to the elevators and pressed the button for Andrei's floor. Meanwhile the receptionist dialled Andrei's suite and advised him that his guest was on his way. When Ian exited the elevator, he saw Andrei walking down the corridor towards him.

"Ah my friend," he announced. "It is so good to see you again." Andrei gave him a manly hug and the two men then shook hands. Andrei pointed Ian in the direction of his suite, "Come, come, my friend." The two men entered the suite. It was a different set of rooms to his last visit, but once inside, Ian was, again, staggered by the size and opulence of the suite.

Whilst Ian was looking around the main lounge area, Andrei announced, "I have just opened this lovely bottle of champagne for us to drink whilst you tell me more about what has been happening in Moscow. When there is bad news, I always like to have a drink of champagne to offset the sadness."

Andrei duly poured two glasses of champagne and offered one to Ian and pointed to a seat. Andrei sat on another seat close by and leaned forward, anxious to hear Ian's story. "Now then my friend, what is all this sad news you have to tell me?"

Ian was not sure that this should be the time to drink champagne, but he still sipped his drink and then explained all that he knew about the Moscow shootings and the conversations he had had with Sergei. Andrei also sipped his champagne and listened intensely to every word without comment.

When Ian had finished his report, Andrei stood up, picked up the champagne bottle and refilled both their glasses. He then sat down again and finally said, "That's a sad story my friend. You say Ivan and two others were killed." Ian nodded. "However, you have no idea who the other two were?"

"No," replied Ian. "Maybe when Sergei spoke to Dimitri, Dimitri might have told him."

"Okay I will speak to Sergei. It's a bad business. I'll make sure the families are properly compensated."

Ian wasn't sure how any financial compensation could make up for the loss of a loved one, but at least Andrei was showing some level of compassion. However, in Andrei's world, everyone knew all the risks! Ian was beginning to realise that whilst the benefits were high, so were the risks!

After a short pause, Ian thought he ought to try and change the subject, so he asked Andrei what he was doing back in Scotland.

"Ah my friend, it was so special. When we were both there, I could just smell the business opportunities the Laird was not fully exploiting. So, after a few days back in Monaco, I telephoned Richard and suggested we meet again as I had some thoughts about how he could still be financially compensated but without the family losing their paintings. Needless to say, he was very interested as he was still feeling very guilty about the proposed sale. So, after a further two weeks of his and his wife's wonderful hospitality, we have agreed some plans. I have also left them with a number of other proposals to think about too. You know my friend, my understanding of the Scottish language is not much better, but Moira, his wife, has greatly improved her knowledge of the Russian language!"

Both men laughed and Ian finally said, "So, Andrei, do you want to be the next Laird of Baltoun?"

"No, no my friend. A new business interest, yes, free salmon and trout fishing, yes and free malt whisky and 'hot toddies', oh yes! What more can a man want?"

"You are amazing Andrei, truly amazing!"

"I know my friend, I know." Again, both men laughed and finished their champagne. Ian knew it was not all as simple as Andrei had stated. Andrei was a very hard and shrewd businessman, but he also knew Andrei would still always try to make sure there was a 'win–win' result.

"Are you flying back to Monaco tomorrow?"

"Yes. It's probably time to activate some of my pension savings. I need to get my people working on getting some of my paintings sold. Then I think I'll need a rest, or even a long holiday. I am getting far too old for all this business activity and hectic travelling. It's a young man's game."

"But you're not old Andrei. You are physically fit and I don't think I've met a man with a sharper business brain."

"It's very good of you to say so my friend, but age is catching up with me fast. Also, the shooting of Ivan, a man I have known for many years, it is all making me realise we are all mortal and maybe I should relax a lot more. The trouble is I love the art business and the excitement. Staying with your Laird fired up this excitement once again. I find it very difficult to let go."

Ian nodded. He knew from the short amount of time he had been working with Andrei, that his own world was now far more exciting too. It was certainly a more dangerous existence, but definitely more rewarding both from an excitement and a financial point of view. He had not checked his Swiss bank account since Andre had set it up, but he did know that if he did decide to buy an apartment closer to Sotheby's office, in London, he would no longer need to go cap in hand to his bank manager for a huge loan.

Ian concluded that there was certainly a lot to be said for Andrei's way of life. He had experienced glimpses of a different art world to that which he had been used to, glimpses of the wealth that could be generated from hard work, knowledge and the right connections, but also glimpses of the dangers that existed in this sort of world. High rewards, but high risks too!

# Chapter 40

Over the next two weeks, Ian was disappointed not to have heard anything more from Andrei. His work at Sotheby's was interesting but not exciting. Each time there was a gap between his activities from being involved in Andrei's world, he felt down and uninspired. Andrei's world was the spark to his life. Sotheby's was safe and secure ... which is what Emma preferred. However, Ian wanted a life that was much more about challenge, excitement and adventure ... Andrei's life!

When Ian arrived at his office, Viktor was waiting for him and he said that his father would like to speak to him. He was asking if you would call at the house after work this evening. Ian agreed to visit about six o'clock, but he then asked Viktor if he knew what his father wanted. Viktor said he didn't, but he did think his father had some papers for him.

After Viktor had left, Ian stood up and wandered over to the office window. He looked out and across to the small courtyard located at the back of the building. As he gazed across the surrounding rooftops he wondered if this meeting was to give him instructions on another assignment from Andrei. He quietly smiled to himself and hoped it was.

Ian left Sotheby's at just after 5.30 pm. He had planned to

get away from work earlier, but his boss, Michael Hopkins, had asked him to stop by to discuss a possible new auction. Conscious of the time, Ian decided to hail a taxi. He climbed aboard and told the driver Sergei's address in Eaton Square.

The traffic was very busy and during the journey Ian stared out of the window and wondered why Sergei had some papers for him. Surely, if Andrei had specific plans, he would have contacted him directly. Still, Ian reminded himself, Andrei was the master of unpredictability.

It was just after six o'clock when Ian's taxi turned into Eaton Square. Ian pointed to Sergei's house and the vehicle stopped right outside the front door. After paying his fare, Ian stepped out and closed the rear door.

As the taxi was driven away, Ian looked around and decided that spring was definitely in the air and the daylight hours were noticeably increasing each day. He remembered the previous two times when he had visited Sergei's home, it had been dark, so it was nice now to see Eaton Square in the late afternoon daylight. He looked again along the row of the large terraced houses in which Sergei's property was located. The frontages were all similar, but nevertheless very impressive. He stepped forward and pressed the doorbell. Within a few seconds the large green door was opened and he was greeted by Sergei. The two men shook hands and Ian followed Sergei into the hallway.

"It's good of you to come, Ian, especially at such short notice," said Sergei, and Ian followed him into his study.

"Please sit down," said Sergei, pointing to the chair Ian had sat on before. Sergei sat down on the other side of his desk. "Would you like a drink?"

"No, thank you. I'm fine." replied Ian. He remembered that Emma was working from home today, so he'd promised to get home earlier than usual.

It was silly, Ian knew, but when he sat in this chair opposite the large frame of Sergei, in such a studious room, he
felt as though he was back in school and had been 'invited'
into the headmaster's study for a ticking off. Afterall, he
remembered those ticking off days very well!

Sergei continued, "Andrei telephoned me late last evening. He was calling from Mexico. He says he would like
you to visit him in Monaco on Saturday. He hoped it would
be convenient."

Ian wasn't immediately sure of his and Emma's plans,
but decided he would make it convenient. He was mildly
annoyed that Andrei always wanted him to undo any
arrangements he and Emma might have already made, but
at the same time he also knew that he would always be well
rewarded. Incidentally, he thought, what was Andrei doing
in Mexico?!

"I'm sure that will be okay," said Ian. He wondered what
the consequences would be if he did ever have to turn Andrei
down! "Do you know what he wants to see me about?"

"No, I don't. He just asked me to speak to you, arrange
the flight tickets and give you this money for your taxis
to and from the apartment." Sergei removed an envelope
from his desk draw and pushed it towards Ian. "Apparently,
Julian, you know he's Andrei's driver," Ian nodded. "He's
currently on holiday, so you'll have enough money here
for the two taxi fares. You will only be in Monaco for one
night. Here are your flight e-ticket details and money."

Ian stretched over his side of the desk and collected the
unsealed envelope. As he pulled it towards him, he glanced
inside. He immediately recognised quite a number of £50
notes and the flight details.

"Thank you, Sergei. Andrei certainly does make it difficult to say no!"

Both men laughed. Sergei wished him a good trip and

Ian left the house. It was just a short meeting, but Ian left excited again. He walked along the pavement with a slight skip in his step. He glanced around him and particularly looked at the various houses in Eaton Square. He mused of the wealth and the many stories these properties were hiding behind their majestic facades. He also wondered what Andrei was going to surprise him with this time. A trip to Mexico? The man is definitely an enigma!

It was about an hour later when Ian arrived home and Emma was in the kitchen cooking their evening meal. After their usual kiss, brief cuddle and chat about each other's day at work, Ian went on to explain about his meeting with Sergei and that Andrei wanted him to visit Monaco for the weekend. He emphasised, however, that he would be back home late Sunday afternoon. He would be only away for one night.

Emma listened to Ian's comments and noted the excitement in his voice and in his eyes. She still worried that Ian was getting too involved with Andrei and about the increasing influence the man was having on his ... and both their lives! She was about to remind him that he had already arranged for them to visit his parents this coming weekend, but decided to keep quiet and instead, to quietly telephone his parents and give them Ian's apologies, citing work as the excuse. She hoped, however, that this was not going to be a recurring issue.

Ian's Saturday morning flight to Nice landed just after midday. As he walked out of the 'Arrivals' terminal he was pleasantly surprised that it was a warm and sunny day. When he had left England there was a chilly wind and showers. He put down his hand luggage and removed the overcoat that he had needed earlier in London. The French locals, he noted, were still very much in their winter clothes. If they think this is cold, he thought, they should try London in March!

Disappointed not to be collected by Julian this time, he joined the taxi queue but was soon whisked off towards the Principality of Monaco. The traffic was surprisingly light and the journey was completed much quicker than he had anticipated. When he arrived at the first set of security controls to Andrei's apartment block, he expected some problems, but there were none. Andrei had obviously informed security of Ian's impending arrival and checks were therefore minimal, just a passport inspection. He paid the taxi driver and gave him a generous tip. When he walked into reception and announced his name, he was surprised again to be immediately recognised and welcomed.

"Good afternoon, Mr Caxton." said the receptionist, a young and pleasant woman, who gave Ian a nice welcoming smile. Ian noted that her English was excellent. "Mr Petrov informed us of your arrival today. I have been instructed to give you a letter." The receptionist got up from her seat and went over to the far desk where she collected a sealed white envelope and handed it to him.

Ian looked at the addressee and it just said 'Private and Confidential' in the top right-hand corner and 'Mr Ian Caxton' in the centre. He wondered what this was all about. The last thing on his mind was the possibility of being presented with a letter ... and presumably from Andrei! This was not at all in his thinking. He thanked the lady, picked up his bag and coat and took the envelope to a seat at the far side of the room. He sat down, tore open the seal and pulled out a typed A4 sheet of paper. Once fully opened he started to read the contents:

*Hello my good friend and welcome to your new world!*

*I have finally decided, at the ripe old age of 74, to retire from the art world. For the next five years, or until my health finally gives up, I am going to have a long, long holiday. Please do not try to find me. However, I will always be contactable on my email address for V. Sokolov.*

*As you know my business has been my life and although I have befriended many ladies, I do not have any family of my own. You my friend and your lovely wife Emma, have been the closest to me in recent times to being family. We have worked well together and I see in you the frustrated and ambitious young businessman that I once was of many, many years ago. Yes, I once shared your current frustrations, that is until I was given the fabulous opportunity to develop my ambitions by a lovely man in Moscow. My gradually accumulated wealth has now given me the ability to present you with the same opportunity. That is the key word here, my friend ... opportunity!*

*When you enter my apartment, you will find several legal documents that I have signed. Firstly, the apartment is yours. I have temporarily transferred ownership to your name for you to use as you see fit. Hopefully Emma will eventually see the quality of life that I am now offering you both. When I die, the apartment will be yours solely and totally, to do as you wish. The only caveat I have asked of my legal people is to insert a clause that says that if I do decide to return to Monaco, which at this stage is definitely not part of my plans, then I will be able to move back in, at least until I move on again, or I die. But as I say, my friend, this is not part of my plans.*

*As for my collection of pictures, you will find that many of the ones you saw the last time you were in Monaco, have now been sold. Yes, my pensions have finally matured! What is left in the apartment and in the lower basement safety vaults, are immediately yours. I hope you will be especially pleased with the one that hangs at the side of the dining room table.*

*To help you with the financing of 'my little home', I have arranged for three million Swiss francs to be credited to your Swiss bank account on the 28th November each year for the next ten years. That date, my friend, was the date when I first met you in the London public house. I saw, that evening, a younger version of myself. You made me smile that evening and I knew you would become 'my friend'. Not a son, but someone special and very close.*

*The shootings in Moscow have saddened me considerably and, whilst I have made financial payments to the widows, I know this is not enough to bring back their loved ones. I do not want to be responsible for similar events ever again and have therefore ceased all my activities and future business connections with Moscow.*

*My lady friends in Monaco are aware of my plans and all have wished me well. Maybe I will even invite one or two of them to join me for a short stay whilst I am 'on my holiday!' Or, of course, there may be new lady friend challenges still ahead for me! Even an old man still has his needs!*

*My plans in Scotland have now been agreed with Laird Richard and I will be calling on him, and his lovely family, for a spot of fishing and 'a wee dram' or two, from time to time. They are a lovely family and I see it as a real challenge to learn a new language, Scottish!*

*Finally, my friend, I will be watching from afar. I will be hoping and praying you have a happy and successful life, just like I have had. I was given a wonderful opportunity when I was about your age, which I took with both hands. I am now giving you the same opportunity.*

*Very best wishes, my friend.*

*Andrei.*

Once Ian had finished reading the letter he just stared at the paper. He could not believe what he had just read! Had he read it correctly? He decided to read it once again, but more slowly this time. When he'd finished reading for a second time, he still could not take it all in. Slowly, a tear trickled down the cheek from his left eye. After a few seconds he was conscious the receptionist was now standing in front of him. He wiped away the tear and looked up at her. When she realised she had Ian's full attention she said, "Mr Petrov gave us additional instructions after you had read that letter, These instructions were that I should contact a member of our security team and they would arrange for you to have permanent access to Mr Petrov's apartment. We understand you are now the new owner, Mr Caxton, and it is my pleasure to welcome you to Harbour Heights."

Ian's head was spinning. What the heck was going on! Surely this was all just a dream! A joke! He didn't like surprises at the best of times, but this! Wow, he thought, and took two deep breaths.

"I will call the security team now, Mr Caxton, and will be back in a few minutes," said the receptionist, who turned and walked back to the reception desk to ring the security team.

Ian heard the lady speak on the telephone but could not really understand exactly what she had said. His heart was now beating very fast. He tried to stand up but quickly resumed his seat. His legs felt like jelly and he thought he might fall over.

"Are you all right Mr Caxton? Would you like a glass of water?" called the receptionist after putting down the telephone receiver.

"No, no. I'll be okay. It's all a bit of a shock. I wasn't expecting any of this." Ian took some more deep breaths and his heart rate began to reduce slightly. His mind was still spinning and he looked at the letter once again. About two minutes later, a uniformed security guard appeared and approached him. He was tall and strongly built, probably in his mid-40s. Certainly not the sort of person one would pick an argument with! "Mr Caxton, my name is Bates, sir. We have been given instructions by Mr Petrov for you to be able to access his apartment, or should I say sir, your new apartment." His voice had a deep tone and he spoke English with a slight mid-Atlantic accent.

When Ian tried to stand up for a second time, he realised his legs were now a lot sturdier once again.

"This was not really what I was expecting." said Ian, waving the letter in front of him. "It's all a total surprise."

Bates smiled at Ian and nodded trying to show his understanding.

"We need to take some hand prints, sir. Access to the apartment is via your palm registering on the entrance door security panel. Could you come with me to our security room please, sir?"

Ian picked up his overcoat and bag and followed Bates. As they passed by the reception desk, the receptionist gave him a big smile. Ian smiled back and continued down a corridor to the security room.

Ian followed Bates into the security room. The room immediately reminded Ian of the NASA mission control space centre in Florida! He was surrounded by a number of close circuit television screens on the walls, filing cabinets, several computers and a number of other metal cabinets with flashing lights. Ian was asked to follow Bates to a separate machine which turned out to be a special type of hand scanner. Ian had to place each hand, one at a time, on the scanner's metal plate. Bates then processed the data reading that appeared on the computer screen located immediately in front of both of them. Ian stared and the 3D images of each of his hands.

Twenty minutes later, Ian and Bates were standing outside the Penthouse apartment. Bates pointed to the security panel. Ian remembered from his last visit that Andrei had unlocked the door by placing his hand on this panel. "Can you place your hand on the panel, sir," asked Bates. "Either hand should work."

Ian calmly lifted his right hand. It was still shaking a little, but he managed to make contact. After two seconds the door clicked and moved slowly ajar.

"It all seems to be working okay," said Bates, "but let's try with the other hand to make sure."

Bates pulled the door to and they both heard the locking click. "Now sir, please try the other hand."

Ian lifted his left hand and placed it on the panel. Again, after two seconds there was the familiar click and the door slowly opened.

"Good." said Bates. "It looks as though we are all set. If there are any problems, just call us on 124 from your internal phone system, 24 hours."

"Thank you," said Ian.

Bates then began to turn and walk towards the elevator, but Ian called him. "Excuse me, but I'm not sure what I am going to find in here, so could you come in with me?"

"Sure. No problem, sir." Bates walked back and then followed Ian into the apartment.

As Ian stepped through the door, he could feel his heartbeat racing once more, this time in anticipation of what he would find. He firstly placed his coat and bag on a chair next to the entrance door and then looked around the huge lounge area. All of the furniture that he had remembered from his first visit seemed to be still in place, but most of the paintings had been removed. Whilst Bates stood just inside the doorway Ian slowly explored the different rooms. Again, some items had gone but some still remained. Ian felt it was all very weird … a surreal experience. The life and excitement he experienced on his first visit was gone. He could not make up his mind whether he felt he was now trespassing or reviewing a property after someone had died. He returned to the middle of the lounge area and suddenly had a cold shiver.

"Everything alright, sir?" asked Bates.

"Yes, yes, I think so. Thank you."

"Anytime, sir. As I said earlier, we are available 24 hours a day, every day. Just dial 124 on the internal phone system." As he was speaking, Bates pointed to a side table near the chair Ian had just placed his bag and coat. On the table sat a small electrical computer unit with a mobile phone protruding out of the top.

Ian nodded and said, "Thank you."

After Bates had left the apartment, Ian was on his own. He continued to stand in the middle of the lounge area and slowly gaze all around him. He then walked over to the dining area and saw a small pile of documents on the table. Without really reading any in detail, he flicked each typed sheet over. At the end of each document he saw Andrei's signature. He tidied the pile back into the original order and walked over to the huge panoramic patio windows. After opening the door he stepped out onto the balcony. The late afternoon temperature had now cooled a little, but Ian really didn't feel it whilst taking in the fabulous view once more. Absolutely stunning, he thought. That had definitely not changed. After a few minutes watching the activity in the harbour and the comings and goings from the cafes and shops below, he returned to the lounge area and then spotted a familiar picture hanging on the far wall in the dining area. He walked over and inspected it much closer.

He leaned back, smiled and then said out loud, "Andrei, thank you. You are amazing Andrei, truly amazing!" He was convinced that he'd then heard the familiar reply of "I know my friend, I know." followed by the usual booming laugh. But when he turned around there was nobody else in the room!

He suddenly felt quite alone ... and lonely. Maybe, he thought, this is how people feel when their best friend has died. He turned around again and reinspected the painting on the wall. The picture's title was engraved on a small brass plate which had been attached to the bottom section of the new oak frame. The brass plate simply said, *Rose in a Glass Vase*!

A minute later he walked back towards the huge patio windows and removed his mobile phone from the inside of his jacket pocket. He then called his home telephone number. After five rings the familiar voice of Emma answered the call and she immediately said, "Hello Ian, where are you?"

Ian's reply began, "Emma, you are not going to believe this …!"